Fauxmance in the Falls

J.E. BIRK

For Comma: Charley, Rachel, Leslie, and AJ.
I'd still be curled up in the fetal position around this book without
you four.

Contents

Author's Note

Hello, favorite reader! Here are a few things to know before you travel to Devon Falls.

This book does deal with the topic of infertility, and there are some scenes of mild violence. If either is a trigger for you, you may want to step away from this book at this time.

I would be nothing without my intrepid early readers. Great thanks to Riley, Megan, Shantel, Katy, and everyone else who first visited Devon Falls with me. Huge thanks to Kari Shafenberg, my editor, who continues to put up with my em-dash obsession.

While I did background research into the legal and medical professions for this book, I chose to alter certain elements of reality to suit the story. Devon Falls is very much a place of my imagination, and I enjoyed suspending some of my own reality while I was writing there.

Huge thanks to all of you for supporting my books, and great thanks to everyone who encouraged me to write Benson's story after reading *Counterpoint.* Giving my favorite frenemy his own story has been a true joy.

Love,

J.E.

Chapter 1

70 Days to the Devon Falls Leaf Festival

I never mind being the villain in someone else's story. —Benson Lewis

Has my life finally hit a new low? That seems like the only possible explanation for why I'm standing in the middle of the town square in Devon Falls, Vermont, staring at a statue that looks exactly like a poop emoji.

I've known for a long time that life in small town Vermont isn't exactly normal. I've been going to school here largely against my will since I was thirteen years old; I'm well aware of the quirks that come with being a resident of this state. At twenty-five years old, I didn't think I could ever be surprised by anything this place has to offer.

People don't put up statues of poop emojis on purpose—right? But I swear, this thing has *got* to be a poop emoji. Swirls of brown metal pop out of a large stone base, and two circular bits of clay built into the sides of the stone definitely look like they're supposed to be eyes.

What. The. Actual. Hell.

This is exactly why I jetted across the Vermont border and down to Boston the second I finished law school in Burlington. But that was less than four months ago, and I'm already back, wearing my best herringbone suit and standing in the middle of a town where every single person I've passed so far was decked out in either overalls or corduroy. I'm sure a cow parking a car and hopping out of the front seat would have gotten less side-eye than I did when I rolled up on Main Street today.

Fuck my life.

My phone rings, shifting my attention away from the absurd sculpture in front of me. I tug my cell out of my pocket, and my eyes immediately widen in surprise. Grandpa's calling me? He never calls.

I mentally will my damn hands to stop shaking as I hit the *accept* button on the screen and lift the phone to my ear. "Benson Lewis here," I say crisply, because Grandpa appreciates formality in all communication.

"Benson. Carter tells me you're in Devon Falls."

"Yes, sir." I peer at the empty streets around me, taking further stock of my surroundings. I'm standing in what has got to be one of the Vermontiest town squares that has ever Vermonted. The large swath of green grass is surrounded by a row of older brick and wooden churches on one side, and a bright white gazebo stands at the center of the space. There's a perfectly charming café across the street, painted purple with pink trim, nestled right next to a drug store called The Devon Falls Farm-Acy. And then, of course, there's the banner over Main Street advertising the town's weekly farmers market.

Are you even allowed to incorporate a town in Vermont if it doesn't have a farmers market? I'm guessing the answer is no.

"Good," says Grandpa sharply. "Listen, I don't think I have to tell you not to screw this assignment up. I can't have Carter trapped up in that godforsaken town for weeks or months on end over a silly land matter; he's too important of an associate for that. You better be up for the challenge of keeping an eye on things there for him."

"Weeks, sir? Months?" No one at the firm said exactly how long I'd be stuck in Devon Falls. Carter just told me to get my ass up here and said he'd email me all the information I needed while I was driving. To be fair, I didn't stop to ask him many questions. I know how lucky I am to be clerking at Grandpa's firm. No way I'm going to fuck up this opportunity by annoying one of his most successful associates.

"Don't ask people to repeat themselves," Grandpa snaps at me. "It makes you sound like an idiot. While we're on that subject, you took the Vermont bar exam, yes? I expect you to pass on the first try, you understand me? The pass rate in Vermont is too high for any grandson of mine to fail it. Don't embarrass me."

My stomach shifts uncomfortably as I think of the weeks and weeks I spent studying to take the bar in a state I don't even want to practice law in. But Grandpa's firm, Lewis, Stillmer, and Gates, is one of the preeminent New England law firms. They do business all over Massachusetts, Vermont, and New Hampshire, and they have offices in each state. I have to be prepared to practice in Vermont if I want to work for my father and grand-father, I remind myself. I have to. I can put up with more time in this state if it means that eventually I'll get my own office at the firm headquarters in Boston. For as long as I can remember, I've dreamed of working in an office just like my dad's, where the skyscrapers of the city loom outside the window and a fireplace cracks comfortably next to his old leather desk.

Speaking of Dad, I haven't heard from him in weeks. "Does Dad know I'm working on this matter?" I ask Grandpa. Sarah, my step-mother, texted me to ask how I was doing, so I'm sure she'll update him soon if he doesn't already know where I am. But I haven't actually seen Dad once since I started clerking at Lewis, Stillmer, and Gates a week or so ago. Not that I'm taking it personally that he hasn't dropped by my cubicle yet. Dad's got almost as much on his plate as Grandpa does. They're busy people.

All I care about is that I'm working with the two of them now. Even though I have the Lewis family name, I always knew it was a long shot that I'd land a spot at our family firm after I graduated. Almost everyone at Lewis, Stillmer, and Gates has an Ivy League degree. The day I signed my hiring paperwork, Grandpa made it a point to tell me that I was the first person with a state law school degree to be hired by the firm in fifteen years.

I didn't miss the smirks on the other new hires' faces. Or the fact that he said it in front of all of them. Loudly.

"Your father's not going to babysit you here at the firm, Benson," Grandpa barks into the phone, and I wince. "It's time to grow up. Can you handle things on your own up there, or can't you?"

I draw myself up to my full height. It doesn't matter that Grandpa can't see me. Confidence, he's always said, is something people can sense. That's why I never let myself appear weak in front of anyone—not even for a second. "Of course, I can handle this," I promise him steadily. "Carter doesn't have anything to worry about."

"Good." Grandpa clicks off the call before I can say anything else. Not that I had much else to say if he'd stayed on.

I may have lived with my grandfather for six years, but we've never exactly exchanged small talk. I think the most intimate conversation we've ever had was about a lacrosse stick he bought me for my birthday one year.

I slip the phone into my pocket and go back to staring at the statue—well, glaring is probably more like it. *Weeks? Months?* Carter definitely failed to mention I could be up here for that long when he sent me on the road this morning. Aaron and Jeremy, my coworkers from the firm where I used to clerk in Burlington during law school, are going to have a field day when they hear where I am.

As if they can sense that I'm thinking about them—and sometimes I wonder, because these two show up in my life at the strangest times—my phone buzzes again with a text. Naturally, it's the group chat Jeremy started for the three of us. I denied it three times, but Jeremy's a persistent little fucker, and eventually I gave up and accepted his invite.

Aaron: Hey, J and I may come down to Boston this weekend. Want to have dinner?

Jeremy: Of course he wants to have dinner! We're his bestest frenemies!

Benson: Frenemy? Did you seriously just call yourself that? Are you five?

Jeremy: If we called you our friend you'd cancel this group chat so fast my phone would probably explode.

To be fair, he's not wrong. Aaron Morin is annoyingly observant, and his boyfriend Jeremy Everett is nosy as hell. Of course they've noticed that I don't really bother with having friends. This is partly because I've never had the time, but it's also because I just don't see the point. People always let you down. Why bother getting close to anyone?

Aaron and Jeremy just keep creeping further into my life, though. I suppose I could have worse people haunting me. Aaron and I shared an office at Sprysky and Gentry, the small firm in Burlington where we clerked together and where Aaron still works. Jeremy was at the front desk, and now he's in law school at Burlington University. Aaron's a Harvard grad, of course—unlike me, who couldn't even get in no matter how hard I worked or how many family connections I had. Still, Aaron annoys me far less than most people do.

Jeremy usually annoys me a hell of a lot more.

I'm not exactly proud of the way I treated Aaron and Jeremy when we first met. Finding out where Aaron went to school was a low blow for me, and I didn't handle it very well. I can never quite figure out why these two insist on reappearing in my life so constantly.

Or why I keep letting them.

Benson: Fine, you're probably right. But it doesn't matter. I'm not in Boston right now. Away for work. Sorry.

Jeremy: Ooohhh, traveling for the fancy new firm! Where are you? Is it Milan? If it's Milan, I have club recommendations!

I snort out a laugh. Jeremy's a long-time playboy who reformed when he met Aaron. I don't even want to know what kind of club he'd suggest I check out.

Aaron: Wow, that's exciting! They're already trusting you with travel! I'm just working on due diligence this week.

I sigh. No point in letting them both think I've got something glamorous going on here. Vermont is so small they'll probably figure out where I am in about twenty minutes anyway.

Benson: I'm in Devon Falls, Vermont.

Jeremy: [gif of man doing double take]

Jeremy: [long string of shocked face emojis]

Jeremy: Say the fuck what?

Benson: I'm working on an important land matter.

Aaron: Oh wow! It's not the fracking thing that's been in the news, is it? Damn, I'd love to work on that.

Jeremy: You're so cute when you nerd out, baby. But seriously, IS IT THE FRACKING?! I'm studying that in property law class!

Great. Now I have to tell them both why I've been exiled to a town with more cows than people.

Benson: Not fracking. I'm here about a leaf festival.

Aaron: I'm sorry. To quote Jeremy: say the fuck what?

Jeremy: I just laughed so hard I legit peed a little.

Benson: Look, it's a serious matter, okay? I'm representing a client with a land claim. The land just happens to be where they hold some dumbass town festival.

Aaron: Wait. Holy shit. Did you say you're in Devon Falls? Like the town near the ski area?

Benson: Yeah, so what?

Aaron: Benson, the Devon Falls Leaf Festival is one of the best-known festivals in Vermont. It's over a century old.

I suppose "one of the best-known festivals in Vermont" is saying something, especially for a state that seems to have approximately twelve bazillion festivals. And Aaron knows this kind of shit. He's a true Vermonter, born and raised in this state. If he says this festival matters to people, he's probably right.

Jeremy: BENSON NOOO!!!!! You can't wreck the Devon Falls Leaf Festival! (IDK what this is BUT YOU KNOW I WANT TO GO NOW.)

Benson: Sorry. Someone's got to take it down. And it's gonna be me.

Not that I mind. I never mind being the villain in someone else's story. It's a role far too many people, like Aaron and Jeremy, shy away from. But I learned a long time ago that being nice to everyone all the time gets you absolutely fucking nowhere.

If you're me, at least. I suppose that tactic works fine for Aaron Morin. But me? I'm the Lewis family mistake: the baby who showed up on the doorstep of my dad's Massachusetts apartment during his senior year of college. I'm the kid my mom gave up and dropped off on a front porch with a baby bottle, a note, and no forwarding address.

Yup. My life is the actual beginning of a Netflix series.

I was born a mistake. I've always been a mistake, and I've always known it. But someday I'll be more than the biggest error the perfect Lewis family has ever known. Someday I'll show my family, especially my grandfather and father, how much I'm really worth.

And I don't care how many leaf festivals I have to take down to do it.

I ignore the continued buzzing of my phone and start scrolling through my email, looking for Carter's directions. I'm trying to figure out exactly what a town hall would look like in this place when a soft, sobbing sound catches my attention. I follow the noise across the square, over to the empty playground, where I find the source of the crying under a bright red slide. I crouch down, carefully pulling up the bottoms of my pants, which are way too expensive to be anywhere near playground dirt.

It's a little kid. A small redheaded boy wearing dirty jeans and a bright yellow sweatshirt, curled up into himself, tears streaming down his face.

Oh, shit. I haven't even figured out where I'm supposed to stay in a town that doesn't seem to have one single damn hotel, and now I'm supposed to take care of a crying kid? But I'm sure as hell not going to leave the poor guy alone here. He sounds and looks miserable.

"Um, hi?" I finally say. I've never been very good at talking to little kids, to be honest. I was away at school when my younger half-brother and sister were this age, and when I was around all they seemed to do was alternate between giggling and wailing. "Do you, uh, need help?" I kneel a little farther, keeping my knees just off the ground.

The kid looks up at me, sniffs, and bursts into loud sobs.

"Oh, fu—fudge," I mutter.

"I lost Ellis!" he howls.

My stomach clenches as my mind flashes to a memory of a day I usually don't let myself think about: the day my grandfather's housekeeper accidentally left me behind in a grocery store. I wandered the aisles and parking lot for what felt like hours, my heart screeching in my chest, while I tried to figure out how to ask one of the giants surrounding me for help.

Grandpa wasn't sympathetic when a cashier finally managed to figure out I was lost and get me home. Far from it. "Only an idiot wouldn't just tell someone they need assistance," he grumbled at me. As far as I know, my father never even knew I was missing. He probably still doesn't know to this day.

No way am I going to leave this kid alone and terrified like I once was. "Okay," I tell him. "Let's stay calm. Who's Ellis? And, uh, you don't happen to know what that statue is supposed to be, do you?" It's a pretty shitty distraction, as distractions go, but somehow it works. The kid stops crying and actually laughs.

"Yeah!" he says. "Guess!"

Well, at least he's not bawling anymore.

Over the course of the next ten minutes, I learn that a) the ugly-ass statue isn't a tree, cow, monkey, mountain, or cupcake, and b) Ellis is the kid's older brother, and he might be at the Farm-Acy. I've just convinced the kid to stand up and take my hand when I hear shouting from behind me.

"George? George, there you are! Dr. Jack, I found him!"

A young guy with hair the color of summer carrots races across the playground. The kid—George, apparently—squeals and runs to him.

"Thank goodness!" Ellis lifts George up into his arms and hugs him tight. "I'm never taking you anywhere again without a leash." He nuzzles George's nose with his own, and George giggles.

"Wonderful! The escapee's been located." A deep voice cuts through my eardrums, and as I look behind Ellis and George, my gaze shifts from their reunion scene to land on something else that immediately catches my attention: one of the hottest men I've ever seen.

He's tall and built, with wide shoulders and arms that make me wonder if Devon Falls has a gym hidden somewhere in between their three restaurants and one aging laundromat. His hair is dark and short, and it lays in perfect configuration on his forehead, exactly matched with his dark brown eyes and angular cheekbones. Everything about his stance screams *power* and *I'm in charge.*

He's every guy I've ever lusted after in a club or bar. Every guy who's ever brushed me off, full-on ignored me, or slept with me and then stopped answering my texts. I'm not exactly ugly, but I'm not on the level of guys like this. I'm on the shorter side and stockier, with hair that's closer to the color of straw than gold and eyes that are more gray than blue. No amount of working out gets me the abs and glutes it gets the other guys in my family.

Men like this don't even give me a second look when they catch my eyes on them. So why's this guy beaming at me?

"You found George! Ellis, good call on checking the park first." Incredibly Hot Guy holds out a hand to me. "Hey there. I'm Jack Lancer; this is Ellis Ryker. Thanks for keeping George company for us."

"Seriously, thank you." Ellis gives George a final squeeze and sets him back down on the ground. "I swear, I turned around to look at the shampoos for two seconds. George, no more running off when I watch you for Mom and Dad."

George nods in agreement. "Hey, kitty!" He takes off across the park after a squirrel, leaving Ellis to chase after him.

"Ellis, I'll post in the town message board that you found him!" Hot Guy, aka Jack Lancer, calls out. He shakes his head fondly. "Honestly, it's a miracle more of the Ryker kids haven't ended up on the backs of newspapers. I swear, half of them have been runners. And with fourteen of them? I've got no idea how their mom and dad keep up."

"I'm sure they—wait, did you say *fourteen*? As in George has thirteen brothers and sisters?"

"Yup," Jack says cheerfully. "Ellis is number four or five, I think? I lose count. Anyway, I didn't catch your name. Thanks so much for helping out with George. Half of my office rushed out to look when we saw Ellis' message in the town Facebook group. We know how far the Ryker kids can travel when something catches their eye. Great job keeping him in one place."

The last thing I need right now is the town reputation as a kid whisperer. "I didn't do much," I mutter. "And my name's Benson. Benson Lewis."

"Really nice to meet you, Benson. Again, I'm Jack. Dr. Jack Lancer."

Oh fuucckkk.

Look, we all have our fantasies. The porn we jerk off to in the dead of night under the covers. The fetishes we don't tell other people about because we secretly wonder if there's something about them that's wrong in some way. And mine?

It's doctors. Fucking doctors. All the way, every day.

No way I'm letting myself lean into this. I've got to get out of here and away from this guy. I'm here to destroy a leaf festival, not lust after the hottest doctor I've ever seen. And this guy's not going to want to have anything to do with me once he finds out why I'm here, anyway.

"Well, I'm glad you found George," I tell him. "I'll see you around, Dr. Lancer."

"What are you doing in town?" he asks as I walk away. "Can I help you find something here?"

"Nope," I call back over my shoulder. "I've got everything I need, thanks."

Everything I need to destroy this place and make Incredibly Hot Doctor hate me.

I keep walking away, and I don't look back. It occurs to me later that I could have probably asked Dr. Jack Lancer what the town statue is supposed to be, but by then I've already decided it's not worth worrying about. I'm not going to be here long enough to bother caring, anyway. Besides, by the time I've left this town, statues will be the last thing on the mind of anyone here.

Like I said, I never mind being the villain in someone else's story.

Chapter 2

67 Days to the Devon Falls Leaf Festival

Do you glare at all sweet, kind, old ladies, or just that particular one? —Jack Lancer

"Dr. Lancer, we're almost out of tongue depressors."

Mom keeps her eyes on her tablet as I'm talking to her. She's probably updating a patient file. I learned the importance of keeping fastidious paperwork from my mother, and she hasn't let me forget that lesson since the day I came to work for her small family practice in northern Vermont. She also hasn't stopped reminding me that it's very important I call her "Dr. Lancer " while we're at the office, but she gets to call me "Jackalove" anytime she feels like it.

She always seems to feel like it when I'm meeting a new patient. She especially seems to feel like it if I'm meeting a new patient and she's annoyed with me.

"Did you tell Malachai?" she asks.

Malachai, our brand-new office manager, just started two days ago. He's already intimidated enough by the complicated phone systems our retiring office manager set up for the practice. No way I'm going to bother him about tongue depressors while he's busy trying to figure out a voicemail setup that NASA astronauts would struggle with. "Mom, Malachai hasn't even found the stationary, let alone the tongue depressors."

She sighs. "Thank goodness Henri hasn't left us fully yet. Let's go talk to her." I follow her out of the exam room and into the front reception area, where Henri Fontaine is talking to Burt Busby, my last patient. Burt's got high blood pressure and an even more unfortunate case of steak addiction.

"My two favorite doctors." Henri beams at us, while Burt lifts a finger to the brim of the Devon Falls Feed Company hat he's wearing and heads toward the door.

"Doc, I'll try to cut down on the meat this month, I swear it," he tells me. "I'm even gonna try that tofu-nonsense Henri here keeps talking about."

"Pick up some of those spices I mentioned before you cook it!" Henri calls after him.

"I ain't ever even heard of cumin!" he replies as he closes the front door to the office behind him.

She smiles at him fondly, shakes her head, and then turns back to me and Mom. "What do you need, darlings?" she asks. Her voice is an immediate balm to any anxiety that the day and my patient's poor choices might have created within me, and I feel another spark of loss that she's leaving Mom's practice—*our* practice, I quickly correct myself—so soon. Henri and her husband, Harry, are staples in my life. Harry's been a local county judge for as long as I can remember, and Henri's been running Mom's practice for almost twenty years. They've been there for every major moment of my existence: the scraped knees, the birthdays, the graduations. But the two of them have been holding this town together for a long time, and if anyone deserves retirement and the chance to travel the world, it's them. They're long overdue for some time to themselves.

Especially since Harry's been falling asleep in court an awful lot lately.

"Well," says Mom, "Jack informs me that we're running low on tongue depressors. But we can find them ourselves! We're perfectly capable of running this office once you're gone, I promise!" She purses her lips and draws herself up, her bob hairdo glinting with blonde highlights that "give life to the gray," as she says. She's barely five feet, five inches tall, with alabaster skin and eyes so blue that our mailman once told her she looks like a porcelain doll, but Mom always manages to be one of the most powerful people in any room she walks into. And the mailman definitely never said that again after she shot him one of her looks.

She's also usually one of the calmest and most logical people I know. It's rare to see her even slightly lose her very collected demeanor. But Henri's impending retirement is definitely pushing her buttons. "Absolutely," I agree with her. "And if we can't find them, I guess I'll just pop by the grocery store and pick up some popsicles. If I eat enough cherry ones I should be able to take care of the potential strep case I have coming in tomorrow."

Mom shoots me a *look* while Henri laughs. "No worries, hons. I'm training Malachai on the ordering systems tomorrow; I'll make sure we get more tongue depressors in *stat*, as all your colleagues on those TV shows like to say. Are you both ready to go? We need to get the office closed."

I frown. "Why are we closing the office early for this?" I ask as Henri bustles behind the front desk and takes my lab coat from me. "Devon Falls holds a town meeting every five minutes. If we closed the office for every single one, we'd never see any patients."

"Amelia said it was important." Henri leans over her computer, easily multitasking in a way that would make most of my graduating class at medical school highly envious. She's nearly six feet tall with dark skin and long, graying dark hair that's currently tied up behind her head. She and Mom are truly a study in opposites.

Sometimes they like to pretend to be sisters when they go out in Burlington, just to see how people react. "And when Amelia says that a meeting is important, we listen."

That's true. Our town mayor may run a church with the motto "Love Yourself," and she may be married to a woman who believes firmly in nudist practices and sometimes forgets to put on clothes in her own law office, but she's on top of everything happening in this town. And she's not prone to hyperbole. If Amelia Shiner says this meeting is important, it probably is.

Most days I'm very glad I decided to come back to Devon Falls, Vermont, to join Mom's practice. I've always loved Devon Falls with every ounce of my being—this town raised me and made me. I wasn't sure about returning, though, after everything that happened with Fiona. This town is small, and the people know me inside and out. Would they judge me? I wondered. Would they decide the divorce was my fault? What would they say when they realized that Dr. Jack Lancer, former prom king and valedictorian, was just another guy who couldn't even keep his own marriage intact?

Devon Falls welcomed me back with open arms, though. Moving back home has been mostly very good for me. Even my best friends Sam and Milo, who still aren't happy I left them behind in New York, agree on that.

But I did not miss our town's obsessions with regular meetings that involve everything from sewer issues to choosing coordinating colors for holiday celebrations. And I'm not thrilled about getting behind on updating patient files to spend an hour or two sitting on a metal chair while Devon Falls decides if we're for or against Labor Day this year.

Still, I never say no to Henri. No one does. Burt Busby would never touch tofu for me, but I bet Henri has him dousing it in cumin by tomorrow.

So, I dutifully follow Mom and Henri out of the door of the old blue Victorian house that Mom converted into Lancer Family Medicine years ago. Outside, I immediately step into a wall of Vermont August humidity. The sun's out now, but a storm is coming. I can feel it. The air is thick with the scent of clouds and change.

"Thank goodness fall is coming," Mom mutters. She's never liked the heat. "Where's Elijah, honey? Is he joining us?"

My nephew, Elijah Maggio, isn't Mom's actual grandchild, but she certainly treats him like he is. It doesn't matter to her that Elijah's actually Fiona's brother's son and is only staying with me right now because of several cruel twists of fate the world has thrown both our ways. Mom treats him like her own anyway.

"His band has practice right now. He texted that he'd meet me at the town hall when it's over."

"How's his first week of school been?" Henri asks.

I sigh. No kid is happy to be back in school while the weather's still balmy and warm, but for Elijah the transition has been especially painful this year. Starting your first year of high school while your dad's deployed on an overseas mission and rarely has the ability to speak with you is tough enough. And then there's the fact that Elijah and school don't get along in the best of circumstances.

"I think it could be worse," I hedge, because I don't like to think about the fact that I'm basically a de facto father right now while my former brother-in-law is off saving the world and my former wife is teaching in Italy. There are days when I still wake up surprised I agreed to have Elijah move in with me while Eric's gone. But then he pops up at my breakfast table, all smiles and messy chestnut hair that looks just like Fiona's, while he talks nonstop about some new album I grew up listening to that he's just discovered five minutes ago, and it's hard to believe he's only been staying with me since July. I don't think I realized how silent and still my large, old house was until Elijah came to live with me.

Does that mean I'm going to be able to help him pass his freshman year of high school? Jury's out, but I don't have much choice. Eric's counting on me, and I'm not letting Fiona's family down for a second time. No way, no how. I'm going to make sure Elijah thrives in school this year.

Somehow.

Mom, Henri, and I fall in step together and walk up Main Street, past the dentist's office and the drug store. We turn and pass by the town square, where people start gathering in droves around us as we all make our way through the white wooden doors of the square brick building that serves as both the Devon Falls Town Hall and the Devon Falls Historical Society.

"Order! Order, please!" Amelia Shiner, our intrepid mayor and the pastor at Devon Falls Community Church, is tapping anxiously at her podium with a gavel. "We have much to discuss. Sit down, everyone."

The room is packed—I've never seen it so full for a town meeting. Mom shoots me a sideways glance filled with question marks. "I wish your father were here," she whispers. "This seems like it might actually be important."

"You mean as opposed to the time we spent an hour debating whether the school mascot, a porcupine, should be wearing a fedora?" I whisper back. But she's right. Something does feel different about this meeting. There isn't the usual chatter and laughter that fills the room before everyone gathers here. My high school buddy Luis, who runs the café and bar in the center of town, isn't even passing around bowls of his famous homemade chips.

Dad might end up being sorry he missed this one. Even if he is missing it to hide out in his precious tomato garden.

The three of us find chairs toward the back of the room and settle in. "Friends, we have an urgent situation at hand," Amelia tells the room. "It concerns the Leaf Festival Center. The town's ownership of the land is being disputed."

There's an audible gasp from the crowd—and I'm not surprised.

Devon Falls isn't known for much. We're down the road from a ski resort. We produce a decent amount of dairy and maple products, and plenty of farm-to-table goods, but you can say that about most small towns in our part of Vermont.

The one thing we do have going for us? That's the Devon Falls Leaf Festival.

Every October, thousands of people show up in Vermont to celebrate as the leaves here turn colors. The Leaf Festival Center is a large plot of land just northeast of the town, and it's been the home of the festival for over a hundred years. It attracts visitors from all over the country for a reason. The stretch of open space in the middle of it serves as the perfect location for fun and games and festival food, and then the land opens up into acres of woods filled with trails that are ideal for walking, hiking, and staring at the artwork the Vermont foliage paints for us every fall. The Devon Falls Leaf Festival is more than just a yearly tradition in this town.

It's a part of who we are.

"What the heck?" Diane Lions gets to her feet. "That land's belonged to the town for ages! The LeBlanc family gifted that land to the community over a hundred years ago! Nobody's taking it away!"

A loud grumble of agreement rises from the room, and Amelia pounds her gavel. "Before this conversation moves forward," she says, "let's all take a moment to remember that the land in question—and all the land we're standing on here, friends—first belonged to the indigenous peoples who were here long before us. Land acknowledgment matters."

There's nodding throughout the room.

"Now, regarding the specific land in question. We all know the history of how that land came to be the Leaf Festival Center, a centerpiece of our town and our town's greatest tradition. When the LeBlanc family gifted it to us—"

"It's not that simple." A man steps forward to stand next to Amelia, and my eyes immediately stop on him. *Benson.* From the park incident.

I've had a lot of time to explore my bisexuality since Fiona and I separated nearly two years ago, and I'm finally figuring out what attracts me to other men. When I first met Benson at the town park a few days ago, my dick immediately reminded me that he has most of it. He's shorter with a stocky, chunkier build, bright blond hair cut close to his head, and light blue eyes that stand out in perfect contrast with the lighter blue stripes in the suit he's wearing. He's definitely attractive, and he certainly ticks the boxes for what I physically look for in a guy.

But physical looks are always just a piece of the puzzle for me, and there's a lot more about this man that's drawing me to him. There's something about the way he holds himself. He's got the same stance he had when he walked away from me in the park: like he's determined to run this room, and he's going to make sure that happens no matter who stands in his way. There's something in his eyes, something I can't look away from—something I can't quite read.

I've always liked mysteries just a little more than I probably should. I've always liked the solve. The discovery. The rush of figuring out the answer to a problem.

I study him more closely as he goes back to speaking.

"Miriam LeBlanc, as some of you may know, had an estranged son at the time of her death. In her will, she gifted the land to the town, but she specified that if her son or his descendants were ever to return to Devon Falls, her land would revert to them. I'm here with Arnie Blake," he says, gesturing to a middle-aged balding man in a polo shirt sitting next to him. "Arnie's recently discovered that he's Miriam LeBlanc's great-great-great-great grandson. The land legally belongs to him. My firm has filed for an injunction to stop any festival activities until this matter can be resolved."

The energy in the room immediately swells as people rise to their feet, shouting and talking over each other. "Who the hell even are you?" someone yells.

"I'm Benson Lewis." I've got to give it to this guy—his voice is sharp but calm despite the fact that he's essentially being screamed at by an angry mob. "I'm here as a certified law clerk for Lewis, Stillmer, and Gates, Attorneys at Law. We're representing Mr. Blake."

The crowd noise swells again. "Harry!" Someone else shouts. Louise Ryker, I think. "Harry, he can't do this, can he?"

Harry Fontaine sighs and shifts in his seat next to Amelia's podium. "As the judge who will hear the case, I can't speak on this matter. Ellie's been retained to represent the town. Ellie?" He gestures at Ellie Nowack, Amelia's wife and our town's most infamous nudist. She has, I note, put on clothes for this occasion. She's wearing shorts patterned with pictures of cats and a pink tank top that was probably chosen to match the magenta streaks in her long, gray hair. It's not exactly the look an outsider might expect from the woman who runs the only law office in Devon Falls, but it's definitely better than the time she tried to show up at a hearing in a bathrobe. "If I'm gonna have to wear clothing, it better damn well be cute," is her motto.

Ellie frowns as she stands up. "Nobody panic!" she says. "We haven't even confirmed this man's lineage yet, and there are various ways we can challenge that will in court. That land has belonged to this town for over a century. We're not giving it up without a fight. We will take this all the way to the Supreme Court if we have to." She narrows her eyes at Benson and Arnie as she says that, and it's easy to see how she manages to intimidate almost every other lawyer within a fifty-mile radius, even though her very limited wardrobe is covered with animal faces.

Arnie flinches slightly when Ellie looks at him, but Benson hardly blinks. He sends her sharp nod instead, and I can almost hear his mental response in my own head.

Game on.

I'm not sure I'd want to be locked in a chess match with either of those two.

The town cheers at Ellie's last statement, and Amelia quickly loses control of the meeting after that as people swarm the podium to ask her and Ellie questions. Henri rushes over to check on Harry, who's listing a little to the right in his chair. Mom nudges me. "Remind me to talk Harry into another appointment," she says quietly. I wish I could tell her that wasn't necessary, but it probably is. Harry's last check-up was clear, but he's slowing down more and more as each year passes. It's just old age, really, and nothing that the fresh food and legal weed the Fontaines grow on their property doesn't help with, but Mom and I will always watch things a little more closely where Harry and Henri are concerned.

"I'm going to go say hello to him and then I've got to head home and catch your father up. Imagine! Us losing the festival!" Mom huffs and heads away to see Harry, and I find myself moseying through the crowd.

Toward the podium. Toward the man who captured my attention a few afternoons ago and never really let go of it. The man who's now standing next to a chair, surreptitiously shaking far too many aspirin out of a bottle as he picks up a glass of water.

The man who, despite his propensity for saving small children in parks, just declared war on the town I've loved my entire life. The man who is now currently glaring at the back at Marion Stevenson, the graying widow who owns the town bakery and gives out free cookies to everyone on Thursdays.

Benson Lewis is a study in contrasts, that's for sure.

"Do you glare at all sweet, kind old ladies? Or just that particular one?" I ask him.

Like I said: I've always liked mysteries just a little more than I probably should.

Chapter 3
64 Days to the Devon Falls Leaf Festival

No, I would not be happier if I were naked more often. —Benson Lewis

I've got to get rid of this fucking headache.

That's my first thought as the town meeting dissolves into a mass of busybodies with nothing better to do on a Thursday afternoon than sit in the world's hottest "historical society" (whatever the hell a historical society even is—why don't they just call the damn thing a museum?) and talk about leaves.

Leaves. Fucking leaves. I still can't believe I just had to make a public statement to a mob about *fucking leaves.*

"Good job," Arnie tells me gruffly as I search my messenger bag for the bottle of aspirin I'm sure I threw in there. "I wasn't sure about your firm having me work with some guy who's barely out of school, but hey, you handled that like a real lawyer."

"Carter Stevens is in charge of your case. I'm not a lawyer yet. I'm a certified law clerk, remember? This was just publicity," I remind Arnie for the sixty-seventh time. I'm still not sure how this guy ended up getting represented by a firm like my grandfather's. He's not their usual type of client in any way. Most of the people who seek out Grandpa's firm are suit-and-tie types, people with corporate jobs and two or three houses in upscale neighborhoods. Arnie tells me he owns a used car lot and lives in Worcester, Massachusetts. I know what Grandpa charges by the hour, and I can't figure out how Arnie's going to pay his bill. And why does a used car salesman from Worcester care so much about a few acres of land on the Canadian border? Arnie's already made it clear he's not planning to move to Vermont, and he's not interested in selling the land back to the town once he establishes ownership of it. Devon Falls isn't exactly a booming place of commerce ripe for placing new mini mall developments. Why bother going to all the time and trouble for some land that you're probably not even going to make a profit from?

But I'm not here to care about Arnie's finances or long-term plans. I'm here to do a job, end a leaf festival, and win some land. So far, so good. Carter made it clear on our phone call this morning that he's not interested in spending any time in Devon Falls if he doesn't have to, and he expects me to take care of shit here.

I can do that. I definitely just took care of shit.

"When do you need me up here next?" Arnie asks.

The honest answer is that I'd like to see him never the fuck again. Conversation with him is like talking to a bar of soap, and the guy never closes his mouth when he eats. "You gave me all the documents you have, right?" I ask him. "Everything you've been able to dig up showing your family lineage?"

He nods and scratches his head. "Yeah. I mean, I think so. I mean, I'll, uh, see what else I can come up with."

I'm not sure where he plans to come up with more birth certificates from the 1800s and early 1900s, but okay. "Fine, do that. You can head back to Worcester for now. Our next hearing isn't scheduled for several more weeks, and I need to research the specifics of that will and your family's connection to the land." We'll need a lot more evidence than what we have now if we're going to win this case. Cat-print clothing aside, Ellie Nowak doesn't strike me as the type of person who walks into a courtroom unprepared. And the town judge may have nodded off twice during this meeting, but I've seen enough of him already to know he's sharp. He's not going to miss a step here, and he's going to rule in this case fairly, whether his ruling works in his town's favor or not.

I've got to make sure it doesn't.

"I'll call you," I tell Arnie, because my head is already pounding. Just thinking about the hours and days of my life I'm about to spend rustling through paperwork in this disorganized mess these people call a town hall is making it pound a whole lot harder. I need a handful of aspirin, a dark room, and a nap. Then I'll have the energy to deal with Arnie again.

"Okay. Remember: we gotta win this. We gotta." Arnie points his finger at me in a gesture that feels a little too intense for someone trying to take back some acres of land that are barely worth the trees on them. I'm still not sure exactly what his deal is or how he suddenly discovered that one of his distant relatives had rights to land in northern Vermont, but it's not really my job to care. If Grandpa and Dad, especially Grandpa, have taught me one thing over the years, it's that.

Are Arnie and his situation weird and sketchy as fuck? Damn straight. But you don't *care* about cases. You win them, as Grandpa always says. And I'm positive that winning this case is what I need to do to finally earn my family's respect.

That means Arnie's right: we gotta win this case.

I nod at Arnie and he leaves, disappearing quietly out of the back door. "Finally," I mutter as I manage to dredge up the bottle of aspirin from the bottom of my bag. I pour a handful into my palm and throw them into my mouth like Skittles, tossing some water back to cut the bitter slide of the medicine down my throat. My eyes stop on the back of the older woman who paused next to me earlier to tell me that while she might hold a free cookie day at her bakery, I sure won't ever be getting any comped baked goods from her.

"Do you glare at all sweet, kind old ladies? Or just that one?"

I almost choke on the nineteen thousand pills in my mouth as I whirl around to see Dr. Jack Lancer standing behind me.

Fuck. Incredibly Hot Doctor is here. He puts his hand on my back as I take another sip of water and manage to get the pills where they're supposed to go. "I'm truly sorry about that. Are you okay?" He moves his hand in a small circle while I finish getting myself together. "Take it easy, please."

Okay. So this is... unexpected. Not that Dr. Lancer has reappeared in my life—it's a small town; I figured I'd see him again eventually—but when I woke up today, I definitely didn't predict that he'd be rubbing my back and speaking to me in soothing tones while I learned how to breathe again.

And *no,* I did not just get a raging hard-on in the middle of a town hall filled with people who want to murder me. Except maybe I kind of did. I adjust the way I'm standing and try to knock the visual of my last viewing of the *Dudes Get Physicals* website out of my head.

I jerk away from him. "I'm fine. Hello, Dr. Lancer."

"Jack!" Some kid appears from within the crowd, ducking under arms to pop up next to my side. "Luis said there's not going to be a festival this year. What's going on?"

Hot Doctor smiles at him. "This is my nephew, Elijah. Elijah, this is Benson Lewis. Benson is representing someone who may be the actual owner of the festival land."

Elijah whips around to face me, and my heart sends out a twinge as I see the guitar case strapped to his back. Is it electric or acoustic? I wonder. My fingers itch to reach and take the case, maybe pluck a string or two.

"You're taking away our festival?" he blurts out.

My temple sends an extra shot of hot, throbbing pain across the rest of my skull, and I can't help but wince. Jack shoots me a look. Concern? Could be, I guess. He is a doctor. But why he'd be concerned about me, the newly established villain in his town, is a mystery.

Maybe he's required to look concerned. Maybe it's something in the Hippocratic oath.

"Mr. Lewis is just doing his job, Elijah," Jack soothes. "He's representing someone who may be a descendant of the original owners of the land. If the land doesn't belong to us, it doesn't belong to us. That's all there is to it."

That's a surprisingly objective viewpoint from someone who clearly lives here. Especially since his nephew's face is falling like it's a crashing elevator.

"Man, I hope we don't lose the festival," Elijah says. "Dad loves it. And my band was supposed to play this year. Is it definitely canceled?"

I should say yes, because there's no way in hell I'm letting that festival happen this year. Arnie's going to have that land back by October. I'm good at my job, and I'm not letting things go any other way. But for some reason the next words that come out of my mouth are, "we'll see what the judge says in court."

Elijah nods and frowns, and he shifts the guitar on his back slightly. And then more words I can't account for come out of my mouth. "What kind of music do you play?" I ask him.

Elijah's face lights up. "At school I'm in the orchestra, so we play a lot of classical. But my friends and I just started a band, and we play all kinds of stuff. Have you ever heard of Nirvana?"

Jack chokes back a laugh.

"I've heard of Nirvana," I tell Elijah. His light brown hair is dipping over his face in a way that looks almost Kurt Cobain-like, and I have to smile. "I used to love their stuff. I played some of it. 'Smells Like Teen Spirit' was one of my favorites."

"Wow, that's so cool! Do you play the guitar too?"

The question sends another shard of ice-sharp pain across my skull. "Uh, I used to. I don't anymore," I tell him quickly. I rub at my temple with one finger, but the pain stays strong.

"Hey, just so you know," says Jack. "My mom and I own a medical practice not far from here. If you're having issues with pain, one of us would be happy to check you out."

"I'm fine," I tell him quickly. "It's just a headache." I learned young not to make a thing of my *silly little headaches.* No one cares if you need to take a few aspirin. No one wants to listen to you whine about your head hurting.

Jack's eyes slide over to the painkiller bottle he just watched me nearly swallow whole, and I decide it's a good time to change the subject. "What else does your band play?" I ask Elijah.

He names off a series of bands with members old enough to be his grandparents. "Hey," he tells me. "You should come by the record store! I work there sometimes."

This town has a record store? They only have two stoplights. "Sure, I guess," I tell him. If I'm going to be stuck in a place with more cows than people for weeks on end, I may as well at least stop by and check out the six records they probably have for sale.

"Great! It's right next to Ellie's office. Mostly I work there during fencing and lambing season. The owner has a sheep farm outside of town," he adds. I guess the look on my face suggests that I have no idea what the hell he's talking about. "Come by when I'm working and I'll show you around. It's the coolest place ever. We've got Weezer on vinyl! It's like the best place ever."

"Don't forget our deal," Jack tells him. "You only get to stay working there if you keep your grades up. Speaking of which, how much homework do you have?"

"Ah, Uncle Jack!" Elijah whines. "Seriously, don't worry about me. I'm fine."

"I'm very glad to hear that. Just don't forget that you have algebra to think about. Don't you want to be ready for that first quiz you have coming up next week? You know you need to get a good grade on that."

Another stab of fire pushes through my forehead. This conversation sounds awfully familiar.

"Algebra's boring. I'd rather be playing the guitar," Elijah grumbles, tugging at the case behind his back.

I stare at his guitar longingly. I remember those days. Those days when all I wanted to be doing was playing music. Those days when I was constantly reminded to do Algebra homework instead. Because learning was more important. School was more important. And I was *falling behind.*

I was always behind, no matter how hard I worked. Not anymore, of course. I've spent a lot of years making sure I'm no longer the kid who's always behind in school. But right now, looking at Elijah, all I can think of are those days filled with constant pushes and reminders to put away the guitar and go be better at the things everyone else in my family was good at.

Eventually, I stopped fighting and put away the guitar for good. It was just easier.

"I know you'd rather be playing guitar." Jack smiles at Elijah fondly. "And I love listening to you play. So do me a favor. Go home and do some practice problems, and then you can play for me while I make dinner. Sound good?"

I inwardly wince as I try to imagine my grandpa or dad saying those words to me when I was Elijah's age.

Elijah frowns as he considers the offer. "Yeah, that sounds good," he finally says. "I'll see you at home. Don't forget to come by the store, Mr. Lewis!" Elijah rushes off, leaving me to wonder exactly what these two are to each other. They definitely seem a lot closer than your average nephew and uncle.

But it doesn't matter. It's none of my damn business anyway, and it's got nothing to do with Arnie's matter.

Which is why I'm here. Getting this land back to Arnie is the only thing I need to care about right now.

"Sorry to drag you into our family drama for a minute there," Jack says, smiling apologetically. "Hey, listen, if you ever want to eat with me and Elijah, you're more than welcome. When we're not at home, we're usually at Luis' café down the street. He makes killer food."

Is this guy seriously inviting me to eat with him? After I just declared war on his town? I'm still figuring out how to answer him when Ellie Nowak appears next to us. The brown cats on her shorts almost match the Birkenstocks she's wearing. It's an outfit that looks vaguely familiar.

I wonder if she and Iris Sprysky, my former boss, are friends.

"Well, son, you certainly made a splash here today," she tells me conversationally. "I assume you'll be here tomorrow, combing through the historical society's files?" I nod. "I will as well. I suppose we'll be seeing a lot of each other in the coming weeks. I wouldn't get your hopes up about winning this one, though. I've lived here my entire life, and I know every inch of this town's legal history back and forward. Plus, I'm very good at my job. But I'll certainly enjoy nailing your ass to the wall," she adds cheerfully.

"Right back at you," I tell her.

"Excellent. Now, son, you seem tense. Tell me: has anyone ever told you that you'd be happier if you were naked more often? Oh, dear. There's Amelia. I must run. I'll see you tomorrow, Benson!"

Jack's not even trying to hide his laughter as I turn around to face him. "What did she just say to me?" I ask him. "Did the opposing counsel just tell me to get naked more often?"

Jack sets his hand on my shoulder, and a rush of warmth circles through me, somehow easing the headache that the painkillers have barely taken the edge off of. "Welcome to Devon Falls,

Benson Lewis. I hope you enjoy your time here," he says. And then he disappears into the crowd.

I leave the town hall/wannabe museum and make my way back toward the studio apartment above the Farm-Acy that the firm rented for me—an apartment that continuously makes me wonder exactly how long I'm going to be in Devon Falls. I can't seem to make my feet take me directly back to the bare and lonely walls of that place, though. Instead, I find myself in the center of the town, at the park, staring a statue that still looks exactly like what it looked like when I first arrived: a poop emoji. As I fight the low drone of thunder that won't quite stop echoing through my temples, Ellie's strange question drifts back through my head.

No, I think. I would not be happier if I were naked more often.

Unless maybe I was naked with Dr. Jack Lancer.

Chapter 4

64 Days to the Devon Falls Leaf Festival

What kind of person purposely orders meatloaf? —Jack Lancer

I step into Byley's Record Shop and immediately hear what sounds like David Bowie's *Reality* album. I did wonder when the kid was going to discover Bowie. I wind my way through disorganized stacks of tapes, CDs, records, and sheet music toward the sound of Elijah's voice.

"Can you even believe what he could do with chord progressions? His solos!" Elijah's saying excitedly to someone. Definitely sounds like he's talking to one of his bandmates. I was going to suggest we eat at Luis' after the shop closes up in a few minutes, but now I'm guessing I might be eating alone tonight. If he's hanging out with his friends Pat and Lindsey, he's probably going to end up eating dinner with them. I follow a few inches of cleared floor space around a display of kazoos—

And see Benson Lewis leaning over the checkout counter, staring at the back of an album cover.

I stop where I'm standing.

It's been three days since Benson made himself an official enemy of Devon Falls and swallowed half a bottle of aspirin in front of me. Since then I don't think much has happened in the leaf festival case. The gossip mill says that Benson and Ellie have both been holed up in the historical society archives researching, but I haven't heard that either one of them has killed the other, and that's not Ellie's style anyway. It's more likely that she'd pop into the stacks nude one day and make Benson panic clear out of Vermont.

"Uncle Jack! Benson's here. Oh, he said I could call him Benson. And he likes Bowie! Isn't that great?"

Benson turns slowly from the album cover to look at me. His eyes have that same striking, penetrating look I remember from when we first saw each other. He's not smiling; I'm guessing that's not a natural look for him. But he's not frowning, either. His face is a pensive mask as he tilts his head up at me in greeting.

"Dr. Jack Lancer," he says. Did he stutter slightly on the term *doctor*? I must have imagined that.

"Benson Lewis, Attorney at Law," I reply, and I don't even try to keep the smile out of my voice. If I'd first met Benson Lewis at a bar in New York, I'd already have tried to pick him up.

"Not yet," Benson corrects me as he straightens up and sets the record down on the counter. "I graduated in May and just took the bar a few weeks ago. Won't get my results back for a little while still. Hey, I'm going to take this one," he tells Elijah.

"Wow, you took the bar quickly after you graduated. That's impressive." I don't have too many friends who are lawyers, but the ones I do have were all quick to tell me what a nightmare studying for the bar was. That seems like an awful lot of studying in such a short amount of time. "Are you nervous at all about getting the results?"

Benson shrugs. "It was no big deal. Vermont's got a high pass rate. I'm sure I'll be fine." I notice, though, that he's tapping his fingers anxiously against the countertop as he says that.

"*Space Oddity* is an excellent choice," Elijah tells him agreeably as he takes the album Benson handed him and starts punching buttons on a cash register that's probably older than him and Benson put together. I'm willing to bet Elijah only found out David Bowie existed a day or two ago, but I'm not surprised he's already managed to cram in the highlights of his catalog. Music is, after all, Elijah's first love in life.

"What are you doing here, Uncle Jack?" Elijah asks as he finishes ringing Benson up and pushes a bag across the counter to him.

"I thought I'd see if you wanted to eat at Luis'," I tell him, and his face lights up. I lived out of Luis' Café and Bar before Elijah came to stay with me, but I've been trying to make sure I feed him home-cooked meals since he arrived. Studies show that eating at a dinner table with kids is good for their stability. I know Elijah would be happy to eat at Luis' every single night, though. He loves it there.

"Yeah!" he says excitedly. "I just gotta turn off the lights and lock up. Hey, you should come, Benson!"

You have to love a kid who's so quick to forgive the man trying to destroy a key element of his home. Give Elijah someone to talk music with, and you've given him a friend for life. Benson looks shell-shocked at the invitation, though, despite the fact that it's not all that different from the one I offered a few days ago.

"Huh? Oh. I. Uh. I mean—"

It's like he's never been invited out to dinner before. Then again, he almost definitely hasn't since he arrived here. He probably can't even eat out in Devon Falls right now without taking a shower in dirty looks. A sudden image of Benson, alone in one of the tiny studio apartments or motel rooms that are the only places you can easily rent short-term here in Devon Falls, eating a microwave pizza and staring at the television, situates itself in my brain. "Come with us," I tell him. "We'll point out all the good things on the menu."

"Which is everything," adds Elijah as he picks up his backpack. "Luis makes the best empanadas. And spaghetti. And club sandwiches."

"Ah, the teenage appetite," I joke to Benson, who's still standing there, looking almost frozen by the idea of eating with us. "Seriously, Benson. Join us."

I know he surprises himself when he straightens up completely, juts his chin out, and says, "okay."

"What kind of person purposely orders meatloaf?" I ask as Benson slides his menu across the table to Ellis Ryker, who sends us both shy waves as he takes our orders and makes a quick promise to drop off more water.

"I like meatloaf," Benson replies gruffly. "Especially when it has ketchup on it."

"Huh. I didn't take you as a meatloaf-with-ketchup kind of guy." Maybe I read him wrong, but Benson strikes me as the type of guy who was raised on things like caviar and goose. My first impression of him was that he had the same sort of background as the upper-class business types I used to meet in high-end restaurants and clubs in New York.

"They used to serve it at my boarding school on Fridays," Benson mutters. "It was good."

Boarding school. I tuck that tidbit away into my Benson-Lewis-mystery-file.

"Boarding school sounds like it sucks," says Elijah absently as he scrolls on his phone. I keep meaning to ask Eric if he lets Elijah have his phone out at the dinner table.

"It was fine," Benson says curtly, and I quickly decide not to go down that path for this conversation.

It looks like an awkward silence might be about to descend on the table, but Elijah sets his phone down and quickly puts a stop to that. "I got an email from Dad," he tells me. "He might be able to talk next weekend. He's not sure." And then, because Elijah is Elijah, he promptly prevents Benson from having to ask any awkward questions by saying, "My dad's in the National Guard and he got called up. I don't get to talk with him much lately. That's why I live with Jack, in case I didn't tell you that."

"Oh." Benson casts me another look I can't read. He keeps touching the side of his head. I think a headache is bothering him again, but I don't want to mention him coming into the office. I hate the idea of seeing him in pain, but I also hate the idea of nudging at him so hard that he pushes away from me completely.

I have a feeling Benson has plenty of skills in pushing people away. And maybe it's just the attraction that hit me in the first few minutes we met, but whatever draw I feel toward him keeps me walking the fine and dangerous tightrope of making sure he doesn't push me anywhere.

With Elijah's help, of course. Not that he has any idea he's helping.

"Jack was married to my dad's sister, Fiona," he says, because it would never occur to Elijah not to spill our family story to a near-perfect stranger. The two of them have discussed Bowie, after all. "They're divorced now, but I used to stay with them sometimes when Dad had to go away. They had the sweetest apartment in New York! But Aunt Fiona's teaching in Italy now, so I couldn't stay with her, and my grandparents don't like me."

Benson looks bewildered by this speech, so I send him what I hope passes for a soothing look while I correct Elijah's last words. "Your grandparents love you, Elijah."

Elijah scowls. "They'd love me a lot more if I got all As. And stopped playing music and dropped out of my band." He shrugs. "At least Dad loves me the way I am. And you and Aunt Fiona."

"Huh," says Benson. He crosses his arms over his chest but doesn't elaborate. I'm still trying to figure out what the hell that interjection meant when Betty Norwal, one of Luis' long-time servers, appears at our table.

"I almost didn't even bring this food out," she tells us loudly. "The nerve of you, Jack Lancer! Eating with this man! And you, a former Devon Falls prom king and member of the Leaf Festival royalty!"

Benson nearly chokes on the sip of water he just took. "The Leaf Festival has royalty?"

"Of course it does. They lead the parade," Elijah tells him seriously.

"Now." Betty sets down our plates and puts her hands on her hips. "I brought this food because it's the duty the good universe gave me as your server. But I'll have you know that I'll be cheering when you're on the first bus back to wherever you came from, young man." She scowls at Benson, nods at me and Elijah, and picks up my empty soda glass. "I'll get this refilled."

"Tell Luis I said hi if he's back there," I call after her.

"Prom king, huh?" Benson asks with a smirk as he picks up his fork.

Damn. He even looks good eating one of the most disgusting foods on the planet. "I'll have you know I excelled at the role," I tell him seriously.

Elijah and Benson end up having an in-depth conversation about Radiohead while Elijah devours a sandwich, an order of empanadas, some fries, and one of Luis' specialty cheesecakes for dessert. Sometimes I'm amazed Eric can feed him on his salary. "Hey, Uncle Jack?" he eventually asks. "Can I go over to Pat's place? They learned something on the drums they want to show me." He turns to Benson again. "Pat's my best friend. They use they/them pronouns. Just in case you ever meet them," he adds.

I should probably say no. It's a school night, and I'm willing to bet he hasn't done his homework yet.

But then my eyes drift to Benson. My mind drifts to the idea of us alone, in this booth, together, for just a few minutes.

"Okay. Be home by eight-thirty."

"Thanks, Uncle Jack!" He throws himself out of the booth and barely gives the two of us a backward wave before he's crashing toward the door.

"He's in an overgrown puppy stage," I tell Benson fondly. Elijah's always been like that to a certain extent, actually. It's a stage I hope he never fully grows out of.

"Hmmm," says Benson absent-mindedly. "He reminds me a little of my sister, Daphne."

I can't imagine Benson with a little sister. I add that new detail to the mystery file and figure this is as good a time as any to press my luck. "Is your family here in Vermont?" I ask.

Benson raises an eyebrow. "You do know you can't 'nice' me into dropping my actions against the town, right? You can't manipulate me like that. That land rightfully belongs to Arnie. I'm going to get it for him."

Pressed a little too hard there, I guess. I put my hands up in the air, declaring my innocence. "Benson, I promise I'm not trying to manipulate anyone, least of all you. I was just asking a question."

His shoulders fall back into position, but at the same time he raises his hand to rub at his temple again.

"You should really see someone about those headaches," I tell him softly.

Benson groans and keeps rubbing. "I swear to fucking hell, this place is going to drive me nuts." He shakes his head. "It's a nice idea and all, this whole peace-love-kumbaya thing you all have going on. But there's no way this town is really as perfect as everyone here wants to think it is. Especially this festival everyone's so fucking in love with." He rolls his eyes and drops his hands back onto the table. "Look, I don't get why everyone's obsessed with a few orange leaves and some trails. But the law is the law, and the law will win out here. Maybe you'd all realize that if you weren't so into being fake-nice to each other all the time."

"Benson, I swear, I'm not trying to be fake with you here—or manipulate you. I promise you that," I tell him. "And just so you know, we're not all nice to each other all the time here. Just ask Elijah's grandparents." That's not a situation I normally talk about, but if Benson needs me to spill some of my dirty laundry before he can start trusting me, that's a price I can pay. Elijah certainly won't mind, and the entire town knows about our family dysfunction, anyway.

We're not particularly good at secrets in Devon Falls.

"What did Elijah mean by that?" Benson asks, and there's a little more give in his tone now. More curiosity than frustration.

"Elijah has a definite aptitude for music. There's nothing he can't do with an instrument. School? He struggles with it. Things there are harder for him. His grandparents moved to Florida last year, and they wanted him to move down with them. When they were here they were constantly fighting with Eric, trying to get him to push harder on Elijah about school. Eric's a single dad, and they have this idea that he doesn't have the time or energy to help Elijah be successful on his own." I sigh. "Fiona and I have played interference over the years, but when she and I were in New York there was no one to do that. It got messy. I moved back to Devon Falls a little over a year ago, and the last thing Elijah wanted to do was go down to Florida to be with his grandparents when his dad left the country, so it made sense for him to stay with me."

"Why'd you come back?" Benson asks quietly.

Because I failed in New York, is the answer that sits on the tip of my tongue; and that's exactly where I keep it as I say, "I decided to join my mother in running her practice. That's been her dream ever since I graduated medical school."

It's not a lie, exactly. More like an incomplete truth.

"So you and your ex both grew up here? That's quite a small-town story, prom king." Benson pushes his now-empty plate across the table and laces his fingers in front of him. He has that same guarded, defensive look he always seems to wear, but now it's etched with something else. More curiosity, maybe.

"We were. Met and fell for each other at fifteen." The usual feeling of disappointment drops into my stomach as I think of what Fiona and I once had. I don't mourn our marriage anymore, but I think I'll always mourn what might have been. At least on some level. "We were married at twenty-two. Stayed married for a little over ten years."

Benson sips at his water. "Do you and her parents get along?"

"Well, that's tricky." If I'm going to crack open more of the Benson Lewis mystery, I suspect I'm going to need to share a whole lot more with him about myself. And I'm curious. I'm curious what his reaction will be if I put even more of myself out on the table here.

Metaphorically, of course. Right now the table is still covered with the remnants of Benson's meatloaf, and I will die on the hill that meatloaf is the one and only terrible thing Luis serves here.

I draw in a breath. This is still something that's hard for me to talk about. It's not easy to figure out you're bisexual in your early thirties. Everyone's got such an ingrained and specific image of you in their head. Telling them is like asking them to erase an entire drawing of you and start it from scratch all over again.

But I know it won't be like that with Benson, at least. He's barely begun to sketch any details of me, if he's even bothered to do that. What I'm about to say to him will be just one more line in a picture that's still a work-in-progress. I like that.

"Her parents liked me fine right up until our divorce," I tell him. "But they're still not happy about me and their daughter splitting up. They've been even less happy about it since they found out I'm bisexual."

Before he can catch himself, Benson's eyes go wide. He gets whatever cool he's lost back together pretty quickly, though. "Are they homophobes?"

"No, not exactly. Well, probably. At least on some level. They'd never admit that out loud. But it definitely bothers them that their daughter was married to someone who also likes men. I sometimes wonder if they think my sexuality had something to do with our divorce. It didn't," I add quickly.

And there's another twist to the gut—because it's been made clear to me, in so many small moments, that the divorce was essentially my fault. And I still don't understand what I did wrong. I'm not sure I ever will.

But at least I can say for certain that the divorce had nothing to do with anyone else.

Benson nods slowly. He stands and tosses money on the table, and I know this conversation is over for the evening. Maybe I've said too much at once. I didn't imagine Benson as being homophobic, but you never know.

Benson grabs his suit jacket from the booth and pauses in place for a moment. "Thanks," he finally says. "For telling me." He frowns. "And by the way, I'm gay. Not that it makes a fucking bit of difference." He turns and stalks out of the café. The bells on the door clang loudly as it slams shut behind him.

"Man." Luis Morales appears next to me. He shakes his head as he throws a dish towel over one shoulder. I've been friends with Luis for years, long before he went to culinary school and returned to Devon Falls to cook us all the best food in town. "Can you even believe that guy? I should have known you'd eat with him." He starts gathering the plates from the table and shakes his head again. "You always gotta fix everyone and everything. But even you can't fix this mess, man."

"I don't try to fix everyone and everything," I call after him as he walks away from the table. He waves back at me in the universal gesture of *yeah, whatever.*

Luis may know me better than most people, but he's wrong about this. I don't think I can fix everyone.

I know I can't.

I couldn't fix my marriage. I couldn't fix *us.*

Chapter 5

60 Days to the Devon Falls Leaf Festival

You have open mic nights in the town square? Can't you just have them in your emo coffee shop like everyone else? —Benson Lewis

"Your headache's back."

Ellie's words slide through my skull like a machete, and I quickly add another aspirin to the pile I just poured into my hand. I swallow them fast and dry, and they burn going down my throat.

Who fucking cares.

"I'm fine," I grumble at her as I go back to staring at the yellowing piece of newspaper that keeps blurring in front of my eyes. Fuck. I can't be getting a migraine. I've gotten good at managing my headaches over the years, but when they turn into full-on migraines all bets are off. And I don't have time for that shit right now. I still haven't found any evidence to corroborate the family lineage documents Arnie's come up with, which are shaky at best, and I still need to further research the town bylaws and go back to the original will and testament document, and this entire situation is not helped by the fact that I'm basically being spied on by opposing counsel.

The same opposing counsel that keeps forgetting she's not alone in the Devon Falls Historical Society archives room.

"Ellie, I—Ellie! We talked about this!" Out of the corner of one eye I can see her leisurely reaching for the corner of her blouse, like she's thinking about taking off her shirt. It's happened before. Apparently, she frequently works nude when she's alone in her office.

"I just keep forgetting you're here too," she told me when I came back from the bathroom the other day to a picture that definitely wouldn't make the cut for network television.

"Oh, please relax. I was just adjusting this ridiculous seam," she says now. "Clothing is simply so confining! I'm certain you'd be so much happier if you didn't keep locking yourself up in those starchy suits and ties every single day. Have you given the idea of nudity any more thought, Benny?"

My opposing counsel also insists on calling me *Benny*, and unlike the assholes who used to call me that in elementary school, she's not doing it to be a jerk. She has got to know Tom Gentry and Iris Sprysky. Tom used to call me Benny all the time.

I kept meaning to ask him to stop, but it's tough correcting a guy who puts oil diffusers in your office to help "calm and center your chi."

"Don't you have an office you can go work in or something? Another case? Shouldn't you be defending a pig against a duck or something right now?" I ask Ellie for the thirty-seven thousandth time since we've started holing ourselves up in these archives together. Surely there's some other legal work somewhere in Devon Falls, but you wouldn't know it from all the time Ellie's spending here with me.

"This case is my top priority. You know that," Ellie says airily as she clicks at the keys on her laptop. "You seem like a nice young man, Benny, but I can't have your client destroying our festival. I simply won't allow it to happen."

I really wish my aspirin would kick in. Another knife drives its way into my skull just in time for my phone to ring.

Grandpa.

This can't be good. He doesn't exactly call me socially. And I just gave Carter the case update yesterday. I rush out of the door before Ellie can start asking questions and find a picnic table behind the building. I answer as quickly as I can, because Grandpa does not like to be kept waiting. "Benson Lewis here."

"I've spoken with Carter," he barks through the phone. "He has concerns, and so do I. We expected more in-depth due diligence from you by now. These people have no leg to stand on."

I wish that were true. "Theoretically, yes," I answer, and I wince as I hear the slight quiver in my voice. "But they're contending Arnie may not be a real heir of the land." I frown as I think of some of the oddities I noticed as I was going through the paperwork Arnie handed off to me. "I'm trying to find some further documents corroborating that he and Miriam are related, but so far—"

"So far nothing," Grandpa says sharply. "I hope you fully understand the importance of this case, Benson. Arnie is a key client to the firm. Don't fuck this up. Don't embarrass me." He hangs up before I can say another word.

"What the hell?" I ask the squirrel who's circling my table hoping for lunch leftovers. In its dreams. I don't think I've even eaten today. "Since when are used car salesmen important to Grandpa's firm?"

The squirrel leaves.

Okay, fine. Maybe it's time to get some more info here.

I wonder if Dad knows anything about Arnie's case. I unlock my phone and take my time thinking through how to word a message. Dad and I haven't talked much lately, and I don't like to bother him. Between Sarah and the twins, he's got enough to worry about.

Benson: Hey, Dad! I'm in Devon Falls. Do you happen to know anything about this Arnie guy I'm working with?

I hesitate, almost rewrite the message four times, and then finally hit *send.*

An hour later he still hasn't responded. But at least I'm not nearly as surprised as I was when I was eleven and my messages went unanswered.

"You need a break."

It's almost six o'clock and Ellie's back in my face, but at least she's fully clothed.

"I think you should come with me to the town square. We're having open mic night tonight."

I squint at her, and not just because this headache won't leave me alone. "You have your open mic nights in the town square? Can't you just have them in your emo coffee shop like everyone else?"

"Certainly not!" Ellie crosses her arms. Looks like I've finally found something that's an affront to her besides clothing: a typical open mic night. "When the weather is nice like this we always hold them in the square. We have some excellent talent. Moira's juggling tonight. And that new band the Maggio boy started is playing," she adds.

"The Maggio boy" has got to be Elijah. Suddenly, she has my attention.

I'm not usually the type of guy to show up for amateur hour music events, but I kind of want to see Elijah play. I've been spending more time in the town record store, which has a surprisingly decent collection, and the kid's good company. He's been playing me some of his stuff, and he's got talent. More than that, he loves to play. I'm sure this open mic night tonight is important to him.

And if some sparks of jealousy shoot through me when I hear Elijah playing the instrument I was forced to give up? Well, he doesn't need to know that. No one does.

And then there's the other reason Ellie's got my attention right now: *Dr. Jack Fucking Lancer.*

My dick perks up just at the thought of him. Mentally, I scold it to stay down. This is why I had to light out of the café like it was on fire last night after Jack told me he's bi. It's hard enough being around the man of your dreams—the one you can never have, because not only would he probably never have any real interest in you, but he's also basically the hero of the town you're about to destroy—when you think he's straight.

Finding out Dr. Jack Lancer isn't so straight after all? *Fuck my life.* I had to get the hell out of that booth before I embarrassed us both by making a pass at him or something.

Honestly, I'm starting to wish he'd turned out to be like every other hot asshole I've ever crushed on who wouldn't give me the time of day. Because all this fucking *kindness* he keeps trotting out is a whole lot harder to handle than indifference. Every time I see him he's asking if I want to grab dinner or how am I feeling or do I have everything I need here in Devon Falls? And sure, the guy probably has an ulterior motive for all this aggressive kindness. He may say he's not trying to manipulate me into dropping the land claim, but there's no way that's not at least part of what's going on here.

Not that it matters. I'm here to do a job, and it's going to get done. I won't be distracted.

I just have to make sure I stay far, far away from Jack's doctor's office. Because Jack in a lab coat... let's just say that's an image I've seen more than a few times while I'm falling asleep at night. I'm not going to find out what would happen if it suddenly manifested itself as a reality in front of me.

I quickly adjust myself in my pants again, because even thinking about Jack with a stethoscope around his neck is enough to do it for me, apparently. Still, I may as well enjoy the view while I'm stuck here in Devon Falls, right?

"Sure, I'll come," I tell Ellie. "Fine."

"What a favor you do us," she says dryly as she begins shutting down her laptop and gathering up papers. "But I don't think you'll regret the choice. Moira's juggling skills are unparalleled. She's up to four balls, you know."

I pack up my crap and follow her out the front door of the historical society and across the street to the town square where I first met Jack. Every time I walk by it or through it I'm shocked all over again by how much it's basically every small-town TV show I've ever seen come to life—to the point where I'd think this was a TV set if I hadn't lived in Vermont long enough to know that town squares are a real-life thing here. Between the large, stage-like gazebo at the center of the square, the playground in one corner, the picnic area in another, and the obligatory farmers market they hold here every Saturday, I spend half my time in the square waiting for everyone in it to break out in song together. Then I'd know for sure I was dropped into a Broadway musical without my knowledge.

People are setting up lawn chairs and blankets around the gazebo. I see Elijah standing on the makeshift stage with some other kids his age, messing with amplifiers and chords.

"Let's find Amelia," Ellie says. "She'll have a blanket we can sit on."

This is the strange thing about spending hours and days of your life locked in a room with the person that you're supposed to be fighting against. Sometimes you forget they're the enemy, and you end up picnicking with them at a concert while your grandfather thinks you're working on destroying the soul of their town. And shit, now I'm thinking about how fucking *pissed* Grandpa would be if he could see me right now.

Coming to this open mic night was a really terrible idea.

"Listen, I think I'm going to go," I tell Ellie. "I—"

"Oh no," Ellie says in a low voice. "Not them. What are they doing back here?" She clutches at my arm dramatically. It's clear she hasn't heard a word I just said.

"Who? What?" Who the hell could she be talking about? How could this town possibly have another enemy besides me within a hundred square miles?

"The Maggios have returned," she says, in the same tone the superhero in a movie uses whenever their nemesis suddenly appears on screen with them.

"The Maggios? But Elijah's playing. Who are you—" *Oh.* I find Jack standing in the middle of the square, not far from us, and suddenly everything makes sense.

The grandparents are back.

"We have to go help Jack," Ellie hisses. Now I'm being pulled across the grass toward an older couple in polo shirts and khakis who are having what looks like a staring contest with Jack. Not one of them is smiling, and I'm guessing Ellie's decided we're going to go stare with them.

"They're supposed to be in Florida," Ellie mutters. "I can't believe they had the audacity to come back here after how terribly they treated Eric before they left. That man is just trying to do right by his son! And for them to suggest that Elijah quit his music, with all the talent he has." I stumble next to her, and she frowns at me. "I'm not sure I should be telling you any of this. You're not really one of us." She taps her lips thoughtfully. "Ah, but I do like you despite myself. You have an interesting soul, Benny. Get ready for some mudslinging here. Conrad and Barbara Maggio don't like to fight fair."

And with that, we come to a stop right in front of the Maggios and Jack.

My dick perks up again. I'm going to have to buy some bigger pants if Jack Lancer's going to keep appearing in my daily schedule.

"Hello, Ellie," Jack says calmly. "Look, Barbara and Conrad are back from Florida." His eyes cross to me and the corners of his lips lift slightly. "Benson! I didn't expect to see you here. Benson's the man leading the case to see who the Leaf Festival land rightfully belongs to," he adds for the Maggios' benefit.

I wait for Barbara or Conrad to send me evil looks and share declarations that I'm destroying their beloved home, but they both keep their gazes on Jack. This is almost definitely the first time I haven't been the most hated person in a conversation since I've arrived in Devon Falls, and I'm not sure how I feel about that.

"I didn't know you two would be back from Florida this fall," Ellie says, in what's clearly her courtroom voice.

Conrad sends her a biting look. "Not that it's any of your business, Ellie, but we heard Elijah was struggling with his classes. Of course, we had to come back." He crosses his arms. "We know Jack's doing his best here, but Eric had no business leaving our grandson with a single doctor who's probably too busy cavorting all over Vermont to pay attention to a teenager. Not to mention that Jack's not even part of the family anymore."

Jack sighs. "Conrad, I'm still not sure how you've heard anything about Elijah's progress in school," he says. "Given that you're not on the high school's contact list."

Conrad crosses his arms. "Son, I've lived in this town longer than you and Eric have been alive. You think people don't tell me what's going on here?"

"That sounds legally problematic," Ellie muses, and he glares at her again.

"Ellie, I don't know why you and Amelia think you can stick your nose in everything everyone in this town does. You want to be part of this conversation? Well, that's fine with me. You can hear everything I have to say to Jack right now if you insist. You too," he says, gesturing at me with a flapped hand. "Whoever you are."

I should tell them all that I'm leaving. I shouldn't be at this damn open mic night in the first place, and I definitely shouldn't be watching my low-key crush have a blow-out with his former in-laws. I should be walking away. I shouldn't care about any of this. None of it is my problem.

But for some reason, my feet stay planted where they are.

"Listen." Conrad shakes his head. "I know you and Eric thought it was best and all, keeping Elijah here through the transition to high school. I understand what you both were trying to do for him. I really do. But Jack, you're obviously not up for this. I'm sorry, son, but it's time he came to stay with us."

"It's nothing personal, Jack," Barbara interrupts as Ellie opens her mouth. "You know we don't think any less of you because of... well, everything that went on with Fiona. Or because of the—the man thing." She shakes her head in confusion while I try to figure out if she actually just referred to Jack's bisexuality as *the man thing.* Sure sounds like it. "It's just that you're obviously unprepared for this! You've never been a father. You don't even have younger siblings. You're a doctor, for heaven's sake. You have a busy schedule and no one to share this responsibility with. We both know your parents are too busy with other things to help, and Elijah shouldn't fall into their care anyway. He's *our* grandson!"

"Grandma? Grandpa! What are you doing here?" Elijah runs up to Jack's side, panting and puffing while two other kids his age appear behind him, equally winded. "You're supposed to be in Florida."

Oh shit. This soap opera just keeps getting sudsier.

"Elijah, love!" Barbara sweeps down to envelop him in an awkward hug that he stiffly accepts. "Honey, we heard you're having trouble in school again. Of course we rushed right back up here to check on you."

Elijah turns bright red as he whirls on Jack. "Did you call them?" He looks close to tears.

Jack places a hand on Elijah's shoulder and sighs. "No. I didn't even know they were coming."

"Well, you should have!" Conrad booms. It's impossible to miss the crowd of onlookers that are starting to gather around us now. "Elijah, I know you don't like the idea of coming to Florida with us, but we're here for your own good. You've got such potential! It's time to live up to it. Time to put away that damn guitar and focus on what really matters."

My stomach clenches as a memory winds its way through my skull.

Grandpa, at the head of the large family dining table, discussing my future with Dad.

"We've got to accept that this boy isn't reaching his potential. It's time we finally took away that damn guitar and sent him off to that school I've been telling you about."

And my dad, looking over at me—sadly, almost.

Then looking away, quickly. And nodding.

My bags were packed two weeks later, and my guitar wasn't with them.

"Elijah," says Barbara. Her voice snaps me right back to the now: to this strange town square where bluebirds sing all day long, until people like me and the Maggios roll up the street. "We know you love Jack, and we all appreciate what Jack's trying to do for you here. But Jack's busy. He clearly doesn't have time to help you with school the way you need to be helped."

"This isn't working!" Conrad adds sharply, shocking his wife so much she jumps slightly. "Jack, we've talked to a lawyer. We'll take this to court if we have to."

"Oh, here we go," mutters Ellie.

Elijah's face goes white. "But Dad said I could stay with Jack!"

"Your father doesn't always know best," Conrad says. "And this isn't a gay thing, I swear!"

Jack sighs and rubs his hand over his face. "I'm bisexual," he mutters.

"Bise-bisex—" Conrad seems to be having issues saying the word out loud. "Whatever it is, that ain't the issue. I swear it isn't! But you're a newly single man! Who knows what the hell you're getting up to night after night. And you've got your patients to focus on."

"The entire town has less than thirteen hundred people in it," Jack says. "How many patients do you think I have?" He's holding on to his air of collected calm, but I can see the frustration starting to rise in him now.

"You don't have the skills for this." Conrad shakes his head. "That boy's failing again, just like he was with Eric, and someone's got to put a stop to it. We couldn't make Eric see reason, but you're not even a blood relation of Elijah's, and we can make you see reason. Our lawyer said so. It's time someone stepped in. Now, it would be different if you and Fiona were still together. If you were in a relationship with someone, someone who could help you out with Elijah when you get busy, someone who could help with tutoring and schoolwork—well."

"Then we wouldn't worry so much," Barbara adds.

And just like that: something happens.

Something I have no real explanation for.

I knew this guy at boarding school who got in trouble all the time for doing ridiculously impulsive things. Shit like suddenly sweeping all the books off a shelf because he felt like it, or starting a food fight in the cafeteria just because the mashed potatoes were in front of him. "It's like my body does it before my brain thinks about it," he told me once.

That's the only explanation I have for what comes out of my mouth next: my body does something before my brain even thinks about it.

"Jack and I are dating," I blurt out. Loudly.

I swear, no open mic night in the middle of a town square has ever gone more silent.

Chapter 6

60 Days to the Devon Falls Leaf Festival

I firmly believe real maple syrup goes on everything. And I do mean everything. —Jack Lancer

I've been surprised by some things in my life.

I was surprised to learn that I could hack it in med school. That I could keep up with everyone there, hold my own, and even show myself to be one of the best there at times.

I was surprised when Fiona agreed to marry me, even though we'd been dating for years at that point.

I was surprised when the doctor first gave Fiona and me the crushing news that started the slow, dragging descent of our marriage into divorce.

But I'm not sure any of those surprises—any one of them—will beat the shock I feel when *Benson Lewis* of all people suddenly outs himself as my fake boyfriend to the entire town of Devon Falls.

"What?" My former mother-in-law's eyes go wide. "But—I don't understand! You're here suing the town! You and Jack can't possibly be dating. And even if you were, that doesn't change anything!"

"Oh, really?" Ellie barks out. "And why wouldn't that change anything? You just said that if Jack had someone to support him while he's taking care of Elijah that you wouldn't be concerned. So is the real problem that Benny here is a man?"

"No! Certainly not!" Barbara crows.

"I'll have you know we support plenty of equal rights campaigns!" Conrad adds loudly. "Why, we even went to a wedding for two women last year!"

"We did!" Barbara nods enthusiastically. "It was lovely," she tells the crowd that's beginning to gather around us.

Ellie barely hides her smirk. "Good to know. Then I don't see why you'd have any sort of problem with Benson helping our Jack look out for Elijah."

"But—I—how long have you even been dating?" Barbara wrings her hands and almost wails the question. "I thought he just got to Devon Falls!"

Elijah's gone silent as he stares back and forth between me and Benson. Benson is white as a sheet, and I have a feeling his brain is only now processing the words that have just come out of his mouth. No way am I going to let him get stuck in a spur-of-the-moment lie he never meant to tell, even if it would help me and Elijah out in a big way. "Not long at all," I say gently. "In fact, I would never want Benson to feel... *stuck* helping me and Elijah out that way. He's very busy himself."

"And how long can he even be here?" Conrad asks. "Aren't you out the door the second this lawsuit is over, son?" Conrad shakes his head. "This is Fiona all over again," he mutters. "I still can't believe you ruined that the way you did."

I'm not even sure exactly what he means by that, since I know Fiona was tight-lipped with her parents about everything that went wrong between us. Still, the words are a knife etching their way across my skin, creating the kind of slow and aching bleeds I've treated far too many times in the past. I always thought those wounds were underrated and underappreciated. If something's not deep enough to get stitches, people assume it's no big deal.

Every knife wound hurts, no matter how deep it cuts.

I've spent a lot of time holding my ground against my former father-in-law since Fiona and I divorced and Eric first asked me if Elijah could come stay with me. It shouldn't be hard to find the words I need to say to him next. It shouldn't be difficult at all.

But any words I could say now are like an ice cube stuck in the back of my throat, choking me while I wait for it to melt. And while I'm waiting for that long and slow but inevitable thaw, Benson speaks first.

"This is a new relationship," he says quietly. "But I like Elijah a lot, and I'm more than happy to help him with schoolwork as much as he needs it. I was the valedictorian of my class at Burlington U Law." He raises an eyebrow. "Frankly, sir, I suspect I'm much more qualified to tutor him in freshman-level Algebra than you are."

"Oh, shit," whispers Pat.

"That's not—I—" Conrad sputters.

"Jack and I haven't talked about what will happen to us after this case is heard," Benson goes on. "But Elijah's told me that his dad should be back sometime this fall. That's correct?"

Elijah nods. "Uh, yeah. Hopefully by October."

"Then it stands to reason that we can cross that bridge when we get there." Benson turns to Ellie. "I assume you'll represent Elijah's father and Jack if Mr. and Mrs. Maggio here should decide to pursue custody of Elijah?"

"Damn straight." Ellie smiles widely. "And I'll do it pro bono. I bet their lawyer won't be working on that pay scale."

"Ellie, for goodness' sake!" Barbara sighs heavily. "You know we're only trying to do what's right here!"

"I do." Ellie nods. "I just think you've got the wrong idea about what 'right' is."

Barbara huffs. I'm still trying to find my words, my voice, my place in this hellhole of a conversation, when Elijah does it for me.

"Grandpa and Grandma, I like living with Jack," he suddenly blurts out. "And I like Benson! And if he wants to help me with school, that's cool." He sends Benson a quick half-smile. "He keeps trying to tell me that I need to be good at math if I want to be a musician anyway."

"Does he?" Conrad perks up, suddenly intrigued. "Huh." He eyes Benson up and down, sending him the sort of look that I've seen take down farmers back when he ran the seed company here. Benson never flinches, though.

"Well," Conrad finally says. "Barbara, I think we can see how this all plays out. We're here now, after all. We can come back and forth to Devon Falls as often as we need to. Keep an eye on things."

She sighs. "I suppose." She loops Elijah into another hug, even though it's clearly unwanted. "I still think you should be home studying right now," she scolds him gently. "But we'll stay and listen to you play." She collects a large bag at her feet and gestures to her husband. "Let's go find the Iversons," she says to him as she breaks through the crowd around us to begin walking across the square.

Conrad sends me a quick glare.

"Like I said, I'm keeping an eye on things here, Jack," he tells me. He pats Elijah on the head, ignoring the way Elijah ducks from under his hand, and sets off after his wife.

Burt Busby peeks out from where he's standing behind Ellie. "You and the lawyer are dating? Well, I'll be a heifer in heat!"

There are murmurs of agreement interspersed with mutterings of things like "I knew it!" and "I saw them at the café together, you know."

I turn, slowly, until I find Benson's eyes. I can't read the expression on his face. It doesn't look like he regrets what just happened here—but maybe he doesn't realize exactly what he just locked the two of us into

I'm not sure *I* fully understand what he's just locked both of us into. All I know is that the damn ice cube in the back of my throat feels like it's finally melted, and I think I know what words I need to say to him next.

"I guess we should probably talk."

"Why did you do it?"

It's a cool night in Devon Falls, and the beginnings of autumn are making their presence known. The sky is falling in pinks and purples and oranges, and Benson and I are leaning against the railing of the walkway next to the bridge at the south end of town. It's the bridge that passes over the waterfall Devon Falls is named after. This waterfall is only fifteen feet high, but when I was young, I was convinced this was the biggest waterfall in the world. No one could tell me otherwise. I don't think I fully understood how anyone could stand in front of this waterfall and not think it was the most spectacular thing on the planet until the day my parents first stood me in front of Niagara Falls.

Even then, I still knew there was something special about De- von Falls.

The sound of the rushing water is all around us, loud but gentle in the background. Benson sinks back against the railing we're standing next to. He doesn't answer me for several moments. "I didn't plan it," he finally says. "And I'm not sure I can explain why I didn't take it back."

"Well, I'll understand if you want to renege now," I tell him quietly. "The town may have bought into your story, but they'll just as easily buy into a story that we didn't last." I sigh. "Especially given my recent track record."

Benson looks at me sharply. "You're not exactly the first person in Vermont to get divorced, Jack."

True. Some days it sure feels like I am, though.

Benson tilts his eyes toward the sky. Night is closer now, and the crisscrossing colors of sunset are slowly dissipating as darkness moves to stamp them out. The open mic night is over, and Elijah's off celebrating his musical success with his bandmates at Pat's house. He wasn't nearly as thrown off by Benson's declaration as I expected him to be. "I think it's great that you're dating," he told me right before his set. "I like Benson. And now I don't have to stay with Grandpa and Grandma!" He was off to get his guitar before I could even answer.

I swear, that kid is like Teflon.

"Would Elijah's grandparents really come after you in court?" Benson asks.

"I don't know," I tell him honestly. "They've done some pretty shitty things to Eric where Elijah is concerned. Called child protective services on him for totally bullshit reasons. Crap like that. He's not a perfect father, but he doesn't deserve to be treated the way they treat him." I shrug. "Elijah's their only grandchild. Sometimes I think things would be a lot better if they had a few more to focus on."

And you didn't help there, did you Jack? I try not to wince as that familiar voice spins through my head.

"So the answer is probably yes, then," Benson says evenly. "And they'd really do it? They'd really make him quit the guitar?"

"If they were his guardians? That I don't doubt for a second," I tell him. "They'd certainly try, anyway. I mean, I understand their concern about his grades. I really do. I just don't think pulling his guitar is the way to get him on track with school."

Benson pushes himself off the rail. "Actually, maybe it is," he says conversationally. "But that sure as fuck doesn't mean you should do it." He shores himself up, and now his posture reminds me of how he looked the day he took on all of Devon Falls at the town meeting. "So we need to make this work, then," he says. "At least until the case ends or we've got a better idea of when Elijah's dad is coming back. Think you're going to survive being in a fake relationship with me? I'm told I'm kind of an asshole."

I push myself off the rail too, straightening until I'm standing above him, looking down slightly at his angled features and the way his eyes shine in the light. What I tell him next is the truth.

"I like you, Benson," I tell him. "I'm very grateful that you stepped in to help me and Elijah out today. You didn't need to do that, and I appreciate that you did. I appreciate that you're still willing to help out. I hope you know you're not trapped in this—anytime you want to step away, just say the word. But in the meantime? It's not going to be a hardship for me to spend time with you."

He tilts his head upward slightly. As his face moves toward mine, I feel a flash of something between us. Energy. Connection, maybe. And for just a moment, I wonder: is something more happening here? Or is what I'm feeling just the magic and beauty of Devon Falls pushing me to imagine things?

I don't come up with an answer to that question quickly enough, and Benson steps away. "I've got to go," he mutters. "Have to get up early. I have a case to win."

"Sure," I tell him. I send him a smile. "I have to open the office, actually. Hey, you want to have breakfast first? Elijah and I are making pancakes at seven o'clock if you'd like to join us."

Benson squints at me slightly. "I guess we have to make it look like we're dating, huh?"

That's the moment when it occurs to me exactly what Benson and I have just gotten ourselves into. Devon Falls thinks that Benson Lewis and I became a couple in the last few days.

Dating. They think I'm dating Benson Lewis.

For the first time ever, my hometown is going to watch me date a guy.

I'm still processing through this, trying to sort through all the varying emotions and changes that have flooded around and over me in the last few hours, when Benson says something so completely unexpected that it jolts me right back into reality.

"You probably use maple syrup on your pancakes, huh? The real stuff?"

"Benson." I pretend to dramatically clutch at my chest. "I would never dream of bringing any sort of fake maple syrup into my household. The blasphemy! I'm raising an impressionable youth right now."

Benson rolls his eyes. "Funny. But fine. I'll see you tomorrow morning. Only if there's real maple syrup, though."

He steps away into the falling dusk of Devon Falls. I watch him step lightly across the bridge, his steps even and his posture low, the profile of his features crisp and perfect, and I resist the urge to tell him that I firmly believe real maple syrup goes on everything.

And I do mean *everything.*

Chapter 7

55 Days to the Devon Falls Leaf Festival

How much happiness does one town actually need? —Benson Lewis

"I'm sorry. You did what the fuck now?"

I groan into the speaker of my cell phone. "I called to talk to Aaron, Jeremy. Not you."

"Well, it's just your luck that he happens to be in the shower then, isn't it? Because clearly, it's *moi* you need right now, not my beloved boyfriend. Who do you think is the expert on messy sexcapades here?"

"I'm not in a messy sexcapade," I grumble at him, but the truth is that I'm starting to wonder if maybe I do need some advice from Jeremy Everett, the former playboy of Burlington, Vermont, if I'm going to get through the next few weeks. Yesterday morning I had fucking pancakes with Jack and Elijah, and no way am I going to admit how delicious they were or how much fun I had listening to Elijah try and convince Jack and me that neither of us have heard enough Blink 182. Then last night I laid awake for hours while the implications of what I'd done crashed all the fuck over me. I ended up making a mind map at one a.m. of all the shit I'd started when I said those five little words—*Jack and I are dating*—and the implications weren't good.

I started a fake relationship with a doctor I have a not-so-low-key crush on.

A doctor who maybe—possibly—likes me back. At least more than most people do.

A doctor who just happens to be one of the key figures in the town I'm trying to legally destroy.

If my family finds out, they'll probably disown me.

If the Maggios find out, they'll probably make sure Elijah never sees Jack again.

Who the fuck knows what the town will do if they ever find out.

If only there were *actual* sexcapades somewhere in this mess.

"Okay, fine. So maybe there's no sex *yet*," Jeremy says. "But I can tell from your voice that this doctor is hot. He's hot, isn't he? I'm right. I know I'm right."

"Jeremy, can I please talk to Aaron now?"

"Benson, baby, I'm just trying to help you out with your fauxmance here. Now. Have you and the good doctor agreed on how much sex you'll need to have in order to establish your fake chemistry? Because—"

There's a rustling over the line, followed by some laughter, and then Aaron's voice appears over the speaker. "So. You're fauxmancing a doctor? I thought you were in Devon Falls to end a leaf festival."

"I am." I groan. "Listen, I never should have texted you about the doctor thing. It's not that big a deal, and don't call it a fauxmance. That's not even a word. I just have to pretend to date the guy, so his nephew doesn't end up living with his asshole grandparents."

"Okay," Aaron says slowly. "But, and don't take this the wrong way, Benson—since when do you care about whether some kid has to live with assholes?"

A mental shot of Elijah playing his guitar at the town open mic night, his face lifted in perfect happiness as his fingers drifted over the strings, wanders through my head. "Since now," I tell Aaron abruptly. "And that's not why I called anyway. I'll figure the stupid doctor thing out myself. I need your help with something else, though."

"The great Benson Lewis needs our help? Has this day finally come?" I hear Jeremy yell in the background. Aaron shushes him.

"What's up?" he asks.

"Maybe nothing. I'm not sure." I frown as I study the ancient census document in front of me. "Listen, does Sprysky and Gentry still have those connections at the Burlington historical society?"

"Yeah, sure. Actually, my coworker Peter's dad runs the place. Why?"

"I have some birth certificates for some people who just... don't seem to exist anywhere else in historical records. I can't find them in any of the documents I've been hunting through. I'm wondering if maybe the people in Burlington have more documents than what I'm able to find here and online. Could you pass me Peter's dad's name?"

"Sure. I'll send you Peter's info too. You've met him, remember? I introduced you a few times."

That vaguely rings a bell. Aaron's forever trying to pull me into his and Jeremy's eclectic circle of friends. I like them all well enough, and maybe I would have taken him up on his invites more often during law school if I had more time. But no way was I going to try to explain to Aaron that the same studying which took him four hours took me eight, and there wasn't usually time left over at the end of the day for hanging out at bars or going to game nights.

It's easier, I've learned over the years, to get yourself a rep as an asshole who hates people than it is to admit that your brain doesn't work the same way as everyone else's.

"Thanks, Aaron," I tell him. "I appreciate the help. Gotta run. I'll talk to you soon, though."

"Okay... but listen. You sure you're okay? Whatever's going on over there sounds like it could get tricky. Do you need me and Jeremy to drive up and see you?"

I need that like I need a hole in the head. "I'm fine. Talk to you soon." I click off before he and Jeremy can start getting all touchy-feely with me, and I dial another number.

Arnie answers on the second ring. "Yoho."

I'd probably be thrown off by that greeting if Arnie didn't use it every single time I called. "Listen, Arnie, it's Benson Lewis. Hey, do you know anything about where your great-grandfather would have spent most of his life? I'm going through all the census data, and so far I haven't found—"

"Wait a minute! I thought Bill said we didn't need anything like that!" Arnie interrupts suddenly. And loudly.

"Bill? Who the fuck is Bill?" I rustle through the piles of papers I'm currently sitting beside in the middle of the back room of the historical society. I don't remember any of Arnie's relatives being named Bill.

Arnie goes quiet. "No, not Bill. I didn't mean Bill. I meant you! Or that Carter guy. That's what I meant. You said this case was open and shut, and the land was going to be ours, no problem."

I definitely never said that. Maybe Carter did. But where the fuck did this Bill name come from? "Arnie, is there more information you need to give me?" I ask him slowly. "You mentioned last time we talked that you were going to try to find some more documentation of your family line. If you've got that, now would be a great time to trot it out."

Because I keep coming up empty.

"But he said we didn't need anything else!" Arnie bursts out. "Bill said—I mean, not Bill!"

If my suspicion meter wasn't already close to hitting its peak in this conversation, it sure as hell is there now. "Arnie, who's Bill?"

"Never mind. I didn't mean Bill!" he says quickly. "Look, I don't have anything else for you. But I'll look more. We gotta win this! You promised! We gotta!" He hangs up while I'm still trying to figure out who—or what—the fuck he's going on about.

I hover my finger over the screen of my phone. Do I call Grandpa? Ask if there's a Bill in this case I should know more about? The last thing I want to do right now is give Grandpa more reason to think I'm blowing the first assignment he's given me.

Dad never texted me back the other day, though, I remember. Maybe it's time to try him again.

Benson: Hey Dad! You know anything about a Bill in the Devon Falls case? Arnie mentioned the name but didn't tell me more.

Most likely he won't answer. He's not directly involved in this case, and he's a busy guy. Still... I hover my finger over the message for a moment before I finally click *send*.

Just then Elijah comes bursting through the door of the historical society, with Jack behind him. His guitar is over his shoulder. "Benson!" he says. "Jack and I were trying to figure out where you were."

I frown at a pile of file folders. "Working."

"On a Saturday. We should've known." Jack sends me a smile, and I try to ignore the fucking twinkle that's behind his eyes as he says it. He looks especially good today, in a salmon-colored polo and jeans that make his ass pop. The only thing hotter would be him in a lab coat, and *no* I did not just think about that image again.

It's been less than forty-eight hours since Dr. Hottie Lancer became my fake boyfriend, and I already can't stop thinking about him naked under a lab coat and giving me a very thorough examination. I adjust myself in my khaki pants and try not to look like I'm thinking about sexcapades with Jack as Elijah keeps talking.

"Jack's parents are having a picnic out at their house," Elijah says. "You have to come! His mom said so."

"That she did," says Jack easily. "She and my dad would like to meet you. Get to know you better."

I suppress an inner groan. Jack told me at breakfast yesterday that he's never been good at hiding things from his parents, and he planned to tell them the truth about our situation up front. We were much less truthful with Elijah. Jack didn't want to put him in a situation to have to lie to his grandparents, so he told Elijah that our relationship was still very new and that we're just testing the waters with each other. "But my parents won't have a problem lying for us," he told me. "The last thing they want is for me to lose custody of Elijah."

Still, I can't imagine that either Lancer parent will be thrilled their perfect son is fake-dating the guy who's in Devon Falls to destroy their beloved leaf festival. I'd rather spend the next hour on the phone talking to Arnie than try to make small talk with these people.

But Elijah's giving me his puppy dog face. "Please come?" he begs. "I just learned a new Foo Fighters song I'm going to play. And my friend Pat's coming, and you haven't really met them yet."

"We'd really like it if you joined us, Benson," Jack says softly. His voice is relaxed, his eyes soft, and how the fuck did I end up fake-dating someone who actually has real-life dimples?

"Okay, fine. I guess." I stand up and stretch, pushing gently at the slight pain in the center of my forehead. The headache that I've had since I first arrived in Devon Falls never quite goes away, but at least it isn't as intense as it usually is right now. "I can take a break, I suppose." I've sort of hit a dead end here, and I know that I'm not likely to make much more progress until I can get in touch with Aaron's connection. Not that I'm telling the Devon Falls faithful that. "Fine, I'll go. But there better not be any lawn games or dumb sh—stuff like that."

Elijah's eyes widen. "But we always play corn hole!" he says, and he starts leading the way out of the historical society. "And we eat ice cream. And Jack's dad's macaroni salad."

"Yup," agrees Jack. "It isn't a picnic without corn hole and ice cream. Clearly, Benson, you just don't know how to picnic properly. Don't worry, we'll teach you. You'll have the time of your life, I promise."

"Sure, whatever," I grumble as I follow Jack out the door. "But honestly, does Devon Falls need a picnic on top of all your other together-ness? How much happiness does one town actually need?"

"As much as we can get," Jack replies as he opens up the passenger door of his Subaru and waits for me to climb in.

"So, you're the boy who's pretending to be my son's boyfriend."

Alan Lancer strokes his thumb and first finger through a graying beard. He's wearing a t-shirt that says MADE IN VERMONT, cutoff jean shorts, and Crocs that look like they probably started off as red but are now a dingy brown color. I didn't think anyone besides Iris Sprysky actually wore Crocs.

Devon Falls loves to surprise me.

"Harry and I have decided we support it." Henri Fontaine, who I've learned is married to Harry Fontaine, the town judge, sets a casserole dish down on one of the picnic tables in the Lancers' backyard, which is really more of a giant field, actually. It's acres and acres of green grass connecting their large yellow farmhouse to electric fences with black and white cows grazing serenely on the other side. "Mind you, I don't generally support lying. But Benson, I appreciate you standing up to the Maggios for Jack like that. Takes a good man to do such a thing." She crosses her arms. "I don't suppose you'd also find it in your heart to drop this ridiculous land claim of yours?"

"No ma'am," I tell her evenly. Apparently, Henri and Harry are also in on our lie; Jack says he doesn't keep things from them either.

She sighs. "I suppose we'll have to learn to appreciate one another's imperfections, then. Alan, am I manning the barbecue, or are you?"

"I've got it this time," he tells her as he opens up a barbecue grill with more rust than metal on the body and starts turning knobs. "Now, Benson, you stay right here and tell me all about yourself. If you're going to be spending time with Jack and Elijah, I need to know everything."

"Alan, don't prod." Jack's mother appears next to me wearing yoga pants and a t-shirt. She quickly sends me some side-eye. "Now, listen here, young man. I'm going along with this charade because it's what's best for Elijah." She sets down the ketchup and mustard bottles she's holding and puts her hands on her hips. "But I'll have you know that if you hurt Jack or Elijah in any way, I'll—"

"Now, now, Dr. Lancer!" Alan swoops across me to interrupt her with a quick kiss on the cheek. "You know how attractive I find you when you go into protective mode, but let's not jump to conclusions here. What Benson has done for Elijah and Jack is very kind."

Dr. Lancer, who Jack says I should call Marie, sighs. "I suppose." She narrows her eyes at me. "I still don't understand your motivations, though. If you're really here to take the land from us, why on earth would you put your work on pause to help Elijah?"

"Yes, I'd be interested to know that too." Jack suddenly appears next to his mother, back from the bathroom with a bag of chips in his hand. "But it's up to Benson whether he wants to tell us that or not. All that matters now is that he's doing an incredible favor for us, and therefore we are *not going to interrogate him at an afternoon picnic,* Mother. You promised."

"I did." She holds up her hands in mock surrender. "Benson, I apologize. I do hope at some point you'll tell us more about yourself and why you've stepped in to help Jack like this, but in the meantime—"

"In the meantime, you're family!" Alan booms as he slaps me across the shoulders. "Festival or no festival. Now, set out some plates and let me tell you how I make my county-famous macaroni salad. The trick is frozen peas! Would you even believe that? I learned it on one of my cooking shows Marie hates. The other trick is...."

"Aren't you glad you came?" Jack whispers into my ear as he passes by me on the way to help his father with the grill. His breath is soft and warm, and it smells vaguely of the fruity gum I noticed he keeps in the center console of his car.

And weirdly enough? I actually am.

"That's what we think it's going to sound like."

Pat, Elijah's buddy from his band, strikes another chord on their guitar in perfect harmony with Elijah's playing. The two of them send each other confident grins. "But we're not sure yet. We still have to work out the bridge."

The blankets of onlookers erupt into applause. "That was lovely!" Marie calls. "Just lovely. You two are becoming excellent song writers."

"We're trying," Elijah says. "But it's fun to mess around with learning covers too." He breaks into a few lines of a Rolling Stones song I recognize.

"'Wild Horses,'" I blurt out before I can stop myself. "I used to love playing that one."

Ellie eyes me from where she and Amelia are sharing a plate of carrots and dip. "Opposing counsel plays the guitar? Benny, you never said!"

"I haven't played in years," I quickly add. Jack, who's sprawled out next to me looking like some kind of sun-kissed Greek statue, tilts his head at me.

"You should try playing something for us," he says softly.

"Yeah!" Elijah jumps up and rushes over with his guitar, eager as always. "Pat brought an extra."

"I did! I'll get it!" Pat runs off while I wonder exactly how many guitars two teenagers need to attend an afternoon family picnic.

"C'mon, Benson," Elijah urges. "We've never played together. It'll be fun!"

"I'm not even sure I remember the chords," I mutter, more to myself than him, as Elijah places the guitar in my hands.

But the second my fingers brush across that fretboard? It's like they never left.

There used to be this sort of magical moment of peace that would fall over me whenever I picked up a guitar. The only time I ever felt truly calm, truly in charge, was when I had one in my hands. Now, as I use the pick Elijah hands me to find old chords I didn't even know I remembered, that same sense of *rightness* washes through me. It doesn't matter that my fingers, which lost their callouses years ago, will ache for hours later. It doesn't matter that I'm hitting some incorrect strings as I move my fingers around. All that matters is the music pouring out of the instrument in front of me. Before I even realize what I'm doing, I'm playing the first notes of "Wild Horses" while Elijah grabs Pat's abandoned guitar so he can play along.

I play like I'm in a trance—through mistakes, through missteps, through forgotten melodies, as Elijah and I, and eventually Pat, move between the Rolling Stones and Bowie and then some old Beatles tunes. It's like I've completely forgotten where I am or where I'm supposed to be—until I hit a really bad note during the chorus of "Can't Buy Me Love," and the discordant sound jolts me back into reality.

A reality where an entire picnic of onlookers is staring at me. I nearly drop the guitar like it's hot lava as they all begin clapping and my face goes red.

"Benson," Jack says. There's an almost reverent tone in his voice. "That was... amazing. Absolutely amazing."

He sits up so that he's leaning toward me on the blanket, his eyes locked with mine. "I can't believe you can play like that," he adds.

"I haven't in years." I quickly pass the guitar back to Elijah. "I, uh, need some macaroni salad."

I have to get off this fucking blanket. I push myself up from it, fast, and head toward the distraction of the picnic table. Maybe if I eat enough macaroni salad—and there's no way I'm ever admitting it, but that is some of the best damn macaroni salad I've ever had—I'll forget how good that guitar felt in my hands.

Or how good it felt when Jack looked at me the way he just did.

I'm halfway across the field and trying not to wonder whether Jack's following behind me when my watch buzzes with a text. I tap the message there, and a sort of numbness washes through me as I read the words.

Dad: Never heard of a Bill. Make sure you stay on that case! Firm needs that win. Don't let yourself get distracted by silly details. Stay on track, bud! You got this!

And just like that, the headache that had all but disappeared while I was playing with Elijah and Pat reappears in my skull in a persistent thump.

It only gets louder and more painful when Jack Lancer appears next to me asking if I want a maple bar.

Because as distractions go, Jack Lancer is the most dangerous one I've ever stood next to.

Chapter 8
50 Days to the Devon Falls Leaf Festival

*Are you going to date me and detest me at the same time? —Jack
Lancer*

"I just saw another strep throat case." I groan and drop my head
onto my desk as Mom pats my shoulder on her walk by me. "I
swear, I never thought it was possible to see this many cases in
one week."

"Thank goodness it's already moved through most of the elementary school," Mom says patiently. "It won't last much longer,
I promise." She falls into a seat at her desk, which is across from
mine in the small office we share. "Starting to miss your fancy big
city cases in your fancy big city hospital?"

Am I? I look at my last messages from Sam and Milo in the text
chain we all share.

Sam: Just treated someone with an actual cucumber stuck up
their ass. Beat that.

Milo: CAN DO IT. Last week my knee patient told me he
tweaked it out on a walk. Later his wife spilled that he did it while
they were taking a naked yoga class together.

Sam: Naked yoga is a real thing??

Milo: Apparently. I'll let you know how my first class goes on Monday.

Sam: Of course you will.

"No, I don't really miss it at all," I tell her honestly. "Things are going just fine here."

The truth, actually, is that life in Devon Falls has never felt more interesting or exciting, strep outbreak aside. It's been less than a week since Benson Lewis announced to the town that we were dating and the two of us started spending time together nearly every single day, and I know I'm enjoying it far more than I should.

I'm only supposed to be doing this to help my nephew. But when the three of us went out to the café together last night and Benson wore these sleek black pants with a bright blue polo shirt that perfectly accentuated his chest and made his eyes look bluer than they ever have... well, let's just say I was *very* careful how I sat in that booth.

"Is the town giving you any trouble?" Mom asks as she leans over her desk.

"About what? Me finally being openly bi in front of them, or me dating the man who's trying to wreck shop on Devon Falls?" Benson isn't the first man I've dated since Fiona and I broke up, but he's certainly the first man I've dated this publicly in front of my entire hometown. And sometimes it's hard to tell if the strange looks we get are because of that or because the court date for the land claim is getting closer or closer.

"Either, I suppose." Mom tents her fingers and frowns.

I shake my head. "Not really. Not openly, anyway. Well, I don't think I'm getting any more free cookies at the bakery anytime soon. But Marion made it very clear that's because I'm dating 'that land-grabbing lawyer,' as she put it. Until the case is over, I wouldn't eat at the bakery anyway. Too much of a chance I'll get a cookie filled with baking soda."

Mom laughs out loud, and I try to figure out what I want to ask her next. Finally, I just decide to come out with the exact question that's been on my mind.

"Mom? Did it surprise you when I told you I was bisexual?"

"Not really. Not anymore than it surprised me when you told me you were marrying Fiona." She frowns. "Do you mind if I ask if it was a surprise to her?"

"No, I don't think so." There were so many times in our relationship where I was convinced Fiona knew me better than I knew myself, and the moment I told her I was bi was certainly one of them. "And she knows I've dated men since we split up. She's told me it isn't a problem for her. Though it's clear that's not completely true for her parents."

Mom scowls.

"I guess... I just..." I'm not sure how to explain the confusion that's cycling through my head lately. How being around Benson lights up something I didn't even know was inside of me. How drawn I feel to him, and how much that feeling amplifies every moment that we spend together. How protective I feel when he rubs at his forehead or tries to hide the pain he seems to be in almost constantly. How proud I felt when he played with Elijah that day at the picnic, just knowing I was probably one of the first people to see him pick up a guitar in a very, very long time. It felt like such an honor. Such a privilege.

I haven't felt this way with any of the people I've dated since Fiona and I broke up, regardless of their gender. I'm actually not sure I ever felt this way with Fiona. And that scares me enough that I wish I could find a way to explain how I'm feeling to my mother. This is the person I've gone to with most of my problems throughout my life, and I need some of her sage advice more than ever at this moment.

But I'm not sure even my superhuman mother can solve the problem that I might be crushing on my fake boyfriend, who also just happens to be the town's archnemesis.

"I think…" I'm still desperately trying to put my thoughts into words when my phone rings. I see who's calling and immediately stand up.

"Can you handle throat cultures for a while? This is Elijah's school."

Mom's eyes widen. "Oh, dear. We're all set, Jackalove. I hope everything's okay," she adds as I quickly hit the button to answer the call and step into the hallway for some privacy.

Me too. But I've never gotten a call from Elijah's school before. Whatever this is about, I have a feeling it isn't good.

"Cheating? Really, Elijah?"

He's sulking on the couch in the middle of my living room, looking every bit the part of an angry and angsty teenager, while I pace in front of him, feeling an awful lot like one of my parents. Except I'm not the parent here. And when I just tried to call Eric, hoping for a little guidance on how to handle this situation, I was told he's out of contact indefinitely.

"It was just a stupid quiz!" Elijah glares at his hands, me, and then the TV in rapid succession. "I don't know why everyone's making such a big deal about this."

"Pat was letting you look at their paper! On a quiz I know you studied for! Elijah, please help me understand what's going on here."

God, are Barbara and Conrad right? Is this a mistake, me having Elijah? Am I going to mess him up the same way I messed up everything with their daughter?

"Please help me understand this." I cross my arms and stare down at Elijah as I hear the back door creak its way open.

"Hey, is anyone here?"

It's Benson's voice. My heartbeat races slightly. What's he doing here?

"Elijah, I got your text, but no one's answering the front door." His voice is getting closer now, and my body is responding the same way it always does to him: it's as if every single cell starts curving itself toward him in a strange dance I can't fully explain and don't understand.

"We're in here," Elijah calls.

"You texted Benson?" I demand, more than a little annoyed. I'm having enough trouble trying to figure out how to be a quasi-parent here. I doubt having my probably-crush, definite-ly-kind-of-nemesis and very-definitely-fake-boyfriend watching me do it live is going to help.

Elijah crosses his arms. "I thought Benson would understand."

"Benson's a lawyer! You think he cheated on tests while he was in school?"

"It was a quiz!" Elijah yells, just as Benson steps into the room. He takes one look at Elijah and me, facing off against one another, and his eyes go wide.

"Something wrong?" He situates himself in the middle of the room, next to the coffee table and right in between us. He slips his hands casually into his pockets, but I can tell he's worried.

"I copied some answers off of Pat's paper on a quiz and now Jack wants to make a federal case out of it," Elijah tells him.

Benson bites his lip. "You did what?"

"He cheated! On a math quiz! And now he thinks that telling me it's no big deal will make the problem go away!" I shake my head.

"Elijah, I need you to take this more seriously. I can't defend you living with me to your grandparents if you're going to get in trouble like this. I can't!"

Elijah glares, and Benson's eyes go a little wider.

"Maybe we do need to talk about you scaling back some of the time on the guitar. Or the record store. I told you we'd have to talk about your hours there if you couldn't keep up with school."

Elijah stares at me in absolute horror. "I can't believe you!" His voice is louder than I've ever heard it. "You sound just like *them*. You're supposed to be on my side!"

"I am on your side!" I'm trying to keep the frustration out of my voice, but it isn't easy. "Elijah. I want you to keep playing music. I don't ever want you to have to stop—you're incredibly talented. But I also have to make sure you finish high school. Your dad gave me a job when he left: to make sure I do right by you. I have to do my best to make sure you're as successful as you can be. And if that means we have to look more closely at your schedule, then so be it."

"Dad wouldn't care about this!" Elijah shrieks, and I think it's his tone that sends me over a cliff I didn't realize I was standing in front of.

"Well, he should!" I'm not proud of how loudly I'm speaking now. "You have incredible potential, Elijah, and I'm not going to let you squander it!"

"You're being such a control freak!" Elijah throws up his hands. "I can't believe this! I thought you were different, Uncle Jack. Is this why you and Aunt Fiona broke up?"

The words are like a punch directly to my stomach. I actually find myself moving backwards, away from him—that's how hard those words land.

And that's when Benson steps in.

"Okay," he says, raising his hands, almost as though he's setting up an imaginary wall between us. "Time out. This isn't getting anyone anywhere. Elijah, I know what it's like to be so frustrated at school that you don't make the best choices."

Elijah and I both turn to stare at him, Elijah in victory and me in surprise. "You do?" I ask.

Benson nods uncomfortably. "I do. But Elijah, you know cheating's messed up, right? And it isn't actually going to solve whatever the real problem is here."

Elijah scowls. "The problem is that algebra is dumb."

"Maybe. But at least that's a fixable problem. Tomorrow we're working on your homework together while you're at the record store. Put in some serious time and effort and we'll jam together afterwards. Deal?"

Elijah looks as shell-shocked as I feel. "Yeah, okay. Deal."

"Good. And you." Benson turns to me. "Stop talking about making him quit music. It's not going to help. Not the way you think it is, anyway."

I nod, dazed. I have so many questions right now. Like how he pulled this parental magic trick out of his back pocket. Or how he can be so sure that asking Elijah to spend less time on his music won't help this situation. Or what he meant when he said he understands what it's like to be frustrated with school. Or why he's here in the first place, standing in my living room, when I know he has much bigger things on his plate right now than my pseudo-parenting emergencies.

"Fine. Okay." That's all I can say, as he stands there making me feel more and more things that I'm uncomfortably sure I've never felt before.

An hour later, the two of us are walking through the town square on our way to the café. Elijah's gone to Pat's house. He said he has some apologies he owes them. I resisted the urge to tell him he was grounded when Benson shot me a look that said *let him go.*

I suppose there's an argument against taking parenting advice from a guy who's about ten years younger than you and barely out of law school. But I can't deny that Benson seems to have a much better handle on this situation than I do. He saved my ass back in that living room, and I know it.

"Thanks for showing up when you did," I tell him as we stroll past the town's statue of two small children dancing around a pile of leaves. Unfortunately, in stonework the whole thing looks more like a massive poop emoji. It gets a lot of selfie action from tourists, and I'm told it went viral recently. "That argument was going off the rails fast. I'm not sure where it all would have ended if you hadn't shown up when you did."

Benson shrugs, looking almost embarrassed. "I'm sure you would have figured it out," he says.

"Yeah? Well, I'm glad you are, because I'm certainly not." I shake my head. "Eric's out of touch again, probably for a while, and I'm just not sure the best way to handle these situations with Elijah and school. School was never hard for me, you know?"

Benson casts me a wry look. "I sort of got that impression," he says flatly.

"Mind if I ask you something?"

"If I do, I'll sure as fuck tell you," he replies mildly. It's hard not to appreciate his honesty.

"Did you mean what you said to Elijah back there? About understanding what it's like to be frustrated with school?"

Benson hesitates for a moment. We've paused across from the I, and people are moving up and down the sidewalk, trading laughter and shots of conversation. "Hello there!" someone calls as they walk by. It's Rose Ellerby, who owns the laundromat. "Benson, I have your pants all pressed and ready. But I'm putting extra starch in them until you drop this ridiculous lawsuit of yours."

Benson rolls his eyes, but he looks like he's trying to hide a smirk. "Be there tomorrow," he calls back. He turns around to face me again. "Yeah, Jack. I know what it's like to be frustrated by school. I know that feeling all too well."

That surprises me more than it should, given the conversation we just had in the living room. "I'm really sorry to hear that," I tell him.

He studies me. "You're exactly the kind of guy I hated back when I was in middle and high school. The kind of guy everything came easily to. I bet you could ace a test without even looking at the material. I'd stay up all night studying and get a B."

That story does sound familiar. I take another step toward him, and now we're so close that I can feel the buzz of energy between us. "That sounds terrible," I tell him softly.

He shrugs. And then he takes another step closer to me.

"Are you going to date me and detest me at the same time?" I ask. I can feel the danger in the sentence. Like I'm standing on the platform for a tightrope, and whatever words he and I say next will decide if I venture out across it.

"I don't hate guys like you anymore." He says the words slowly, with something like a smile inching up over his face. The energy in the air is more than a little palpable now. I can feel it dancing between us, and I know he does too. I lean a little closer to him, testing the boundary of whatever's shifting between us. He moves toward me, and I know if I just leaned a little more, if I just let my body go where it wants to go, I could discover what it feels like to have my lips against his. My skin flush with his. All this drive and desire and chemistry I've never felt before—I could have it, all of it. If I just moved a little closer.

But then it happens.

Benson takes a step back, suddenly grasping at his temples like his head is in a vice. He hisses aloud, and I wonder how long he's been nursing this headache without saying a word. Was he hurting this much the whole time he was brokering and bartering agreements between me and Elijah?

I have to make sure this doesn't go on. "Benson, you have got to get this looked at," I tell him urgently. "Let me take you back to the office now. I shouldn't examine you, given our current relationship, but we can call my mom. Once you've got some pain management in place, we can—"

"Jack, stop."

It takes me a moment to realize Benson's glaring at me. "Huh?"

"I said stop. Leave me the fuck alone, okay?" He winces as he rubs harder at one of his temples. "Don't try to fix this like you try to fix Elijah, okay? I know you like to think you can make everything better, but you can't. You can't fix me."

His words stop me in my tracks, and I'm still trying to figure out how to respond when Ellie comes rushing up to us. "I've got it!" she yells loudly. "Definitive proof. Your boy Arnie is no relation to the LeBlancs. You have to drop your injunction immediately!" She thrusts a piece of paper into Benson's hands. He studies it for a moment, eyes narrowing, before he turns and starts walking quickly across the park.

"Where are you going?" I call out to him.

"Where I should have been this whole time," he calls back. "Work."

I spin to face Ellie. "You really found it? Proof that the land belongs to us?"

"I believe I did." She crosses her arms, looking like a cat with a mouse trapped between its paws. "I hope you haven't gotten too attached to that mercurial fellow there, Jack. I do enjoy his spirit, but I don't know how much longer he'll be around."

I turn again to watch Benson. He's jogging swiftly now, headed toward the street. I have no doubt he'll hole up in the historical society and spend the rest of the night there, investigating whatever evidence Ellie's just dug up.

I watch, and I wonder: what does it really mean to fix someone?

Chapter 9
44 Days to the Devon Falls Leaf Festival

But I don't want to go back to high school. —Benson Lewis

"No, Carter," I explain with as much patience as I have left to give the conversation I'm having with the associate in charge of the Devon Falls case. He's made it clear since we first began working together that he wants to deal with a leaf festival land case about as much as any associate with an Ivy League diploma and a thirst for money wants to talk about leaf festivals in an area of Vermont hardly anyone has ever heard of. "It's a death certificate. For the man who's supposedly Arnie's great-grandfather, but it's dated ten years before Arnie's grandfather was supposed to have been born."

The silence on the other end of the phone is the kind of silence you'd expect from a lawyer who's just been told he's at least eighty percent fucked.

"Are you kidding me right now?" he finally says.

"I'm not." I sigh as I squint at the screen of my laptop. It's a little bit fuzzy around the edges. Whether that's from the fact that I didn't sleep last night—my brain wouldn't stop spinning around this damn certificate Ellie dredged up from somewhere—or the headache that feels dangerously on the edge of being more than just a headache... well, that I can't quite say. And I don't have time to worry about it right now. "Listen, Carter, I've got it handled. A guy I know connected me with someone who got me access to the Burlington Historical Society Archives." Which are all digitized, of course, because Burlington's managed to find its way into the current century. Unlike Devon Falls, where microfiche and plastic sleeve protectors seem to be the height of technology for preserving historical documents. "I'm going to take a fucking microscope to that thing. There's got to be something there that corroborates our evidence or disproves theirs."

Carter's silence says a hell of a lot. "Listen, Benson," he finally mutters. "Do I need to come up there? I can't let a clerk screw this up under my watch. This suit was supposed to be a cakewalk, and it's an important one to the firm. So I'm told, anyway."

"I've got this," I promise him. "I'm in the digital archives now, and I'm going to give Arnie a call to see if he has any additional information. We'll get this figured out. Hey, listen," I add casually, because I don't need this question getting back to my grandfather. "You don't happen to know why this case is so important to the firm, do you?"

"Why the fuck would I know that? It's your family who's running the place."

He hangs up, and the edges of my computer screen go a little bit fuzzier.

Five hours later, I'm wondering what the hell I'm going to do if I can't create the outcomes I promised Carter earlier. This archive Peter's father gave me access to is *massive*, actually, and the more I dig through it, the more and more that death certificate starts to look legit.

Which it can't be. It just fucking can't be. I can't fail in my first assignment for Grandpa and Dad's firm. I just can't.

I decide it's time to do what I've been avoiding doing all day: I'm going to have to call Arnie Annoying Blake.

He answers on the second ring. "Yoho!"

Shoot me now. "Arnie," I tell him abruptly. "Look, we need to talk. The town has a death certificate for your great-grandfather. It's dated ten years before the birth certificate you gave us for your grandfather. This is going to cause us huge problems in court if we don't have solid evidence disputing it. What can you tell me about your great-grandfather? There's not much info on this certificate the opposing counsel drummed up. I need evidence that he was alive after—"

"I don't understand," Arnie interrupts suddenly. "I just talked to Bill Cummings! He said we have all the documents we need and everything is in place. They can't have a death certificate. They just can't!"

There's that name again: Bill. But at least now I've got a last name to go with it. "Arnie," I say, "that's the second time you've mentioned someone named Bill. Who is this guy? Is he helping you with your family research or something?"

Arnie's quiet for a moment. "Yeah," he finally says. "Yeah! Uh, helping me with my family research. That's who he is!"

His answer doesn't explain much about why he couldn't just tell me that in the first place. If I were working for Iris and Tom still, back at Sprysky and Gentry, they'd definitely ask more questions. Probe more. But I've been around Grandpa and Dad long enough to know they don't work that way. As Grandpa says, we're here to win cases, not get all up in people's business. Get what you need to win the case and get out.

What I need right now is proof that this relative of Arnie's didn't die when a stupid piece of paper says he did, and I quickly tell Arnie that. "Get your guy Bill on this if you can. I'm digging through everything I can find, but so far, I haven't found any proof that this guy existed past the date on his death certificate, except your grandfather's birth certificate. And a judge isn't going to like that."

"I'll get proof!" Arnie replies. "I can do that. I swear it." At least he's got a sense of urgency. That's what I need to hear right now. "We're gonna make this happen!" he crows, and he immediately hangs up.

Then he calls back two seconds later. "What did you say I need to find?" he asks.

How, I wonder again, did this guy get involved with someone like my grandfather?

When he hangs up, I stare at my phone for a long moment. My vision's still blurring, but I haven't gone full-on migraine yet today, so that's something. I scroll through my contacts until I come to the number I'm looking for. Then I just sit for a minute, trying to decide whether or not to hit the call button.

My dad and I have never been all that close. I spent the first six years of my life being raised mostly by nannies at my grandfather's house while he was finishing law school and getting his feet under him working for Grandpa. And then I only lived with him for a few years before I was shipped off to boarding school in southern Vermont. Even when we did live together, I was definitely around nannies and babysitters a lot more than I was with him.

But he's a good guy, my dad. Like Grandpa, I know he's always wanted what's best for me. The money he spent on my boarding school alone proves that.

I think of Elijah for a moment, and I wonder: did my dad cave right away when Grandpa told him I needed to give up the guitar? I can't see him standing up to Grandpa the way it sounds like Elijah's dad stands up to his grandparents. Then again, it's not like I know my dad all that well. Not the way his "real" kids do.

I take a breath, and before I can overthink things any longer, I press the button on my phone. The name DAD stares at me from the screen as it rings and rings and rings. Eventually his voice message comes on.

"This is Linus Lewis. Sorry I missed you, but—"

I hang up fast, because what the fuck would I say in a message? *Dad, I might be screwing up in my first assignment for your firm—the one place I've wanted to work my entire life? Dad, I have a headache and it really hurts? Dad, I think I had a moment yesterday with this doctor I'm crushing on? Oh, and by the way, I'm pretending to be his boyfriend right now, and you and Grandpa would definitely not approve?*

I drop my face to the desk below me and moan.

"Benson! Benson, are you okay?" Fuck, there's my doctor now. Looking tall and hot in a pair of fitted jeans and a t-shirt that stretches perfectly across his pecs. And as if that wasn't enough, he's wearing a look that gives me an immediate chub, somehow. A look like he's concerned. Like he cares.

What the actual hell is wrong with me? I know I have a doctor kink, but a doctor looking at me like he gives a shit has never given me a hard-on before.

"I'm fine." I tilt my head up. "What do you need? I'm working."

"You've been working all day." Jack's still giving me that look, and it's starting to be a problem for my pants. "Elijah's school has their fundraiser night at the Thai restaurant tonight, remember? The owner's performing his standup routine, and all the proceeds go to Elijah's band. You told Elijah you were going to come."

"The guy who owns your Thai restaurant does standup?" I feel like I should remember that conversation. Then again, my head is more than a little foggy right now.

"Yeah. Elmore Tran. He's great. He does a really solid routine about people who want him to figure out a recipe for maple syrup curry. Hey, are you sure you're okay? You look a little green, and—"

"I'm fine," I interrupt at the same time I mentally order my dick to stand the fuck down. "But I don't want to go back to high school. Especially not tonight. Tell Elijah I can't make it, okay?"

Jack frowns. "Benson, Ellie told me what she found. Look, if that document is real and the land does belong to us—"

"It doesn't," I interrupt. "It can't, because I have a job to do here, and I'm going to do it, Jack. And that means I can't waste time watching stand-up comedy while I eat drunken noodles."

Even if that scenario does actually sound *really* good right now.

Jack nods, his face pinched. "I understand," he says softly. "I get how important this all is to you. Guess we'll just have to brave the Maggio grandparents on our own, then." He rolls his eyes.

"Wait. Elijah's grandparents are going?"

"Yes." Jack sighs. "They got wind of the cheating thing—surprise, surprise—and made sure to text me to tell me that we'd discuss it tonight. Believe me, I don't want to go back to high school right now, either. But Elijah has to attend this, and it will look more than a little strange if I don't show up with him."

Devon Falls is doing something to me, I swear. Because old Benson? He would not have given a shit about that speech Jack just gave. He would have shrugged, waved, and gone back to work.

But Benson who lives in Devon Falls? Somehow, I'm grabbing my jacket. "One hour," I tell Jack. "I'll go for one hour."

His face lights up, and I end up having to cover my groin with my coat all the way to the restaurant.

Thai for Two isn't far from the apartment where I'm staying, so I get takeout there a lot. It's better than most of the Thai food I've had in Boston, actually. Devon Falls may be lacking in restaurant quantity, but it's not lacking in quality. I even liked the bakery before I filed that injunction and made myself persona non grata there.

"Jack! Benson! Over here!" Jack's father waves us over to a large table where he's sitting with Jack's mom, Elijah, and the Maggios.

So, it looks like we're diving right into this party. I follow Jack across the room, taking note of the makeshift stage that's been set up in one corner of the room. I hope the show starts soon. I suck at small talk in the best of situations, and this definitely isn't the best of situations.

"Benson, I'm so glad you came!" Jack's dad beams at me while his mom shoots me a kind but guarded look.

Elijah breaks into a wide smile. "I'm so glad you guys are here," he says. His eyes are darting back and forth between his grandparents and his pseudo-grandparents, and I don't doubt the sincerity of his words for one moment. "Mr. Tran's going on soon. And then—"

"And then we need to have a talk with you, Jack," Conrad Maggio says. "Elijah tells us this *man* of yours is tutoring him?" The way he says *man* is almost comical. Jack's parents look like they can't decide whether to burst out laughing or jump across the table and start a fistfight.

"Benson," Jack corrects him smoothly as he gestures toward me. "His name is Benson. And yes, he's helping Elijah out."

"It's been great so far, Grandpa!" Elijah pipes in. "He knows how to explain things I don't get, and then after he teaches me, we play guitar together. We're working on 'Stairway to Heaven' right now, and—"

Elijah stops just as he realizes he's said the wrong thing. His grandparents' eyes have both narrowed in my direction. "Elijah, honey," says his grandmother sweetly. "Can you go to the counter for me? Fetch me another iced tea." Elijah starts to balk, well aware that he's being sent away, but Jack gives him a quick nod and he reluctantly gets up from the table.

"Jack, just what on earth is going on here?" Conrad hisses the moment Elijah is out of earshot. "Elijah needs someone helping him who will focus on math, not that silly guitar! How do we know we can trust this fellow, anyway? He's suing the town, for crying out loud! You can't tell me this is actually getting serious."

And just like that, I've having one of those moments again. One of those Old Benson vs. New Benson moments. One of those strange, impulsive moments that took over me the day I landed myself in this strange arrangement with Jack Lancer and his family. I'm sure no one at the table is more surprised than me when I pipe up and join the conversation.

"Sir, you can't help who you fall for."

I lean over to wrap my arm around Jack's waist, doing my best to ignore the flash of excitement that moves through me as our bodies connect. "Jack and I are very serious," I add. "And Elijah's already improving in algebra." This is true, actually. It turns out Elijah struggles with a lot of the same mathematical concepts I struggled with as a kid, so I'm finding I know exactly how to teach them to him differently. "With all due respect, you need to give this some time. Jack and I are figuring this out, I promise. We—"

"Are a good team," Jack interrupts me gently. My hand is still around his waist, and he's turned to look directly at me now. Our gazes are locked. His eyes are more hazel than brown, I realize. I want to dive into them. I want to swim in the depths of layers and strength and kindness there. And since when do I think shit like that? I like romance as much as the next guy who got sucked into *Bridgerton*, but I can't remember the last time I spent two seconds thinking about what was behind the color of someone's eyes.

"Yeah," I reply, my voice husky in my ears. "A team."

Then Jack's leaning toward me again. And I'm pressing my face toward his. But unlike the other night, neither of us turns away. His lips push against mine, just for a moment. But a moment is all I need to know this kiss is nothing like any kiss I've ever been a part of before. This is somehow soft and succulent and sweet and urgent and needy all at the same time. This is what I've always thought every kiss I've ever had should feel like. This is what they've always looked like in the movies and on TV. But mine never felt like anything more than something that met a basic physical need, and I quickly gave up believing that kisses could be anything other than that. At least in real life.

Eventually, the two of us break apart, but our eyes stay locked. I have no idea what to say. Did Jack just feel what I felt? Do I want him to have felt what I felt? What would that even mean?

"If you'll excuse me, I need to use the bathroom." Conrad flees the table without a backward glance for either of us. "I'm going to go see about my iced tea," adds Barbara. She casts Jack a strange, almost curious look. "I'll be right back."

"Wow." Jack's father wolf-whistles as soon as they're both gone. "The two of you sure have been working on your acting skills!"

Jack nods, still looking at me. "I guess we have," he says quietly. My stomach turns over, hitting my chest, and it's a huge relief when my phone rings. "Gotta take this," I tell them, jetting away from the table just as fast as Conrad did.

I don't make it outside in time to take the call, but there's no missing the voice mail sitting in my inbox. It's Grandpa, and he's pissed as hell. Shouting about how he expected better than this when he sent me up here. How he should've known better than to think I could hack it at his firm. I've got two weeks to fix this, he says, or he's sending Carter up. Words like "disappointment" and "lazy" are thrown around like sprinkles on the birthday cakes I never had as a child that my twin siblings get every year on their special day.

One for each of them, actually.

I've barely hung up when the fuzziness that's been hovering around my vision begins to get wider. I rush home as I shoot a text to Elijah and Jack that I have to leave. I hit my bed just in time for a crushing, iron, vice-grip of pain to lace its way around my head and stay there, holding me in its unrelenting grasp for so long that I lose complete track of the rest of the mess my world has become.

Chapter 10

43 Days to the Devon Falls Leaf Festival

Do friends spoon each other when they're sick? —Jack Lancer

"Hey, Dr. Lancer? Sorry to bother you, but your nephew's here to see you." Malachai Flynn, the office manager Henri's been training, is standing in the doorway of my office looking nervous. Malachai always tends to look nervous around me. Mom, too. I wish I understood what we could do to make him more comfortable here. So far, he's proven himself to be a very capable employee and, even more importantly, a genuinely nice guy. "He'll settle in," Henri keeps telling us. "He's young, yet." She's right about that. The guy's still in his early twenties and in college. I try to remember that when he's staring at me like he's a lost little deer and I'm a giant Mack truck barreling down the highway toward him.

"Thanks for letting me know, Malachai." I smile at him as brightly as I can. "You can send him right in." I'm nearly done with updating patient files for the day, and I'm more than happy to have Elijah's company on the walk home. But I'm surprised he's here. This is usually the time when he and Benson study and jam together.

Elijah comes bursting into the room, his chestnut hair popping off his head in wild curls that mimic his frantic expression. Fiona's hair used to do that, too. She always said her hair was like a mood ring.

"Uncle Jack, I think something's wrong with Benson!"

"What?" I sit up quickly in my chair. "Why do you think that?"

"You know how he left the restaurant early yesterday? Without saying good-bye?"

Oh, I definitely do know. I've been telling myself that he must have gotten busy at work because of that phone call he took. Because the only other alternatives, that he was either just as affected by that kiss as I was or not affected at all, are too much for me to process right now. "Yes. I remember," I tell Elijah slowly.

"Well, today he didn't meet me at the record store. Or even DM me that he wasn't coming! Benson always shows up when he says he will. Or he messages if he needs to change the time. Always!"

I could point out that neither of us have known Benson all that long, but that would be skirting the point. The truth is that in the short time Elijah and I have known Benson, he's proven himself to be very reliable. I'm worried now, too.

"Did you try texting him or calling?" I ask.

Elijah sends me the kind of look only a disrespected teenager can give. "Uncle Jack, I may not be the smartest person at school, but I'm not *dumb*. Yes, I called him. He's not answering. I went by the town hall, too, and Ellie says she hasn't seen him either."

Okay. Now I'm officially starting to get very, very worried. Benson was rubbing at his temples again last night. If he's struggling with migraines, as I've suspected for some time he does, this could be very bad. I grab my jacket and messenger bag. "C'mon."

"Where are we going?" Elijah demands.

"To make a house call," I tell him.

Benson's renting an apartment on Main Street. The lights in the apartment are off, but his blue Toyota sedan is in the parking lot behind the building. Not a good sign.

"Benson?" I knock softly at the door, trying to be conscious of my volume. For several moments there's no answer, and I start making contingency plans in my head. I think I can break down the door if I have to.

"What if we can't get in?" Elijah asks anxiously. He's stepping back and forth between one foot and the other, and it strikes me how close he's gotten to Benson in the short time they've known each other. No surprise, really, given that he's missing his dad and that he and Benson have so much in common. I hope he's not going to be heartbroken when Benson leaves Devon Falls. The way my stomach clenches at the idea of Benson leaving only makes me knock harder at the door. There's a shuffling on the other side, and I hold my breath as the door swings open.

Benson stands before us, looking as wrecked as I could ever imagine seeing him. He's barely standing upright, and there are dark circles surrounding his sagging eyes. He's wearing a wrinkled pair of jogging pants and a shirt that looks like he's sweated through it, and his facial expression screams of absolute misery. I simultaneously feel extremely guilty for knocking on his door and extremely glad that I did.

"Benson," I say softly. "Migraine?"

He nods, immediately wincing at the head motion. And that tiny little movement is all the cue I need to start taking charge.

"Elijah, I need you to run to the drug store," I tell him quietly. I list off a series of items that Benson likely needs.

"Be right back," Elijah whispers, though I never warned him about being quiet. He's far more astute than his grandparents give him credit for. He runs off down the hall and I step into Benson's space, examining him with my eyes. "How long?" I ask.

"Since the Thai restaurant."

Shit. Almost twenty-four hours, then. "Have you taken anything?"

"Just aspirin." He winces at the ray of light peeking around the door from the hallway. "Don't have anything else," he mumbles. I'm going to make sure we correct that the second he's well enough for conversation. But right now, all I want to do is make him feel better.

"Okay," I tell him gently. "We'll fix it, Benson. I've got you. You're not on your own anymore."

He stares at me, squinting, and I notice his eyes are wet. "I'm really glad you're here," he says hoarsely.

I startle slightly. I know Benson well enough by now to know those probably aren't words he says often.

I guide him gently into the apartment, which is a small studio with a double bed in one corner and a combination kitchen/living room taking up most of the space. The curtains are closed tightly. They're mostly light-blocking, at least. I surprise him, I think, when I guide him over to the sofa and help him lay down there. "I'm going to get you some water and change your sheets," I whisper. "Have you been able to keep food down?"

He shakes his head slightly.

"Well, I sent Elijah for applesauce and electrolytes. We'll see if we can fix that." I can feel his eyes track me as I make use of what his small space has to offer. I find a glass of water and help him sit up long enough to take a few sips. When he shakes his head at me, I don't push for him to drink more. I find clean sheets and quickly make his bed, then grab some sweatpants and a Burlington

U Law shirt from his dresser. "C'mon," I urge him. "Let's get you into some more comfortable clothes."

He holds onto my shoulders as I help him step out of his pants. I look away to give him as much privacy as possible, but Benson draws my attention back to him when he says, "this isn't really how I envisioned you getting in my pants for the first time."

The corners of his lips are turned up in a hint of a wry grin, and my heart speeds up. Has he really had those thoughts too? Now is not the time for that conversation, unfortunately. "Me either," I tell him, keeping things light as I help him into the fresh pants and shirt.

I get him settled into bed and then dampen a washcloth with cool water. Some migraine patients are sensitive to any kind of touch when they have episodes like this, but Benson sighs with happiness when I lay the cloth across his forehead.

I sit down gently on the side of his bed. "When Elijah gets back we'll try food and more water," I tell him. "Get excited for that applesauce."

Benson grimaces. "I'll try it," he promises. "I already feel better than I did. Thank you, Jack."

I gently take one of his hands, and when he doesn't object, I hold it while I rub my thumb against his palm. "Thank you for what?" I ask. I'm not sure what I'm being thanked for. Changing someone's sheets and getting them some water when they're ill are about the most basic things you can do for another human.

"No one's ever really done this before. You know. For me," he mutters. "Not lately, anyway."

"Do you get migraines often?" I ask him.

He sighs. "I used to get them a lot more when I was younger. I thought they were going away. But lately they've been getting worse."

"Who used to take care of you when you got them?" I ask.

He shrugs into the sheets around him. "I think my nannies did. Well, some of them anyway. Until they... couldn't anymore." Benson grimaces again, and I decide this isn't the best time to have this conversation.

"You're going to be okay," I tell him. It's a universal line I've used a million times in my career. Some patients believe it. Some don't. From Benson's expression, I can't tell where he stands.

"It was worse last night," he replies. "In the middle of the night. It was so bad. They've gotten worse lately, like I said. I was here, in this bed, and the pain was so awful I started to wonder if I was going to live through it. And I kept thinking... kept thinking that I didn't want to die by myself in a studio apartment. Alone. All by myself." He closes his eyes against pain I can't see, and suddenly I need to be holding more than just his hand.

"You're not alone," I tell him. I lean over farther and graze his cheek with the fingers of my other hand. It's a test to see if my touch hurts, but all he does is lean farther into it. And just like that, I know I'm doing the right thing. "You're not alone right now," I repeat. "And you never have to be alone again. Not if you don't want to be. You have me now. Me and Elijah."

Benson has settled his cheek deep into my hand at this point. He's almost nuzzling it. "Not forever," he mumbles. "Just for now. Just for pretend."

"No way," I tell him. "You and Elijah have played Bowie togeth-er. You don't think he's gonna keep you around forever?" A hint of a smile creeps back across Benson's face. "And me. I'll be there for you even when all this is over. I promise. Just like you've been there for me when I needed you. You're stuck with both of us for life now, Ben."

I'm not sure how he'll react to the nickname that just slipped out of my mouth, but all he does is study me. "Okay," he finally croaks. Uncertainly. Like he wants to believe my words but isn't sure that he can. He sighs. "Whatever happens... like I said, I'm really glad I'm not alone right now."

Something in his voice breaks me a little bit, and it's that break which pushes me to ask a question that both logic and reality suggest I probably should not ask. "Do you want me to lie down with you?" I say hesitantly.

I'm pushing another boundary here. A boundary we both know is clearly set. Sure, we kissed at the Thai restaurant, but that was supposed to have been for Conrad and Barbara. There's no one here but the two of us now. I'm not sure what will happen if I lay down on this bed beside Benson and tell my brain to stop insisting that I back away. But Benson just looks at me and slides over slightly. "Please," he whispers. "Yes, Jack. Please."

I slide under the covers with him slowly. At first we're both hesitant. I'm hesitant about how to touch and where to touch, especially given Benson's current state. I want to make sure I'm not hurting him in any way. Finally, I say, "if you want me to hold you, you just have to let me know." I'm not worried about Elijah walking in on us. He thinks Benson and I are together, anyway. He thinks this is real. He's not going to think there's anything strange about me holding my boyfriend while he's ill.

Benson takes a long breath and lets it out slowly. I can feel the movement of his chest through my entire body. "I want that," he says.

That's all he has to say to spur me into action. I carefully roll him slightly so I can slide one arm under his body, and then I cover him with the other until I'm spooning him. My face is against his neck, our breathing perfectly in sync as though we've timed it. For the first time since I knocked on Benson's door earlier, I feel at peace.

He's safe. He's here with me. He's in my arms.

He's going to be okay.

The connection between us, the one I can't seem to place or explain, feels stronger than ever. I held Fiona like this hundreds, thousands, maybe even millions of times in our years together. But it never felt like this. Holding her never felt like it had this level of purpose, and I'm still not sure exactly what to do with that knowledge.

Benson closes his eyes. He tucks his arms around mine like he's wrapping himself up in a blanket, and the feeling of *rightness* and *fullness* inside of me only gets stronger every time he pulls me closer to him.

I hold him until his breathing evens out and I can tell he's falling asleep. And when he fully drifts off, the rise and fall of his chest even against mine, I don't let go.

He comes awake slowly the next morning. He slept through the night, I think. I didn't get much rest. I dozed, always on the edge of sleep, but I knew I had to be awake to hear if he called out. If he needed me.

Neither of us has moved much. There's been some gentle shifting, but overall, we're in the exact same place we fell asleep in.

He peeks one eye open and turns slightly in my arms to study me. "You're still here," he says. His voice is husky, and I should definitely not find that hot.

"Still here," I tell him. "How's the pain level?"

He twists his neck back and forth like he's trying to decide. "Mostly gone... I think."

"Good. I'm going to grab you some applesauce and some Gatorade. We'll see if you can keep something down. How's that sound? Are you hungry?" Thank goodness Elijah came back with supplies last night before I sent him to stay with my parents. Benson definitely needs calories and electrolytes right now.

Benson's still looking at me like he's not sure what to make of the fact that I didn't disappear in the middle of the night. "Yeah," he finally says. "I think I am."

He has more of an appetite than I expected, as it turns out. His hand shakes as he goes to lift the spoon to hold up the applesauce, though, so we end up in a somewhat strange position where I'm essentially holding his hand and helping him feed himself. I'm expecting snarky remarks about him not being a toddler, this being Benson and all. But all he does is look at me gratefully. In between his fourth or fifth bite, he says, "I'm sorry you had to do this. Really sorry."

"There's nothing to be sorry for," I tell him. "This is what friends do."

"Friends, huh?" Benson locks his eyes into mine, and I know we're both thinking the same thing.

Do friends spoon each other when they're sick? Do fake boyfriends do that?

Benson ends up eating almost a cup of applesauce and drinking half a bottle of Gatorade. "I feel one hundred percent better than I did yesterday," he says as he sits up against the headboard of the bed. "Good work, Doc."

"This is just good old-fashioned nursing. You still need to be examined," I tell him as I wash the bowl and tidy up the apartment. "Elijah texted me, by the way. He says he hopes you feel better. He dropped off the supplies last night, and then I sent him over to my parents' house. Mom's got you scheduled for an appointment tomorrow, by the way."

Benson scowls. "I'm fine," he mutters.

I come back to the bed and plant myself on the edge of it, the way I did last night. "I'm glad you're better now. I just want you to be better long-term. You don't have to suffer like this anymore, Benson. Mom wants to help. So do I."

He looks at me with his patented stare: the one I've come to learn is taking me apart and then putting me back together again. And then, before I can react or think, he leans across the bed and kisses me hard.

Every nerve in my body immediately stands on edge. It's like I'm reliving the same moment we had the other night but with twenty times the intensity. I can only assume from his sudden urgency that Benson, a man who could barely move twelve hours earlier, is feeling the same thing. His lips are crashing against mine, his skin sparking against my skin, his breathing desperate and wild. For just a moment I lean away. "Are you sure you're not in pain?" I ask, panting slightly in between words. I need to be sure.

"Fuck, no."

That's all I need to hear. I lean back into the kiss and let his lips have mine. It isn't long before I feel him sliding his hands underneath my shirt. His fingers caress the bottom of my stomach, and I know without a doubt that whatever's happening between us right now is going to go further. "Don't stop," I urge him as I slip my own fingers under the hem of his t-shirt. His skin is hot against my fingertips, and the touch is somehow invigorating and terrifying at the same time. Our tongues are exploring each other madly as Benson tugs up the bottom half of my shirt. I let go of him just long enough to help him get rid of the difficult piece of cotton, and soon I'm half naked before him.

"Holy shit," he whispers when the shirt is fully gone.

"Thanks, but I'm not that impressive."

"Sorry to tell you, dude, but you are very wrong."

Benson claps his mouth back against mine. As I begin slowly working my hands farther under his shirt, he grabs at them. "Stop," he says, as he pulls away from me. "I mean, leave the shirt, okay? I don't look like you."

"Wait, what?" I take his cheeks in my hands. "What do you mean you don't look like me?"

"I don't have the muscles. I don't have a six pack," he says. And now he gives me a look that's half-annoyed, half-amused. "Let's be honest. You look like you work out all the fucking time."

"The gym in town is actually pretty decent," I defend myself. "And I don't go there to get a certain look. I go because working out helps me with stress and anxiety. But I know that's not the case for everyone. Listen, Benson." I rub my thumb against his cheek and hope he knows how much I mean every word I'm about to say. "I don't give a shit what you look like under that shirt. I want to touch you. All of you. Everywhere. That's all I want right now. I want to see every fucking inch of you. And I want to rub my hands over every fucking inch of you."

Benson's eyes go wide.

"I'm gonna love rubbing my hands over your entire body, no matter what it looks like," I add. "No way in hell I won't."

Benson freezes in place for a moment before he drops his hands to the bottom of his shirt. And then he tugs it up gently over his head, slow and sweet. And soon there's nothing between his chest and mine, and every part of his body is just as perfect as I knew it would be. My dick, which was already half-hard, is now straining against my pants. "You're so hot," I whisper, before I push him back and down against the bed, tackling his lips again while I cage his body with my own. He gets a hold of the button of the jeans I slept in last night, and now he knows how hard I am. How much I want him. I slide two fingers into the waistband of his sweatpants. "Are you sure?" I ask carefully. Because I have to know. I have to be certain.

"Geez, Jack." He flips over the denim right in front of my cock and it springs further to life. "Stop talking. I want you."

Okay, then.

Soon we're fighting a war against our clothes. It's me against his boxers, and him against my difficult jeans that we finally have to work together to get off. But it isn't long before our dicks are moving against each other, finally released from their cloth cages, and he's every bit as hard as I am.

"You're so gorgeous," I tell him.

"Whatever, Soldier of Fortune."

I laugh as I let my hand drift to his dick. I grasp it slightly, and he thrusts upward into me.

"Oh fuck," he says. "I may not last long."

"Do you think you're the only one with that problem?" I tease the tip of his dick with my finger as I nibble at his neck. "Got any lube?"

He moans and points at the bedside table. "Yup. I'm a good little boy scout."

Thank goodness. I keep one hand on his dick. He has one hand on my ass, and I can feel the other hand slowly drifting closer to my cock. Eventually, he takes hold of it just as I grab hold of the lube. "Benson!" I call out. Every stroke of his finger against me is a little touch of magic. A little touch of something unimaginable. I've had guys' hands on my dick before—not many, but enough. It's never felt like this, though. I've never felt like my entire body is an engine, primed and ready to burst past a starting line. I stumble with the lube cap as we take turns teasing and torturing each other.

"Holy fuck," Benson says, his voice more of a whine. He's panting into my shoulder. "Now," he adds urgently.

My thoughts exactly.

I drip lube across both our dicks, crisscrossing it slightly. When we're both good and ready, I grasp us together in one hand. "Are you sure?" I ask again.

"Stop asking me that." He tackles my mouth with his, his swollen lips closing against mine as he places his hand on top of my fingers. "Yes," he adds.

And then it's on.

It's like we're in a race to get off with each other. I rub our dicks together, sliding them back and forth through a field of skin and soft sweetness and rightness and electricity. This is everything I've ever wanted in bed, everything I didn't quite realize I didn't have, and I don't know what to do with that. Because this is just rubbing, just friction. Right?

But it's not. This is so much more. This is connection. This is fireworks. This is that moment at the leaf festival when all the colors crown and shine together and you feel like you've been thrust into a scene that the universe has created for you and you alone. This is something so beautiful and golden and bright that I want it to last forever.

But my dick is quick to remind me that won't be in the cards. "I'm so close," I whisper to him. He is too. I can feel it. I can feel it in the way he's shaking beneath me. God, I hope everything about this feels as good for him as it does for me.

"Jack," he says. There's a whimper on the edge of his tone, and I know then that I'm not alone.

I touch my lips to his ear. "Come with me," I whisper. It's an order and a question and a hope wrapped all in one. He gasps, just as I feel every nerve on my body climb to the edge of a cliff, and then I explode as I feel him fall off the cliff with me. We're vibrating together, two sparks that have fully ignited, and as we both spill across my hand and his stomach, it feels as though the flame that spark has ignited will never go out. We shudder in each other's arms, holding on tight while we tumble down the rest of the cliff together. When we finally land, softly, I fall across his body, holding him.

Oh god, I think as I drop across his chest. Now what? What's he thinking? What does he need? What have I just done?

Those are the thoughts that come first. But then Benson sighs and folds his arms around my body. He pulls me against him, and I know one thing for certain.

Whatever just happened between us? I want it to happen again.

Chapter 11

36 Days to the Devon Falls Leaf Festival

I've never had an urge to go into a doctor's office and beg one of the doctors to strip down to just his stethoscope. —Benson Lewis

"Well. I don't think a courtroom in Devon Falls has been this packed since the dispute between the Rykers and the Shoalskis. The Rykers painted the Shoalskis' heifer shed bright pink in the middle of the night."

Most of the time when Ellie says shit like that, I can't tell if she's joking or not. "It was a prank war," she adds. "It escalated after the Shoalski kids dyed one of the Ryker kid's poodle chartreuse. Poor thing looked like a member of a defunct 80s rock band for all of show season."

Now I know she's not kidding. I also know that I probably don't want to hear the rest of this story. Especially not on a day when I woke up with a to-do list of eighty items running through my head and a heart rate that feels slightly above normal.

It's the day of the injunction hearing to stop the leaf festival from moving forward this year. And while I'm fairly sure the injunction will be granted, I can't say that for sure anymore. Not since Ellie unearthed that death certificate. I haven't found any other evidence disproving that document, either, and Carter wasn't pleased when he showed up in town yesterday. "I thought you had access to some giant historical archive?" he asked. "What the fuck, Benson? You told me you had this on lock. What the hell have you been doing in this boring-ass town for days on end?"

I managed not to stutter as I thought about the two days I lost while working on this case: one because I was black-out sick with one of the worst migraines I've ever had in my life, and another because I was in bed with my arms wrapped around the doctor who nursed me through that migraine.

Fuck, I'm hard again just thinking about it.

It's been a week since Jack and I got off together in my studio apartment in what I can unequivocally say was the best sexual experience of my life. Too bad Jack's been pretty unhappy with me since then.

For one thing, I skipped out on the doctor's appointment with his mother. The last thing I need right now is my fake boyfriend's mother studying every single mole on my body while I'm trying to research the most important case of my life.

For another thing, I've been avoiding Jack since it happened. I still see Elijah for our tutoring and jam sessions, but I've been skipping dinners and breakfasts with them and blowing off Jack's texts. I told him I needed to focus on the hearing for the injunction, and we could talk about "us" as soon as the hearing was over.

Which means that my stay of execution is going to end very soon, because today Henry Fontaine will hear our firm's case. Today's the day I either fail my family in the most epic way I have so far, or the day I land a crushing blow on a town that seems to grow on me more and more every day I spend in it. And what the fuck is up with *that* I couldn't say. All I know is that this morning when I walked over to the coffee shop, Belinda Ryker (she's the third or fourth Ryker kid, I think—I can never remember) handed me my order without me even asking for it and then cheerfully told me that she heard my dry cleaning order was ready and did I know that the farm-to-table store was running a special on eggs? And when I popped into Luis' café to pick up a breakfast sandwich, Betty Nowal insisted on telling me all the tips she knows about tutoring students in math from back when she worked at Devon Falls Elementary, because she heard I was helping out Elijah and wanted to make sure I knew she "supported that endeavor despite who I work for." And then on the quick walk I took through town to settle my nerves I walked by Lancer Family Medicine, and... well. Let's just say I've never had an urge to go into a doctor's office and beg one of the doctors to strip down to just his stethoscope before today.

"Benson." Carter nods as he appears next to me, carrying a recyclable cardboard cup from the coffee shop. "Not a bad latte for a town that's never even heard of valet parking. Are you ready to watch me work some magic?"

Next to me, Ellie eyes him with distaste. "You mean, is he ready to watch you take credit for all the research and work he's been doing here for weeks?"

Carter scoffs. "Ma'am, Benson knows he's lucky to even have this job. Can't believe I'm working with a state school graduate," he mutters as he walks off toward our side of the courtroom. "Damn nepotism."

"Well." Ellie coughs. "This seems like a real nice firm you're working with, Benson." She holds out a hand to me. "Whatever happens today, I just want to say no hard feelings. I've enjoyed working with you all this time, despite the fact that you're basically a porcupine wrapped up in a bag of poison ivy."

I smirk. "Same, I guess. Despite the fact that you can't figure out how to keep your damn clothes on."

Ellie eyes the summer dress she's wearing distastefully. "I tried to wear my bathrobe today, but Amelia wouldn't hear of it."

"Order! Order!" Harry Fontaine bangs his gavel against an ancient wooden desk. The Devon Falls courthouse is an old but stately brick building, and the inside looks like it hasn't been updated much since the early 1900s. The benches are made of carefully carved wood complete with detailed edges and etchings, and I'm betting the desks and tables in this place would fetch a lot of money at an antiques auction.

Carter's staring at the hard-backed chair he's expected to sit in like it's a metal spike as I walk up and take the seat next to him. "Haven't these people ever heard of ergonomics?" He growls as he lowers his way into the chair, grimacing. "Listen, rookie. You know how important this hearing is, right?"

"I know what a preliminary injunction hearing is, Carter," I mutter. "Even Burlington U Law covers that."

"Just reminding you that you better make sure our shit is in order today," he adds. "If this injunction isn't granted, our case is effectively over."

It's a little bit of an exaggeration, but it's somewhat true. This is the hearing to stop the town from taking any action toward planning and executing the leaf festival, which is scheduled to take place in just about five weeks. If we're granted the injunction, everything pauses, and it's all that more likely we'll win the case to take the land back.

If the injunction isn't granted, the leaf festival moves ahead, which could hold up the trial. Such a ruling would also send a huge signal that our case is in trouble.

And honestly? As much as I hate to admit it, I feel like this could go either way. I haven't found anything to fully disprove the death certificate, but I've been through every damn archive I have access to enough times to know that there's nothing corroborating it either. My heart rate goes up again as I imagine the coronary Grandpa's going to have if we lose. He'll probably fucking fire me. No, he'll *definitely* fucking fire me.

Is it possible for your family to disown you when they barely owned you to begin with?

"Order!" Harry calls again. He bangs the gavel one more time, and the room goes silent. "Let's get this started, shall we?" He sends a nod to Ellie, then one to me, and completely ignores Carter's presence.

The crowd in the courtroom has been steadily growing since eight-thirty this morning, and I have no doubt that Ellie's right: this hearing is probably setting some kind of record for attendance. As Harry begins going over the details of the injunction, I let my eyes drift toward the back of the room. Not because I care who's here. I definitely don't. I have much more important things to care about.

But when my eyes stop on the dark, tall doctor who's standing near the last row of seats, his perfect shoulders and pecs high-lighted by the fitted blue shirt he's wearing, I let them stay there for just a minute. He locks eyes with me. Then he nods slightly. Smiles.

And just like that, every cell in my body simultaneously calms and jumps at the same time.

I don't think a basic preliminary injunction hearing in Vermont has ever been rife with so much tension. Especially when Irene Cooley, who teaches performance arts at the school, stands up and starts yelling at Harry.

"You can't grant this injunction!" she shrieks. "I must start train-ing our dancers! Do you remember the horror that befell little Mirabell Sanders when she didn't practice properly leading up to last year's Performance of the Moving Leaves?"

"Irene, she fell out of step with the orange leaves and ended up with the red ones," Amelia reminds her. "Let's not get hyperbolic, here."

"It was madness!" Irene insists.

Harry calls for order again, and Irene ends up having to leave the courtroom when she has another outburst about how long it takes to create leaf-and-popcorn strings.

If Harry Fontaine is surprised when he's presented with a death certificate and a birth certificate that can't simultaneously exist and are both proven to be authentic, he doesn't show it. If he's surprised that neither Ellie nor our side has come up with anything to disprove the other side, he doesn't show that either.

I doubt Ellie has any idea how he's going to rule when he finally announces his judgment. I sure as hell don't.

"Obviously this is a case that runs close to hearts here in Devon Falls," he tells the room. "But Arnie has shown probable cause for the preliminary injunction to be granted to maintain the status quo. Devon Falls simply cannot move forward with holding a major festival on land which it may or may not have legal ownership of. All planning and execution for the Devon Falls Leaf Festival is therefore enjoined until the hearing on the permanent injunction."

"What the hell does all that lawyer nonsense mean?" Burt Busby yells from the back of the room.

Harry takes off his glasses and rubs at the bridge of his nose. "It means the festival planning will need to immediately be put on hold," he tells the room.

There's a gasp from the room. "But Harry!" someone shouts. "The festival is six weeks away! You know the planning takes time. If we can't start planning, there won't be a festival this year! We need to organize the vendors and plan the leaf walk."

"I need time to re-learn the Twitter again and start our marketing campaign!" someone else calls out.

"The leaves, Harry! Think of the leaves!"

"Never mind the leaves. Think of my profit margins. All those tourists," mutters Luis.

"Order!" Harry calls again. "After weighing the evidence, I must order the preliminary injunction be granted until there is time for this case to be heard in full. However!" He puts a hand up as the crowd springs to life once more. "If any further persuasive evidence is found, I would encourage either party to return to court and request another emergency hearing. What's clear to me right now is that one of these documents is real and one is not." He holds up the birth certificate and the death certificate and draws his eyes back and forth between me and Ellie. "And until we know which is which, we don't know who this land belongs to. But I must err on the side of caution and protect the presumptive property owner's right. I invite counsel to provide further briefing and submit declarations or other evidence in anticipation of the hearing to assist the court in ruling on these important questions of fact. Court is adjourned."

"Like it matters who the land belongs to," Carter mumbles next to me as he starts packing up his briefcase. All around us there's outraged shouting and yelling, and I definitely see Marion from the bakery crying softly at the back of the room.

"What do you mean by that?" I ask sharply. The hammer in my head is back. It appeared right around the halfway point of the trial, and right now it's powerful enough to put up a wall in a new house.

Carter scoffs. "Such a damn rookie. All that matters, rook, is that we win. That's all that ever matters."

He clearly expects me to easily agree with him. Hell, *I* expect me to do that. But for some reason, I just stand there, watching Marion cry.

Carter frowns in disgust and shakes his head. "You don't actually feel sorry for these people, do you? It's a stupid leaf festival, Benson. Damn, you really are the black sheep of your family.

You're nothing like your grandad, that's for sure. C'mon. We need an action plan. There's no way I'm staying in this town one more second than I have to." He turns and starts making his way through the emotional crowd, and he clearly expects me to follow.

I wait until he's out the door to start gathering my things. Mostly to piss him off.

"Congratulations," says a low voice.

The hammer in my head slows slightly at the sound of that voice. I turn to find Jack Lancer standing next to me.

"You should be pissed," I remind him.

"I'm sad for the town," he says quietly. "But Harry ruled the right way. Until we know for certain who that land belongs to, we shouldn't be planning a festival this year."

As usual, he's objective. Clear. Thoughtful. A calm port in the middle of the raging storm around us. "I don't think too many other people here agree with you," I tell him.

"No, maybe not." He sends me a wry smile. "I'd stay away from the bakery for a while longer."

"Will do." I sigh. "Gotta catch up with Carter." Even though the idea of spending any more time with that guy makes me want to heave. At least Arnie isn't here. Carter decided he'd be more of a distraction than a benefit to the injunction hearing, and I certainly didn't disagree.

Jack runs a hand lightly up my right arm. I'm wearing a suit jacket, but a shiver still runs through me. "The injunction hearing is over now. Does that mean you're ready to talk to me?"

Truthfully, I'm not sure I'll ever be ready to talk about what the fuck happened the day Jack Lancer came to my apartment, cared for me like no one ever has, and then proceeded to light my world on fire. But the result of this hearing means I won't be leaving Devon Falls just yet, and the guy is still my fake boyfriend. I can't ignore him—or our situation—forever.

"Yeah," I finally manage to squeak out. "Yeah. We can talk."

"Good." He leans in toward me, his breath a whisper as his mouth comes to a stop by my ear. "Gotta keep up appearances for the town," he says. Then he brushes his lips all the way across my cheek until his lips are resting against mine.

He kisses me softly, and for a minute I forget I'm standing in the middle of a courtroom filled with people who can't stand me. I completely forget that I'm the villain in the current story of Devon Falls.

Because right now I feel like a hero. A hero in a very different story: a story of something happening between me and Jack.

A story with an ending I can't figure out, no matter how many times I flip to the last page.

Chapter 12
34 Days to the Devon Falls Leaf Festival

Apples turn you on now? What will you do when you see a pie?
—Jack Lancer

"I don't understand why we're not just buying apples in a store like the rest of the damned world does."

Benson's staring at the apple orchard we're walking through with the same look of distrust and skepticism that he gives most things in the world around him when he first encounters them. Strangely enough, that look is one of the things I'm coming to really appreciate and enjoy about him. Here's why: when one of the hundred things he's inherently skeptical or mistrustful of proves itself to be beautiful or important or good in any way, that look switches to one of reverence and wide-eyed wonder. Like he can't believe the world could have such delightful joy in it.

I'll watch Benson look skeptical and distrustful over and over and over again to see his face light up with passion like that. And that's a feeling I've been trying not to explore too closely since he basically stopped speaking to me a week and a half ago.

It doesn't matter, I tell myself. He's here with me now. In the Devon Falls Apple Orchard, of all places. He's even holding hands with me, because we're surrounded by other locals picking apples on this cooling but sunny September day. His palm is warm and soft against mine, and I try not to sink my fingers deeper into his with every step we take.

And I try not to examine that urge too closely either. The injunction hearing two days ago was a firm reminder of just how finite Benson's time in this town is. I know his firm could have shipped him out right away had his side lost the hearing.

Whatever these strange and inexplicable feelings I have for him are, they have an unknown expiration date. And whatever we have right now isn't real. It's all manufactured for the benefit of my former in-laws. I have to keep reminding myself of that.

"Apple picking is a big tradition in the Maggio family," I remind Benson quietly as we step between some Macintosh trees. I gesture to the bucket he's holding in one hand and step forward to snap an apple off a low branch with a quick twist of my wrist. "Eric and Fiona used to go with their parents every year. Eric still takes Elijah every year. Thanks for coming with us today. I know it means a lot to him."

Benson's face softens as he looks around to find Elijah, who's laughing with Pat as they move around a tree together hunting for the best, brightest apples. "Yeah. Well. I know things kind of suck for him right now," he says brusquely.

I sigh. "Eric going out of touch again has been hard on him. It was nice of his grandparents to suggest we all go apple picking together. Especially since it's looking more and more like Eric won't make it back this year before apple picking season is over."

Benson frowns, pushing his tongue between his teeth as he concentrates on getting the perfect grip on an apple. He manages to pluck it away from the tree with one perfect sweep of his hand, and his face quickly lights up in that expression of pure delight and brilliance.

And fuck. Now I'm getting hard. In the middle of a damn apple orchard.

This could be a long day.

"You know, Jack," Benson says as he drops the apple into our bucket. "I used to think guys as fucking wholesome as you only existed in irreverent comedies and children's TV shows. I can't decide how I feel about the fact that I'm wrong."

"I'm just a normal amount of wholesome," I tell him as I hunt for another apple to pick. "Ask my friends Sam and Milo. They saw what I could get up to in New York. Especially after my divorce."

Benson looks at me sharply. "Interesting. Still, I don't think any normal person works this hard to get along with their former in-laws. Especially when said in-laws treat them the way yours treat you. I definitely don't think a normal person would agree to go apple picking with them."

It's on the tip of my tongue to point out that his family seems to treat him like absolute shit, and yet he jumps every damn time they tell him to. I still can't believe some of the things that came out of his mouth when he was ill. It definitely sounds to me like his family left him to suffer with untreated pain for years on end—and that's something I've been wanting to talk to him about ever since we spent that day in bed together. I'm considering whether now is the time to mention to Benson that his family sounds categorically abusive when we're interrupted by none other than my former in-laws.

"Jack. Benson. Good to see you." Conrad Maggio approaches, bucket in hand, and sets it down long enough to shake hands with me and Benson. "Benson, I'm sorry to see your firm insists on moving forward with the leaf case."

"I'm sorry to see that your town does," Benson says evenly.

Conrad gives him a sharp look. "Yes, well. Elijah's algebra grades are up, I noticed. That's something to celebrate."

"It is," Benson agrees. "Although I'm not sure how you know that, sir, given that you have no legal access to his grades."

"Now, you listen—"

"Conrad, we're all very pleased that the tutoring sessions are going so well," I interrupt smoothly. "And thanks for suggesting we all go apple picking today. I know it's helping Elijah to keep his mind off how much he misses his dad."

Conrad's face softens as he looks over at Elijah, who's somehow ended up in a wrestling match with Pat in a pile of slightly rotting apples in the grass. He's going to smell like a cider factory, and I can't help but grin at the thought. In moments like these he looks a lot younger than fourteen. It's nice to know he still has some childlike innocence left.

"I'm sure he misses his aunt, too." Conrad sighs. "Goodness knows we do. I know you and Fiona had a tough breakup, Jack, but was it so bad she had to run off all the way to Italy?"

"Maybe she was trying to get away from some oppressive, over-involved parents," Benson mutters, barely under his breath.

"Did you say something, son?"

"I said maybe she wanted really good gelato."

I nearly snort out loud.

"Are you ever going to come clean about what happened there, Jack?" Conrad crosses his arms. "I know our Fiona, and she never would have let her marriage fail if she could save it. Now, mind you, I warned her when the two of you were getting together that she had to be careful."

I open my mouth to defend myself, and the same thing that seems to keep happening to me when Conrad gets under my skin happens again. My throat and mouth go dry, and I lose all the words to explain why my marriage failed so terribly.

Maybe because I never had those words in the first place.

"Don't take me the wrong way. I knew you were a smart one. Knew you'd be successful and all that. But Fiona, I said, you have to watch out for those men who think they've got the world under their thumb. I'm not saying it was your fault, not entirely, but—"

"With all due disrespect, Mr. Maggio," Benson interrupts smoothly. "It sure as hell does sound like you're saying it was entirely Jack's fault."

Conrad's eyebrows go up. "Hey! I've got a right to know what happened in my daughter's marriage. Especially since it went up in flames the way it did. I've got a right to know that Jack's going to take better care of my grandson than he did of my damn daughter!"

Those words are like a truck coming straight toward me in the dead of night, and I choke on the air they take out of my lungs. *You didn't take care of her. You didn't do enough.*

You failed her. And you're going to fail Elijah.

You couldn't fix things with her. You'll screw things up for Elijah, too.

"I... don't... um." And now I'm stammering in the middle of an apple orchard, wrecked by a divorce that's old enough to be in preschool. I should be past this—I know I should. So why can't I tell this man what he needs to hear? Why can't I tell him that Fiona and I did our best, and sometimes things just don't work out?

Because you don't believe that yourself. And you know it.

"You know what?" Benson says suddenly. "Time out here. This is supposed to be a day of people walking around smiling happily and pulling apples off trees even though they basically taste disgusting unless they're in pie. Am I right?"

"Son, apples are a product that generates—"

"And we're all here because we're supporting Elijah. Right?"

Conrad nods reluctantly. "Yeah."

"Then let's leave the family bickering out of the orchard for one damn day, okay? Conrad, go spend some time with your grandson. Maybe tell him to get off the ground before he ends up as a spokesperson for Mott's. Jack, let's go take a walk." Then he sets down our bucket, holds out his hand, and waits patiently for me to take it.

The sun hits a spot in the trees just right, reflecting shards of light through shades of red and green and brown, brightening the path before us as I slide my hand into his.

We end up sitting together under some apple trees next to the pond that edges up against the orchard. It's a small pond, beautifully picturesque, complete with a family of ducks that are currently circling the water and picnic tables dotting the banks. A family is sitting on the other side of it with a package of the apple danish they make in the gift shop here. Two tiny children run in circles around a blanket while a baby sleeps in its father's arms.

Benson and I sit in silence for some time, just watching them. Well, I'm watching them. Benson seems to be just exploring the backdrop around us, looking over everything with practiced eyes. Every now and then his look shifts from skeptical to fascinated, and my heart jumps slightly.

"Fiona and I made out for the first time here," I tell Benson.

He looks over at me, clearly startled. "Yeah? Really?"

"Yeah. Well, over there, anyway." I point to one of the picnic tables. "I was apple picking with her family. Conrad liked me back then." I sigh. "It was the same year we were Leaf Festival royalty together."

"Of course it was," Benson says evenly. He snorts. "And here I always thought my life was out of a Netflix show."

I see an opening here, and I can't help but step toward it. "Oh yeah? You tell me your Netflix series, I'll tell you mine."

Benson studies me carefully, like he's weighing the risks and rewards to this potential conversation. "Okay," he finally says. "You go first, though."

"Sure." I sit up slightly and lean on one arm so I can look directly at him. "You know the first part. Golden boy, perfect life, marries his high school sweetheart. Becomes a doctor, goes to New York. Lives the perfect life. But."

"But," Benson repeats patiently.

"But then Fiona and I found out we couldn't have kids. And it was my fault."

Benson's eyes widen. "Holy shit," he whispers. Then he adds, "I know I'm not the doctor here, but how can something like that be your fault?"

I sigh. "Yeah, that's not exactly in medical terms. That's how it felt, though. Fiona and I had always planned on having children. Always. Even had names picked out. We tried for years, and one day we finally got the news that my body wasn't going to be up to it. And it was like the whole world crumbled in front of me. Us."

"Geez, Jack," Benson whispers. He leans over, his face close to mine. "I'm so sorry. The Maggios don't know?"

I shake my head. "No. We would have told them, probably. If things had gone differently."

Benson nods. Waits. And eventually, I find the words I've never said to anyone else.

"I'd done my OBGYN rotation. So, I knew what we needed to do. I changed diets and got specialists lined up and made all the necessary appointments. Started investigating adoption and foster care options. I knew how to fix our problems. I knew what I had to do to make sure we could start a family."

Benson tilts his head at me slightly. "And Fiona didn't want all that?"

The same frustration I felt back then bubbles inside my chest, and I have to fight to keep it from leaking into my voice. "She kept accusing me of moving too quickly. She said she needed time to digest the news and grieve. We didn't *have* time, though. Infertility treatments can be long and drawn out, and adoption can take years sometimes. I was just trying to make sure we had the future we'd always planned on. She didn't see it that way."

"So you broke up because she wanted to slow down with finding solutions and you didn't?"

"I guess so. I still don't understand exactly why she was so angry with me." I think of Fiona's face that day, the day we stood in our large, open floor plan in New York, staring at each other. Just feet away from one another, and yet so far away. Millions of miles, it seemed. "I was determined to find a way for us to be parents. Treatments, sperm donors, adoption—I was going to do whatever it took. But then one day I looked up... and Fiona was standing there, telling me to stop. She accused me of not listening to her or what she needed. She said she was starting to wonder if maybe we weren't meant to be together."

"Oh, Jack." Benson takes one of my hands in his. He rubs his thumb against my palm, moving in slow circles, and I think of the day I did the same for him when he was down with that migraine. "Fuck. I'm so sorry."

I shake my head. "We tried therapy. So much damn therapy. But the therapist just kept accusing me of not paying attention to the needs of my marriage, and honestly, the last thing I needed right then was someone else blaming me for all our problems."

"So you do think the divorce was your fault," Benson says softly.

"Everyone else certainly seems to think so." I jerk my hand out of his. "Sure, I couldn't do much about my stagnated sperm. But even my best friends, Sam and Milo, acted like I should have been handling things differently. Conrad and Barbara didn't know everything that was going on, but they certainly blamed me." I shake my head. "All I wanted was for us to be parents. That's all I wanted. And I still don't understand how I fucked everything up."

I should have fixed us. I was supposed to fix us.

The words that never really stop running through my head move through it once more, and I wince against them.

"Do your parents know?"

"You know what a hard time I have keeping things from them." I send him a quick grin, and he rolls his eyes. "They know the basics. Not all the details."

Across the pond from us, the family begins packing up their belongings. The two little kids hover by the duck pond, while their mother stands behind them, ready to grab hold of shirts and pants if anyone looks like they're getting too close.

"I was legit left on my father's doorstep when I was a baby," Benson blurts out.

"What?" I turn to stare at him.

"I know, right? And you thought HBO had dramatic nonsense on lock." He shrugs. "But it's true. One night stand. Mom took off, Dad got stuck with me. He didn't even know I existed until I showed up on his doorstep. He was about to start Harvard Law and follow in my grandfather's footsteps, so I lived at my grandpa's house until I was six. He wasn't around that much, though. I was mostly raised by nannies."

I want to ask so many questions. Did he have headaches when he was little? Did he ever see his father? Does he ever see his father now? But I feel like I'm standing next to a wild deer in the forest who's let me come close enough to pet it, and I'm watchful of every sudden movement or sound I make.

"I went back to live with my dad when I was in elementary school, but then I was still mostly with nannies and whatnot. And since it turned out I sucked at school, my dad and grandpa shipped me off to a special boarding school in southern Vermont as soon as I was old enough to go."

So many things suddenly click into place in the story of Benson. The forgotten guitar. His understanding of Elijah's struggles. His determination to prove himself. "That must have been lonely," I say carefully.

He shrugs again. "Not that different from being at home, actually. Then my father got remarried."

Every Cinderella re-telling ever flashes through my head, but Benson quickly interrupts them. "Before you get the wrong idea, my stepmom's always been good to me. And I like my twin half-siblings a lot. But the four of them... they're a family. *Just* the four of them. I've always kind of gotten in the way. I've known since the twins were born that they'd always be my dad's *real* kids. The ones he meant to have. The ones he had at the perfect time with the perfect wife in the perfect house." Benson frowns as he tugs at a piece of grass. "It used to bother me. The vacations they'd take without me while I was away at boarding school. The pictures of the four of them that covered the house whenever I'd come home for visits. I always knew I was a ghost in their space, haunting everyone's presence with my mere existence. Sarah, my stepmother, tried to make me feel like I was more than that, but I've always known otherwise." He rips the piece of grass from the ground, taking a large clump of dirt with it. "And the twins are both fucking geniuses who will get into the schools my dad got into that I never did."

"Benson, you're brilliant!" I tell him quickly. "I can tell that just by the way you work with Elijah.

"I fucking work hard for everything," Benson says slowly. Deliberately. "Because I have to. So I've done nothing but work basically my whole damn life. And I don't think I minded that much until we fucked around the other day and it was the best damn sex I'd ever had."

The family across from us finishes packing up, and now we're alone with the trees. And the ducks.

"Best ever, huh?" I can't help but tease. I move my body closer to his, easing my arms around him. "Are you saying you want to do it again?"

I decide not to bring up the pile of childhood trauma he just laid out across the grass. Not now. That was a lot for him to say out loud, I know. When he wants to talk about it more, he will.

And I also know that now is not that time. Now, I think, he wants to talk about something else. He *wants* something else.

And I want to give it to him.

His Adam's apple bobs as he gulps, hard. "You know I won't be here forever, Jack. We're going to have to fake break up. I'll go back to Boston."

"I know," I tell him. I wake up almost every single damn day thinking about that. "So maybe we should enjoy whatever time we have. Because honestly? That was the best damn sex I've ever had too."

And just like that, it's *on*.

I roll him over onto his back, unbuttoning his pants while he grasps my head to his and we hold onto each other in one of the most intense, dangerous, hardest kisses I've ever been a part of. "Someone could see," he whispers in my ear, just as I start on his zipper.

"Keep an eye out," I urge him.

"Like that'll be easy." He moans, already hot and ready for me, his dick hard in my hand as I pull it through the hole of his boxers. I don't give him any time to process what he's doing before I kiss him once more, push myself down his body, and swallow his cock.

He thrusts upward into my mouth, and I snake a hand down into my own pants, getting just enough clearance to feel myself harden further with every moan that Benson makes. His dick is perfect in my mouth: long and thick but not too thick, his tip wet on my tongue. I use one hand to hold onto his base while I lick and tease and do every single damn move I can while I listen for the cues of what he loves best. I'm jacking myself so hard it hurts, and I'm so close, and then—

"Jack!" Benson nearly howls the word, but I don't pull off of him. I stay where I am, taking everything that he has to give me as he thrusts into my mouth and spills hard. I come in my own hand, making a huge mess. And I couldn't care less.

"Holy crap," he says as I fall down on the ground next to him. "And here I thought you wearing a stethoscope was going to be hot. Who knew you'd be this hot in an apple orchard."

"Wait a minute." I sit up. "Stethoscopes turn you on?"

Benson's face goes red. "Uh, I didn't mean to say that. I didn't say that! You never heard it. I just meant—"

"Do you have a doctor fetish, Benson Lewis?"

"I'm not confirming or denying that," he says. "All I'm saying is that I may never look at an apple the same way again."

"Apples turn you on now? What will you do when you see a pie?" I ask him as I find some tissues in my pocket and work on getting myself cleaned up. But I've already got an idea. A great idea, actually.

Well, maybe it's a great idea. Is anything a great idea when it involves a fake boyfriend who is also the enemy of your whole town *and* someone you just spilled some of your deepest, darkest secrets to?

Probably not.

"It's definitely your fault if apple danish gives me boners from here on out." Benson finishes adjusting his pants and sits up. "We should get going, huh?"

"Yeah. At least it's a good sign that Elijah hasn't texted us. Maybe that means he and his grandparents are getting along. Did I tell you they mentioned getting us all ski passes for when they come back to visit this winter?" I sigh. I really, really hope Eric's back by then.

"I keep forgetting there's a ski area nearby." Benson takes the hand I offer to help him stand, and I pull him up off the grass with me. "Is it any good?"

"It was a mess for a long time, but the new owner's turning it around. He just bought it a few years ago; Bill Cummings is his name. He's been really great about working with the town, and the tourism money definitely helps support us in the seasons when we don't have leaf festivals going on. I guess we'll have to lean on it a lot more if we lose the festival." I shrug.

Next to me, Benson's gone eerily quiet. He's staring at me, wide-eyed, like he's seeing a ghost. "Benson? You okay?"

"Did you say Bill Cummings?" Benson asks. His voice sounds oddly strangled.

"Yeah. That's the guy who owns the ski area. Benson? What's the matter?"

"I'm fine." He schools his face back into its usual evenly skeptical expression and starts walking again. "Let's get going, okay? I have lots of work to do back at the town hall."

I follow him, and I plan.

Because I'm not sure exactly what just happened, but I'm going to put a look of amazement back on his face if it kills me, damnit.

Chapter 13
33 Days to the Devon Falls Leaf Festival

You know I'm not going to drop this case even if you put me in stirrups, right? —Benson Lewis

"You had sex with the hot doctor! I *knew* you were going to have sex with the hot fauxmance doctor."

I groan. "Jeremy, this is exactly why I called Aaron, not you. Stop answering his fucking phone. And stop using the word fauxmance!"

"Benson Lewis, I'm hurt. After all the hours we've spent looking over billing documents together, I'm honestly shocked that you don't miss me more."

Honestly, I do miss him a little—not that I'd ever tell him that. Jeremy Everett is one of those life forces that sort of nudges his way under your skin whether you want him to or not. And I must miss Aaron Morin too, because after I spent the night pacing my apartment and trying to figure out what to do with that bomb Jack dropped on me in the apple orchard yesterday, I woke up and found myself calling Aaron.

Something in our connection clicks and then the sound gets a little less crisp. "Benson?" says Aaron. "You're on speaker. I'm making breakfast."

Of course he is. I'm sure those two adorable fuckers eat breakfast together every damn day. My stomach twinges as I think of the text Jack sent me this morning. *Come over for waffles?* I ignored it because I was pacing. And also because if Jack sees me right now he'll know something is wrong and I can't tell him what's wrong. Especially since I'm not sure what's wrong or if there even *is* actually anything wrong.

What the actual fuck is my fucking fucked-up life right now.

"Tell us what's going on," Aaron says. And I guess it's a testament to how few people I talk to that I start spilling the whole story to my former archnemesis and his boyfriend.

They wait patiently while I jump around from topic to topic like a grasshopper on speed.

"Okay," Jeremy says when I'm done. "So let me make sure I understand this. You're maybe falling for the guy you're in a fauxmance with, and also it's possible that the owner of a ski area has devised a plot to try and strip the Devon Falls Leaf Festival Center from the town?"

That's basically the long and short of it, but I'm not admitting the first part. "I just told you to stop calling it a fauxmance. You definitely made that word up. And you can't fall for a guy you have no future with. Jack and I are done after I leave this town. But yeah, I guess we're having sex now."

"I'll have you know that the word 'fauxmance' is codified in ye good old Urban Dictionary. And Aaron and I had no future once," Jeremy says. I don't know the whole story of how those two ended up looking like the final scene of a Disney fairytale, but I do know that Aaron is Jeremy's best friend's brother and that Jeremy used to be one of the biggest players in all of Vermont. So, I'm guessing they probably do defy some odds.

"Nice that the two of you worked it out," I tell him. "Anyway, I didn't call you about the thing with Jack." I'm not sure why I even told them about it. Something about talking to Aaron and Jeremy makes me do weird things, like *speak openly.* "Right now I'm trying to figure out what to do about the Bill Cummings situation."

"Right," says Aaron brusquely. "Let's examine the possible options here." I can hear the clinking of silverware, so I pull out a protein bar to scarf down while they settle into their lovers' breakfast. "Option A: this is a different Bill Cummings."

"Possible, but seems unlikely," Jeremy says cheerfully.

"Right. Option B: this is the same Bill Cummings and he is working with Arnie, but that's only because the land rightfully belongs to Arnie and he wants to help out."

"Because every Vermont ski area owner happens to know a used car salesman in Massachusetts with heritage connections to some land basically next door to their ski area," Jeremy puts in.

My thoughts exactly.

"Option C," Aaron goes on. "Bill Cummings has a vested interest in that land no longer belonging to the town."

"Ding ding ding," says Jeremy. "I mean, that's the plot I'd write if this were my Agatha Christie novel."

"You know who Agatha Christie is?" Aaron asks.

"Agatha Christie is basically ubiquitous in society," Jeremy tells him patiently. "Plus, I dated a guy who had her entire collection. He liked to surround his bed with her books while we messed around."

"Wow. There's a lot to unpack there," Aaron says.

"I know, right? He even had a poster of her above his bed. And let me tell you, trying to come while Agatha Christie is staring at you directly between—"

"Could we focus here, please?" I interrupt.

"Oh, sorry," says Jeremy. "Right. So, anyway, we're leaning toward thinking there's something fishy here. Benson, I hate to ask this, but do you think your family is involved in whatever's going on? Arnie is their client. And you mentioned before that he's not exactly a typical client."

Unfortunately, this is the exact question I was up most of last night asking myself. "Here's the thing," I finally say. "I don't know much about how my family's firm actually runs. I didn't intern or clerk there. This is my first time working for them."

"So, you really hope they're not that type of firm, but you can't be sure," Aaron finishes simply. And I kind of love him at that moment for not asking anything about why I've never worked for my own family before. Explaining that my grandfather wasn't sure I could hack it and didn't want me embarrassing him? Well, that's nothing I feel like saying to the Harvard Law graduate on the other end of the phone. "But they're also your family, so you're in an awkward situation here."

"Maybe I am. Maybe I'm not." I sink into the couch in the tiny studio I've called home for weeks now and twirl my finger around a loose thread hanging from the edge of the armrest. "A case is a case, right? You win the fucking case. That's how my family works. If the goal here is to prove the land is Arnie's, then what does it matter why Bill Cummings is involved? Who cares? If the land belongs to Arnie, it belongs to Arnie."

"Fair point," says Jeremy. "But what if it really doesn't belong to Arnie? There's a strange death certificate involved here, Benson. What if more's going on? Do you really want to take that land away from Devon Falls if it rightfully belongs to them?"

"That's the job sometimes, isn't it?" I ask. "Our job is to present the best possible case for our clients. That's it. Full stop. Lawyers are officers of the court. Our goal is always to win the case."

Those are the words I keep repeating to myself, anyway. They're the words my grandfather and father burned into my brain years ago. And they're true. I'm sure of it. They have to be true.

Don't they?

Aaron sighs. "Listen, Benson. We both know that's how plenty of firms and law offices operate. But that's also how plenty of law offices choose *not* to operate. I work for Iris and Tom because I don't want to operate that way."

An image of Iris Sprysky and her always-above-board firm flashes through my head. "I don't work for Iris and Tom anymore," I remind him gruffly.

"No, you don't. And Tom told me recently that after I pass the bar, assuming I do—"

"Of course you'll pass the bar!" Jeremy crows confidently.

"Thanks, babe. Anyway, Tom told me that after I pass the bar, I'm going to learn pretty quickly that only I can decide what kind of lawyer I want to be. No firm, he said, can decide that for me. I wasn't sure exactly what he meant. But I think—"

"Yeah, yeah," I interrupt, because I know exactly where this is going, and I'm determined to cut things off before this conversation turns into even more of an unwanted therapy session than it already is.

"I'm just saying that you may have to make some choices, here."

"But we don't know that yet!" Jeremy pipes in. "Right? Option A and B are still on the table. So I guess the question is: do you want to know what's really going on with this land claim? Or do you want to bury your head in the sand and just lawyer shit up?"

"That barely made sense," Aaron says, laughing.

"It totally made sense!" There's more scuffling on the other end of the line, which gives me time to do some thinking.

If law school has taught me anything, it's how often ignorance can be bliss. Sometimes, I've heard over and over again, you're better off not knowing everything about your clients. Sometimes, it's easier to keep yourself in the dark. And I know for sure that's what Grandpa, and probably Dad, would want me to do here.

So why is it that I can't stop thinking about Marion, the bakery owner, crying in the back of the courtroom the other day? Or imagining a high-school-aged Jack marching as the fucking leaf royalty in the Devon Falls Leaf Festival parade? Or hearing Ellie's voice, telling me how important the Leaf Festival is to the town and how she can't let them lose it?

Eventually the scuffling stops, and the phone line goes quiet for a moment. "Benson?" Aaron finally says. "What do you want to do?"

"I think," I finally say, "that I can't bury my head here. I think I need to know if Bill Cummings has an interest in this property. Knowing that he does may not change anything," I add. Because if the land rightfully belongs to Arnie, then it rightfully belongs to Arnie. The law is the law. "But if it does change something—well, I need to know that. I'm not about to perpetuate a fraud on the court."

"Then it's on," Jeremy says confidently. "Stack those Agatha Christie books around your bed, because the three of us are on this case."

By the time I head over to Lancer Family Medicine to meet Jack that afternoon, I've got a plan. Well, *we've* got a plan. I'm going to do some low-key reconnaissance here in Devon Falls to find out exactly who Bill Cummings is and how the ski area is connected to the town. Jeremy and Aaron, or my "hot crime-solving assistants," as Jeremy has begun referring to them, are looking into any connections Bill might have to Arnie or my family's firm. "You don't have to do that," I told them gruffly. "I can handle this on my own."

"Yeah, we do," Jeremy said. "You can't look into any of that stuff closely without risking someone in your firm or family finding out. And dude, family shit is hard. I get that. So let us help you, okay?"

It's a nice gesture from someone who once put salt in my coffee. To be honest, I didn't know how to respond. Aaron noticed.

"Now you just say thank you," he instructed me.

Which I did.

And then I hung up the phone immediately. I'm not sure why saying the words "thank you" makes me feel like I've had sandpaper dragged across my tongue, but it does.

So now I'm headed to the Devon Falls doctor's office with a lot on my mind. Not the least of which is why Jack asked me to meet him at his office. We're supposed to eat at the café tonight, so I'm not sure why we couldn't just meet there. Jack better not have signed me up for a surprise doctor's appointment with his mother. I'm in no mood for that shit right now.

I open the front door to the large blue Victorian house with yellow trim that Jack's mother turned into her practice years ago. A skinny guy with messy brown hair and lightly tanned skin looks up from the front desk where he's sitting.

"Hi! You must be Benson. I'm Malachai. Jack told me you'd be meeting him here. He said you could go back to Exam Room A."

Exam Room A? My hackles immediately go up. "Is his mother there too?" I ask. I maybe kind of growl the words, and then I feel badly when Malachai flinches. "Sorry," I add quickly. "It's just that he's been trying to convince me to come in for an appointment, and I—"

"Oh, no worries," Malachai says, shaking his head. "Dr. Lancer—I mean Jack—is the only one back there. Everyone else left for the day already. I'm heading out now, too." He hoists a heavy book off the desk. *BIOLOGY*, say the dark letters across the front of it. "I've got class."

"Nice. Where are you going to school?" I ask. There aren't all that many colleges close to Devon Falls.

"Just the local community college," Malachai says. The tips of his ears go a little red. "Nothing fancy like Burlington University."

If only my grandfather could hear him say that. Not that he'd give much of a shit what a secretary thinks of the school I went to. But it's nice for me to remember that not everyone looks down on my alma mater. "Hey," I tell Malachai. "Don't say shit like that. School is school. Good for you for working on your degree. What are you studying?"

"I'm in pre-nursing. But..." Malachai trails off. "I mean, enrolling was probably dumb. I barely have time to study. And I want to make sure I do a good job here, because I really like working here and I need this job. And now I'm telling you my whole life story. Sorry," he adds as his ears go even redder. "Sometimes I don't know when to shut up."

"It must be tough," I tell him. "Working and going to school at the same time." As fucked-up as my childhood was, I know it gave me plenty of advantages other people didn't have. The ability to focus solely on school and not have to work to survive while I was getting multiple degrees was definitely one of them. "Good for you, man."

"Thanks. I mean, uh, thank you." Malachai looks startled by what I said. I'm a little surprised too, to be honest. I swear, I never used to be as fucking friendly as I am now. Does Devon Falls put nice pills in their water? Are Aaron and Jeremy finally rubbing off on me?

"I'll head back and find Exam Room A," I tell him.

"I hope you have a great night," he says brightly. "Dr. Lancer said he had a surprise for you!" He throws some more books into an old backpack and heads for the door, leaving me to wonder what the hell kind of surprise my fake boyfriend could have planned for me.

I walk back through the front hall of the building and quickly find Exam Room A. I knock at the door. *This better not be a set-up,* I warn the room label in front of me.

"Come in!" says Jack.

I push the door open. And... wow.

"Holy shit," I whisper. Because standing in front of me is Jack. Wearing a lab coat over his shirt and jeans. With a stethoscope around his neck, and his hands clasped in front of him. And behind him is an exam table.

With the stirrups up.

"Mr. Lewis," says Jack brusquely. "I'm going to need you to take your clothes off for this examination." My dick springs up instantly in my pants.

"You know I'm not going to drop this case even if you put me in stirrups, right? And what am I having examined?" I ask hoarsely.

Jack steps forward slightly. "Well," he says. "According to your file, you've been having some trouble orgasming. Naturally, we'll want to look at that. But no worries, Mr. Lewis. Anytime you want to end this examination, all you have to do is say stop." He eyes me carefully. "Is that clear?"

Is it clear that Jack's about to help me re-enact porn scenes I've jerked off to millions of times? "Yeah, it's clear," I answer in a strangled voice.

"Excellent. Then clothes off, please. I'll lock the door." He moves across the room, stopping next to me as I unzip my pants. "Remember," he whispers in my ear. "Anytime you want to pause or end this, all you have to do is say stop."

Like hell I'm using that word.

In record time I've got my clothes off. The room is slightly chilly, but my cock barely notices as I climb up onto the exam table and lie down.

Jack steps up to the edge of the exam table. His lab coat is hugging his hips, his lips red and wet, and there's no way I could be any harder if I tried. "Are you comfortable?" he asks. I nod. "I see you have an erection."

I nod again as he leans over to pull two plastic gloves from a box. The tension in the room ratchets up as he pulls the right one on and then the left one, letting each one smack against his hand like a rubber band. "I'll need you to put your feet up in the stirrups so I can examine you properly."

I gulp hard, wondering how this moment can even possibly be real, as Jack helps me slide my feet into the stirrups. The cold hard metal there is covered with oven mitts decorated in cow spots. I suppose that sight should take me out of the moment, but it doesn't. Nothing fucking could, I don't think. Cows themselves could come storming through this room, and I'd still have my eyes glued to Jack Lancer, who is currently pulling up a stool to sit right in front of where I'm spread out entirely before him, as naked and vulnerable and turned on as I'm sure I've ever been.

"I'll need to take your temperature first," he says. "Are you comfortable with me taking your temperature rectally?" I nod yet again, fast. Jack and I haven't had many conversations about anal sex, but I'm a bottom all the way. I've had limited experience with sex, and most of it hasn't been very good, to be honest, but I've had enough decent sex to know that I love having a guy slip his dick just inside my hole. I love the push of pleasure meeting pain. I love the pressure. The fullness.

Jack's covering a thermometer in something that looks like lube. "Do you like having things inserted into your anus?" he asks as he turns back to me, holding the thermometer up. "We'll need to discuss this if we're going to discuss why you're having problems orgasming."

I swear, if he says the word *anus* again I'm going to come all over my stomach. And why are anatomically correct terms such a turn-on for me? That's something I'll worry about later, I decide. "I love it," I tell him honestly, and the strain in my voice is very real. "It definitely... definitely turns me on."

"Well, we'll start with the thermometer and get your temperature, then." Jack fixes his eyes on mine as he slowly, deliberately, begins to push the thermometer inside of me.

It's not overly large, but I still gasp as he pushes it past the opening of my hole and it begins to hit nerve endings. "Yes," Jack whispers, as he leans over me and slides the thermometer back and forth, in and out. "I can tell you like that. Would you like it if I touched you while this thermometer was inside of you?"

"Oh fuck, yes. Yes, doctor." I shiver slightly as I say the words, and the corners of Jack's mouth turn up.

"I'll have to test your reflexes there, then. Stay as still as you can, please." He moves the thermometer a little farther in, and I try not to cry out when, at the same time, he gently brushes a gloved hand across the top of my dick and then slides it down over my length. "You seem like a very healthy man, Mr. Lewis," he says. He begins to twist the thermometer around inside of me, and I shout as he hits more and more sensitive places. He bumps up against my prostate with the tip of the thermometer, and I call out as he rubs his other hand around the bottom of my dick.

Jack slowly pulls the thermometer from my body. "Completely normal," he says softly. "Now, Mr. Lewis. I think I may have a treatment for you. But it would require me testing your reflexes by putting something much larger inside of you." He pushes off his lab coat and slowly begins to unbutton his pants. "It's a treatment we haven't fully discussed, so I'll need your express consent before continuing. Would you like me to try the treatment?"

My mouth is so dry I can barely speak, and I'm certain I'm not going to last long enough for Jack and I to actually finish this scene he's constructed for me. I close my eyes against the flood of images around me. "Yes." I nearly choke out the word. "Yes, I really fucking would."

"Okay, then." I listen to the sounds of Jack's zipper moving. I think I hear him open up a condom packet. Then there's the pop of a bottle, and the snap of some gloves, and soon I feel the flesh of one of his fingers snaking its way inside of me.

I jump up against him as the sudden sensation pushes me closer to the edge. "Relax, Benson," he whispers. "Relax."

I open my eyes to find him over top of me. He's easing my legs out of the stirrups as he teases and tortures me with one hand. He places his other hand behind my neck, lifting me gently until we're staring directly at each other.

"Are you sure?" he asks. He's added another finger at some point, but by now I'm one giant nerve sensation, and I hardly notice where the pressure and pain bend and merge and break together. He brushes a finger against my prostate, and I cry out. "Yes!" I yell out. "Please, Jack, get the fuck inside of me!"

He leans over and attaches his lips to mine as he pushes his way into me in one hard thrust.

The next few minutes are lost to me in sparks of light and sensation and pure electric feeling. Jack's so big inside of me, and every time he hits my most sensitive of places I think I'm going lose it—but then he backs the pleasure gently away before throttling it up again, creating waves of sensation that get bigger, sharper, and wilder with every ride I take over them. "Benson," he says, and his voice sounds higher and even more desperate than mine has. "Benson, I—"

"Jack, I'm coming!" I call out. He moves a hand over the tip of my dick, taking hold of the sides of it gently, and that's all it takes. I come so hard and so fast it's almost painful, just as I feel his body stop and stutter inside of me. Over and over and over again, it stutters.

And then, just like that, the waves subside. The ocean calms and falls back, and Jack half-falls across my chest, his breath coming in heaves.

I can't seem to speak, and Jack doesn't expect me to. Instead he lifts me up off the table, cradling me in his arms, and carries me gently over to a couch off to the side of the room. He lays me down on it. I'm barely aware of what's happening, but I think he cleans me off and pulls a sweatshirt over my head.

And then he moves me gently, ever so slightly, just enough so he can slide behind me and hold me close to his chest, spooning me.

"Holy shit, Jack," I finally manage to say. "How long have you been planning that?"

He laughs, but he doesn't answer. I'm drifting off in his arms, though, when I think I hear him whisper, "there's that smile I love to see."

Chapter 14
26 Days to the Devon Falls Leaf Festival

Anything I say to Benson right now won't end well; I know that much for sure. —Jack Lancer

"Dr. Lancer? Dr. Lancer! Your coffee's ready."

Belinda Ryker is staring at me oddly as she holds out my low-fat caramel latte. "Dr. Lancer, are you okay?"

"I'm fine, Belinda. Thank you." I flash her a smile and take the coffee quickly as I wonder how long I've been standing in Falling All Beans staring off into space. All I know is that I placed my order and then found myself wandering in the memory of Benson Lewis, stretched out on my exam table... and damn, here I go again. Now I'm walking down Main Street half-hard, wondering if I'm ever going to stop replaying that scene in my mind.

It doesn't seem likely, to be honest. I've had some good sex in my life, but I can be honest and say that was *the best* sex I've had. Ever. Including the foursome I had right after my divorce when I was, as Milo put it, "grieving through my dick."

I can't seem to wrap my mind around everything that happened in that exam room. First there's the fact that I, of all people, staged a sex scene *in my family's medical practice.* Wait until I tell Sam and Milo; Sam's going to have kittens. Milo, on the other hand, will probably applaud. Then there was the look on Benson's face as he stepped into the room... the way he held onto me while I was pushing him into that table... the blissed-out smile that took over his entire face as I held him on the couch.

And fuck, now I'm definitely hard. This won't do. I'm on my way to church, for crying out loud. Thank goodness it's Amelia's church, where the windows are covered in rainbows and the youth group has regular conversations about healthy relationships and sex positivity. No one at the Devon Falls Community Church is going to shame me for having a boner.

Still, I'm more than a little concerned that I can't even order coffee and walk to a church service without thinking of Benson Lewis. I've never had a fake boyfriend before, but I'm fairly certain that becoming *this* obsessed with one falls into a dangerous level. How's all this going to shake out when Benson leaves? What did I push both of us further into this week?

At least I think it was both of us. Benson seemed happy enough when he left that night—well, as happy as Benson Lewis ever seems—but I haven't seen him all that much since then. He's working double-time on the case as we move closer and closer to the land ownership hearing. I was surprised when he agreed to come to church with us this morning. But then, Elijah and Pat are playing with the choir. And Elijah used those puppy dog eyes of his when he asked Benson to come. Those things should be labeled a dangerous weapon.

I stop in front of the town hall and historical society and take a moment to collect myself. When my pants are slightly less tented, I let myself through the door and head between the display cases of the historical society toward the back archives room. It may be Sunday morning, but I know from his texts that Benson's been hard at work here since six.

Benson's voice is coming from the back room. His words get louder and more distinctive as I get closer, and I don't like what I'm hearing.

"Grandpa, I just need to find further documentation to show that—yes, sir, I know you took a chance sending me here." Benson's voice sounds high and almost panicky now. "Listen, Carter and I made a plan and I'm sticking to it, I promise." He stops suddenly. "Where did you hear that? Carter told you what?"

I push open the door gently, because eavesdropping really isn't my style. I'm not going to listen in on Benson's conversation without him knowing I'm here. He whirls on me, eyes wide. "It isn't like that, sir! I'm just—"

I can't hear exactly what's being said on the other end of the line, but I can hear just enough to know that it's shouting. Loud shouting. Loud, very disappointed shouting.

Benson closes his eyes and listens to all of it, and I fight the urge to grab the phone from his hand and chuck it across the room. Finally the voice on the other end of the conversation goes quiet, and Benson takes a breath.

"Sir," he says, "I promise you, I'm working hard here. Actually, I have a new lead I'm looking into. Another name's come up, and—"

Then the shouting gets louder. Much, much louder.

I watch Benson's entire body sink in on itself as he listens. His shoulders fall, his eyes drop, and his back and legs seem to collapse under his weight. The Benson who once spoke at our town meeting, the Benson with that strikingly confident presence, is disappearing with every word his grandfather says. And now I'm getting *very* close to ripping that phone from his hands.

I don't have to, though. Because then Benson pulls the phone slowly away from his face, and it's all too obvious he's been hung up on.

I clear my throat. "That," I say, "sounded terrible."

If I learned one thing during my divorce and the aftermath, it's that sometimes it's nice to have the obvious confirmed for you.

Benson swallows hard as he slips the phone into his pocket. He blinks as he looks away from me, and all I want to do right now is take him in my arms and hold him tight. I want to tell him he doesn't need his pressure-packed family to love him or believe in him. He doesn't need to prove himself to them.

Can you say all that to your fake boyfriend? Damn if I'm not going to try. "Benson," I say. "Listen, I know that—"

"I can't go with you." Benson takes a seat at the long table in the center of the room where he and Ellie work whenever they're here. I think this place has basically become his office in Devon Falls, but all that sits here is Benson's gray laptop and a plain black travel coffee mug. No hint of his life or personality or interests are anywhere to be seen. "Tell Elijah I'm sorry, but I have to miss seeing him play. I'll make it up to him." He starts jiggling his mouse, and I can see it quivering in his palm.

"Benson." I sit down in the chair next to him and reach for his hand, but he pulls away from me. "Whatever your grandfather just said to you, remember—"

"He said exactly what he needed to say to me, Jack," Benson snaps. "He said that I've got a job to do here, and I'm not fucking doing it. And he's exactly right. I can't keep playing house with you and acting like I live in a place that has a damn poop emoji in the middle of the park. It's time I got myself together and got my head in this game." He keeps his eyes on his computer as he starts typing madly.

"It's a statue of leaves," I remind him gently.

"Well, it looks like a fucking poop emoji!"

"I mean, yeah. It does. You're totally right. And I get that you're busy with this case," I add. "I know how important it is to you. But this is just an hour, and maybe—"

"Stop, Jack!" Benson whirls on me now. "Stop fucking acting like we're together! Stop acting like whatever's going on here is real, okay? Because I have real obligations, obligations to my career and my family, and those obligations are not in line with your goals or obligations, let alone this town's. And guess what, Jack? When this is all over in a few weeks, I *am* going to win. I'm not going to let my family down."

Generally, I'm fairly good at parsing my words and thinking before I speak. You don't do multiple rotations in busy New York emergency departments without figuring out that measured language in times of stress matters. But all of that level-headed thinking and planning my words carefully goes out the window when I say what I say next. "Benson, I appreciate how much this case means to you. Truly, I do. But I don't understand these obligations you think you have to your family. These people left you with nannies when you were sick! They shipped you off to boarding school without a backwards glance. I couldn't believe the way your grandfather was talking to you just now! And where the hell is your dad in all this, anyway? Does he talk to you like that too? Is everyone in your family that abusive, Benson?"

Benson's pale face reddens. Just slightly at first, then slightly more, as if I've inflated his anger the way someone inflates a red balloon. I'm just starting to think that I should apologize, that I really have crossed a line and gone too far this time, when he speaks. His words are clipped and curt, and it's clear he's more than angry.

"You don't know shit about my family," he says slowly. "And even if you did, you've got a hell of a nerve lecturing me about them. Aren't the Maggios around somewhere for you to bow to? It's fucking amazing you're even letting Elijah play today. How many times have they texted you begging to make him bow out? How many times have you almost caved?"

His words would probably get to me no matter what, but they hit all that much harder because Conrad did text me last night, asking me if I checked Elijah's grades before I gave him permission to play this morning.

And I did almost ask Elijah to bow out of the performance after I looked at his grades and saw he has a C in English right now. I might have told him he couldn't go if Amelia hadn't been going on and on at our office a few days ago about how wonderful it was to have him playing at the church.

Anything I say to Benson right now won't end well; I know that much for sure. I stand up and push my chair in. "I don't think we should talk about this right now," I say shortly.

"I don't think we should talk about this, ever." Benson turns back to his laptop. "Because how I act with my family is none of your damn business. And how you act with yours is none of mine." He looks up at me again, his eyes dark glass against his pale skin. "Because we're not together. We're not anything to each other. Not really. Right?"

Our evening together in my exam room flashes through my head just long enough for my insides to twist as I say, "Nope. No, we're not."

"Honey, are you okay? You're doing that thing with your face that makes you look like you just ate Ellie's goulash," Mom says to me as we slide into a pew next to Ellie, Henri, and Harry, who's already nodded off against a stack of hymnals and a program with a #transrightsarehumanrights sticker across the front.

"My goulash is excellent!" Ellie tells her, clearly affronted.

"Tell that to the forty people who got food poisoning after the last church potluck dinner," Henri mumbles.

"My oven was acting up," Ellie defends herself. "But Jack, you do look a bit like you took a bite of something rancid—definitely not my goulash—before you joined us here today. That wouldn't have anything to do with the fact that my opposing counsel was pacing the town hall in circles and talking to himself when I stopped over to pick up my shoes on the way here?"

"You had to pick up your shoes at the town hall?" Henri asks.

"Amelia insisted I wear them into the building today." Ellie sighs. "I simply cannot convince her that a church which considers itself open and inclusive should be willing to cater to attendees who prefer not to wear footwear. Or garments in general."

Mom coughs.

"Anyhoo," says Ellie, "spill the tea. What's going on?"

"I don't understand that expression," says Henri. "What tea? Why would I want to spill my tea? I don't go around trying to spill anything."

"Oh, it means to share the gossip," Mom tells her. "I finally asked one of the Ryker kids what it meant when they kept saying it at the office. I thought they were thirsty or something. Oh! And I finally found out what 'sus' means!"

"I'm going to get some fruit punch," I mumble, and I slide quickly off the bench and into the crowd of other people trying to get to the punch and cookies table in the back. Amelia used to have the snacks served after the service, but then someone accidentally put them out ahead of time and we all quickly discovered that sitting in a building with questionable heating and air conditioning for an hour is a lot more enjoyable if sugar and carbs are involved.

I smile and nod hello back at faces I barely see as I make my way to the punch. I'm in the middle of pouring my second cup—and why adding fizz to liquid sugar is so delicious is something that I understand scientifically but still never cease to be amazed by—when someone taps me on my shoulder. I turn to find Ellie standing behind me.

"You heard him talking to his grandfather too, I'm guessing?"

My eyes widen, and she quickly gestures for me to follow her outside. We step out into the mid-fall clouds of northern Vermont as organ music begins to swell inside the doors behind us.

"You heard that?" I ask.

"First time I tried to get the shoes," she says quietly. "I left to give him some space and came back later. I assume you were there in the interim?"

"Must be," I mutter. I sigh. "I tried to talk to him about his relationship with his family. Let's just say it didn't go well."

Ellie nods sharply. "Sit down, Jack." She plops down on the hard cement of the church's front steps and pats the seat next to her. I sit too, because I learned long ago that trying to argue with Ellie is a very poor use of anyone's time.

"You tried to tell him he doesn't need to impress them," she says.

"I mean—well, kind of. Yes, I guess so." I frown as I try to figure out how to lace my thoughts into words. "I understand his drive to win this case. That I understand. But his family seems to have such control over him. And you heard the way his grandfather speaks to him!" I stop there, not sure what Ellie knows and not willing to betray Benson's confidence.

Ellie crosses her arms and stares out at the town square. "The legal world can be an unforgiving place, Jack," she says. "Highly, highly unforgiving. There are a lot of people in our field who believe very strongly in the kill-or-be-killed mentality. A lot of snobbery. Did you know that Benson's grandfather and father both went to Harvard Law?"

"I didn't."

"Benson did not," she says. "I can only assume because he didn't get in," she adds. "And I assume, as someone in a profession that also places a high level of importance on educational pedigree, that you can understand how that might weigh on a person."

I can, and I can't. My parents never pressured me to go or not to go to any particular school. Mom was thrilled when I became a doctor, but I know she would have been equally thrilled if I'd become a farmer or an accountant or any other thing I wanted to be. But another piece of that Benson puzzle I forever seem to be putting together clicks into place, right in a spot that I haven't been able to discern yet. I can see the shapes there more clearly now. "He's never been able to prove himself to them," I say slowly.

"Nope. Never. That's my guess, anyway." Ellie frowns. "And I don't get the impression Benson's got a wide circle of friends. I guess some folks might find him prickly. Now don't get me wrong," she says, putting up her hand to stop me when I open my mouth to defend him. "I like that little porcupine exactly the way he is. All I'm saying is that I'm guessing Benson doesn't have too many other people to look to for belonging besides his family."

"So you're telling me to cut him some slack."

She sighs. "People aren't hardwired to be alone, Jack. We're hardwired for love. We're hardwired to be a part of things bigger than ourselves. You can't blame Benson for looking for that from his own family. And you can disapprove of his choices all you want, but I doubt very much that any of them will change. At least until Benson sees that he has a chance to find those things somewhere else."

"But he does have that chance—" I start to say. And then I stop myself. Because no, he doesn't. Not really. Benson and I have become so close so quickly that sometimes I find myself all but forgetting what we really are to each other: just a person who needed a split-second favor and another person who gave it to him.

Nothing more, nothing less. And for all the moments that push me to believe we could be more, I know the practicalities of our situation. Benson has bigger plans, bigger dreams than Devon Falls, Vermont. And I'm not sure I'll ever want to leave the home that took me back in and held me tightly after the world kicked my ass a whole lot harder than I ever knew it could.

Ellie stands and stretches. "You doctors always like things to be black and white," she tells me simply. "Lawyers like nuance, exceptions, fine print, special cases, and wiggle room. Not everything is corrected with the right prescription and some rest, Jack." She tugs at the cardigan she's wearing. "Damn thing's so itchy," she mutters before she opens the door to head back inside the church.

She has to be wrong. Doesn't she? Sure, there are plenty of things out of our control in this world. But so many things are *in* our control. Things like sticking around for your family's interminable verbal abuse. Things like exploring family planning options when you're one half of an infertile couple.

Shouldn't we always do everything in our power to fix the things we can fix?

It doesn't take me long to find Benson after the church service is over. He's sitting in the archive room, his eyes on his laptop and his fingers planted on each side of his forehead. His face is wrinkled and his eyes are pinched with pain.

"Headache?" I ask.

He glances up at me. There are dark circles rimming those same pain-pinched eyes, and I have to fight the urge to pick him up right out of his seat and carry him off to bed.

"It's not bad," he says, almost defensively. "Nothing like a migraine. Just a headache."

"Headaches can be pretty terrible, though. Especially when you're having trouble managing the pain." I step into the room, crossing the creaky old wide floorboards like I'm approaching a spooked animal, and I feel as though I am. Benson's watching me warily, as if he's internally assessing whether he needs to fight me, flee, or do something else entirely.

I sit down in the hard backed old chair next to him. It's at least thirty years old and not particularly comfortable, and I briefly wonder if Amelia would let me look into putting some office chairs in here. With how much time Benson and Ellie are spending in this space, they need some better lumbar support. "It's tough sometimes," I say, and I keep my words careful and measured, this time following my years of training in talking to patients. "Working with my mother. It took us some time to get used to being in the same office. And she and I were close before I came to work with her. I can't imagine how hard it would be if we didn't have that relationship to fall back on during the tougher moments."

Benson glances around at me before he closes his eyes. "This was supposed to be my chance," he says, his voice almost grainy. "Grandpa wouldn't let me clerk for him. Their firm usually doesn't hire state school clerks. I think Sarah talked him into hiring me. Or maybe it was Dad. I didn't care. All I cared about was getting the chance. The shot. And I'm fucking it up, Jack." He swallows hard. "I feel like I'm making all the wrong choices. I'm not even sure what those are most of the time anymore. I was always so sure of things before I came here. I had a fucking plan, Jack. A plan that I followed, no matter what. Even when it didn't work, I followed it, and I didn't care who got in my way." He swallows hard again, confusion and pain written all across his face. "What's wrong with this place?" he asks softly. "What's it doing to me?"

I pull my chair slightly closer to his. "Who's in your way right now, Benson?" I ask him.

He looks up at me, his eyes dark and intense. "You really want me to answer that question, Jack?" There's a feeling in the air now, like the barometric pressure is dropping. Like there's a storm coming, but what type of storm it is remains unclear. Will it be the kind of Vermont storm that wrecks everything in its path, taking out key pieces of landscape and washing out the rivers that nourish us? Or will it be the kind of storm that brings clarity to the air, washing the earth clean?

I don't know the answer to that. But I know that the last time I loved somebody, that love ended in a bonfire I never even saw being lit. It was a bonfire I couldn't seem to stop no matter how hard I tried. I know that I've been aware I was bi since I was in college, but up until recently that's all been very hypothetical. I know that whatever I felt for Fiona and whatever I've felt for any person I've dated since her pales in comparison to the feelings racing within me now.

This is a storm that I'm fairly certain could destroy me. And maybe Benson too, based on what he's just told me.

I should answer Benson's question. I should tell him that he's all I see in my tunnel vision these days. I should tell him that no matter how hard I try to stay away from him, or how hard I try to stay realistic about our future together, something within me keeps navigating back to him. I should do and say so many things right now.

But I don't. Instead, I lean across the battered table and tackle his mouth with mine.

The air pressure in the room instantly drops as he responds to me. He grabs my face in his hand and holds onto me as our tongues and lips dance together in a choreography that is both entirely unknown and intensely surprising. This is what it's like every damn time we kiss, and that in and of itself is perhaps the most magical thing about kissing Benson.

His hands are moving down my body now, pushing at my shirt, looking for the buckle of my belt. I'm so focused on the electricity pulsing back and forth between where our mouths meet that I almost don't notice he's got my pants completely undone until he drops to his knees before me, a blond angel with the devil in his eye. He gestures for me to sit up and slides my pants from beneath me, keeping his eyes glued to me the whole time.

"Doctor," he says, and damn, Benson Lewis is pushing me to realize a fetish I never knew I had. "I think I owe you for that last exam you gave me." Then he leans over and swallows me whole, and all thoughts I'd had before cease to be. It's like I'm trapped in my own endorphins as Benson licks and sucks and tugs and gently pulls at all the right places. I'm reduced to one giant nerve as I grip his blond hair in mine and gasp. "Ben," I pant out. "Not going to...."

I glance down to see he's got his hands inside his open Khakis, and he's stroking himself as he sucks me up and down with perfect timing and rhythm. He sends me a quick nod that flips a switch in my brain, and I let myself go in his mouth with a cry so loud I take a moment to hope no one has stopped by the archives on this Sunday afternoon. Because there's no way I could stop myself now, as wave after wave of pure pleasure washes through and across me. When we've both finally fallen back to earth again, his body is limp, his head across my knees. I lift him carefully, placing him in my lap and using the box of tissues on the table to clean him up as best as I can. He's like a ragdoll in my arms, and I relish the feeling of taking care of him, of setting him to rights again. Benson, I know, is not a man who easily lets himself be dependent on others, and I don't take this moment for granted. I know exactly what a gift he's giving me here.

We sit there for a long while, not speaking. The pressure in the air has settled now, but if anything, what just happened between us has made it all too clear that more storms are coming. Bigger ones. Storms of uncertainty. Storms of the unknown.

And in spite of myself, I hope for them. I wish for them.

"I should go back to work," Benson says eventually. I think of Ellie's words and know better than to argue with him. I lift him up carefully off my knees and help him tidy the space around us. "Bill Cummings?" I ask as I pick up a piece of scrap paper with the name sprawled on it. "He's got something to do with the land? I didn't even think he was from Vermont."

Benson's focused on his laptop screen. "His name has come up a few times in relation to the case. It's probably nothing. Hey, what do you think of him anyway? You didn't really say when you mentioned him at the apple orchard."

I frown as I try to figure out how to explain my feelings about Bill Cummings. "Most people in town like him a lot," I finally say. "Including my parents. The ski area was going under when he swooped in and saved it. That's the only major tourism draw we have up here besides the leaf festival, so it felt like a bit of a miracle." I pause, trying to put the rest of my thoughts in order, and Benson waits for me to finish.

"But something about him has always rubbed me the wrong way," I go on. "I don't trust him. The guy's a businessman through and through. Why invest in a ski area with such an uncertain future? The land up there is so limited. There's no room for expansion or additional accommodations. Devon Ski Area will never be another Stowe. I'm just not quite sure what his end game is, I guess."

"You don't trust the good thing that everyone else trusts," Benson finishes for me. He says the words simply, without judgment.

I frown. "Yes. I suppose that's it."

Benson nods and turns back to his laptop again. "I get that," he says, more to his computer than to me. "It's hard to imagine that anything can be as good as it looks."

His words follow me home, through the light rainstorm that begins just as I exit the historical society.

Chapter 15
22 Days to the Devon Falls Leaf Festival

Ben. Jack called me *Ben.* Again.

Ben.

That's the word that's looping through my head on repeat as my phone dings with a video call from Aaron Morin. I press the button to take the call and Jeremy Everett's blue eyes beam out at me.

"Benson! How's sex with the hot doctor going?"

My face answers that question for me, I guess, because Jeremy starts applauding. "Woot woot! Get it, buddy. Man, it's good to see you smile. Weird, but good. Do you know that I spent the first three months we worked together thinking you were born incapable of forming any other facial expression than a scowl?"

"I had some difficult coworkers," I reply easily, and he laughs as Aaron makes his way to the screen and waves.

"Hey, man," he says. "You got my text?"

I nod grimly. All the text said was *Have some information for you.*

Jeremy's bright grin dims. "It's not great. Shit is shady, bro."

That's what I was afraid they were going to tell me. "Crap. Because things don't look great on my end either." I sigh. "I should probably go first," I tell them.

I give them the cliff notes of the low-key research I've been doing into where Bill Cummings fits into the Devon Falls community. The town confirmed what Jack told me: Bill Cummings is beloved here. Just when everyone thought the Devon Ski Area was going under for good, he swooped in and saved the day. Betty at the café called him a "prince among silver foxes" as she dropped off my meatloaf a few days ago.

But then I started doing some further digging into his business plans here, and that's when things started coming up that looked shady, to borrow Jeremy's word.

When Bill Cummings bought the ski area, he also put in a bid to buy a giant plot of farmland to the east of the ski area. It doesn't take a genius to imagine that he'd planned to scale up the failing property and grow it into a much larger resort. But the sale fell through when the owners backed out, and suddenly he was left with a money pit of a ski area and no place to expand.

"He was deep in the red with that place last year," I tell Aaron and Jeremy. "And he's got cash to spare, but not enough to keep hemorrhaging on his investment. And guess where the only other usable land close to the ski area is?"

"Gee, let me guess," Jeremy says wryly. "Wouldn't happen to be the leaf festival land, would it?"

The answer is so obvious I don't even bother to reply.

"But why not just offer to buy the land from the town?" Aaron asks. "It sounds like he's got the money."

"The town would never sell it," I tell him, thinking of the tears in the courtroom the day Harry granted the injunction. "And he knows it." I sigh. "I need to go talk to him. That's the only way I can get a real sense of what's going on here."

Aaron grimaces. "Well, before you do that, there's something else you really need to know, Benson."

Great. Exactly what I want to hear.

"Bill Cummings used to use your family's firm almost exclusively for representation. Right up until a few months ago, when he suddenly cut ties with their practice."

Fuck.

To be fair, the fact that Bill Cummings was represented by our firm isn't all that strange. Grandpa's firm represents lots of business moguls throughout New England. But combined with the oddities of Arnie's claim and the fact that Bill Cummings has a vested interest in that land no longer belonging to the town? All that makes the connection between my firm and Bill Cummings hard to overlook.

"I hate to write the most boring mystery novel ever here," Jeremy says, "But it sure is starting to look like Bill planted Arnie here to take that land from the town and called in a favor from your grandfather to represent Arnie. Right after he maybe cut ties with the firm itself to make sure the town didn't get suspicious about him being involved in all this."

That all sounds plausible, unfortunately. "Bill Cummings would need the town's goodwill to do anything at all with that land once Arnie claimed ownership of it," I agree reluctantly. "So, he'd definitely want to be careful about making sure his fingerprints were nowhere near this. I wouldn't be surprised if he's got plans to sweep in as the town's savior again, with promises to buy it from Arnie and then share parts of it with them or something." My stomach is churning now with all the possibilities of what Bill Cummings might be planning here. "Have you found any connections between Bill and Arnie?" I ask.

"Nothing so far," Aaron says. "But we're going to keep looking. If we're right about this, though, so far Bill Cummings is doing a fairly solid job of covering his tracks. I'm surprised he didn't do more to cover up his connection to your grandfather."

"Nah, he'd want it on open record that he cut ties with our firm. He's probably planning to eventually tell everyone he did that as a show of support for the town or something."

"Super shady, bro," Jeremy whispers to the screen. "Fuck. What are you gonna do, Benson? Are you really going to go talk to this asshole?"

"I think I have to. It's the only way I can get a real sense of whether we're on the right track here. Coincidences happen in real life, right? Maybe everything we've found so far is just that—coincidences."

The looks on their faces mirror the skepticism that I know is probably written all over mine right now.

Like my grandfather always says: facts are for lawyers. Coincidences are for suckers.

"Be careful, Benson," Aaron says. His look is intense. "You don't even know this guy. Can you talk to your grandfather or dad first?"

I think back to my recent communications with my father and grandfather. "If my dad knows anything, he's not talking about it," I say slowly. "And Grandpa? Honestly, I already know what he's going to say."

Or yell, rather.

Stay on the case. Don't get distracted by silly details. Win win win.

"If the land claim is fake, do you think he knows?" Jeremy asks incredulously.

I frown. "Honestly? No. Grandpa runs a money-first business model, but he's proud of the reputation of our family firm. I don't think he'd do anything to put that in jeopardy. It's much more likely he'd just agree to take Arnie's case and make sure not to ask any questions he doesn't want the answer to. And I just can't see my dad ever approving of a case involving a land claim unless it was completely aboveboard."

And if they don't know the whole story of what's going on here, what would their reaction be to finding out they're representing an elaborate scheme? The more I think about all the possible answers to that question, the more somersaults my stomach does.

"Well, let's not get too far ahead of ourselves." Aaron, as always, steps in to sooth and calm down the conversation. "Benson, if you talk to Bill Cummings, just be careful. If we're on the right track with what's going on here, this guy is getting a little desperate. You never know what a desperate person will do."

"I'm not going to do anything dumb," I promise them. "Just visit the ski area and ask a few questions about the land. I'll keep the conversation light. I'll be careful. I promise."

"Okay. We'll keep looking into any possible Arnie-Bill connections," Aaron says. "But Benson, what are you going to do if our suspicions end up being confirmed? Are you going to step away from the case?"

"He has to!" Jeremy all but yells. "He has to make sure the town knows what's really going on here. Otherwise, they might lose the land to these jerks. And I had big plans to kiss you under a giant pile of poop-emoji shaped leaves there this fall, babe." Sounds like someone's been on the Devon Falls Instagram page.

But he's right. No one besides me, Jeremy, and Aaron knows what's really potentially at play here. And unless one of us tells Ellie, she's not likely to discover any of these strange connections on her own. Why would she ever think that one of Devon Falls' most beloved benefactors may be out to destroy the town's greatest historical tradition?

"Dude, you have to tell the town," Jeremy insists.

"'There's nothing to tell them yet," Aaron reminds him. "Not until we have a better idea of what's going on. And proof. But

Benson, you may want to start thinking about exactly what you want to do if—and likely when—you find that proof."

A few hours later I wind my car through hilly, forested roads on the way to the Devon Ski Area. I've got an appointment to meet with Bill Cummings, secured through his personal assistant, and I've spent the last twenty minutes of this drive rehearsing what I need to say and working up every ounce of confidence I can find for this conversation. And trying to get Aaron's words out of my head.

You may want to start thinking about exactly what you want to do if—and likely when—you find that proof.

I know that I'm breaking one of the cardinal rules of being a lawyer right now: I'm asking questions I don't already know, and may not want, the answer to. But every cell in my body is screaming at me to keep driving this car toward the ski resort, and every time I try to turn around, a face appears in my mind: Jack Lancer.

And so I keep driving.

I make the final turn my GPS orders me to take and pull into a large parking lot flanked by three enormous buildings: a lodge, a small hotel, and one labeled with EQUIPMENT RENTAL AND LESSONS in large letters. Behind the lodge I see chair lifts stretching up above rolling green hills. All of them are abandoned and out of use, which immediately surprises me. A lot of big Vermont ski resorts are filled with people in the off-season. They boost a plethora of activities: golfing, hiking, ziplining, and shit like that. But the Devon Ski Area just looks like a ghost town right now.

I shut the car door slowly behind me and start the walk to the lodge, my heart beating loudly in my throat. The lodge is an older building that looks like it was probably built in the 1950s. It needs a new coat of paint, and I can see cracks in one corner of the foundation.

I push open the heavy door to the building. There's not a person in sight, and now I'm more than glad I called ahead and made an appointment with Cummings' secretary to meet with him.

Inside, dark wood ceilings loom large, and ornately carved furniture sits vacant in a dust-covered sitting area that looks like it could be right out of a Stephen King novel. A shiver runs through me involuntarily.

"Benson Lewis." A booming voice behind me has me spinning in place. I turn to find a large, tall gray-haired man in a polo shirt and khakis watching me. He's smiling, but it's a smile that doesn't quite move beyond the corners of his mouth. Then he grips my hand in one of those hard and firm handshakes that's clearly meant to show me who's going to be in charge during this conversation.

Like I'm going to let myself be cowed by a fucking handshake.

"I'm Bill Cummings. Welcome to my paradise." He gestures to the room around us. "It may not look like much, but that will change soon. Let's go back to my office to talk, shall we?"

I nod shortly and follow him past a bar area covered in dust cloths and a restaurant that looks like it hasn't been operational in this century. Eventually, we end up at the door to a large office that overlooks the changing leaves of the mountains behind a huge set of picture windows. Bill sits down behind a desk that I know costs more than most people in Devon Falls make in a month. He's definitely making some interesting choices about where he invests his money in this place.

He gestures for me to sit on the other side of the desk and settles into his large captain's chair. "I apologize for not being able to offer you any refreshments. As you can see, I'm the only person around until we open for the season. May I ask what this meeting is about? All my assistant was able to tell me was that you're part of the Devon Falls Leaf Festival land case."

"That's right." I lean back in my seat, determined to show him a relaxed, casual presence. I don't want to give any hint of unease or nervousness here. "I'm part of the team representing Arnie Blake. He's the rightful owner of the land."

"So he says." Bill eyes me carefully. "I can't say I hope you win your case, son. That festival means a lot to the town. Therefore, it means a lot to me."

"I assume that's why you're no longer using my firm for representation." I keep my words innocent and light.

"Yes." Bill nods. "The people of Devon Falls have been nothing but good to me. I owe them a great deal for their hospitality. It would have been a terrible conflict of interest for me to continue using their services once they began representing Arnie Blake."

My heart speeds in my chest. I have to play this next part of the conversation very, very carefully. "Is the town aware that you were once represented by our firm, Mr. Cummings?"

He booms out a laugh. "I'm not looking for cookies or applause here, son. If the subject should come up, I'll certainly share with them openly that I'm no longer using your firm's services." He arches an eyebrow at me. "Are you implying that you and your firm are planning to make that information more public?"

I know when I'm playing a game of chess, and I know when someone's just moved a pawn in front of me. I'm trying to figure out what my next move should be when Bill Cummings moves out of turn. He leans across his desk, folds his hands in front of him, and stares me down.

"I've always liked your grandfather. Good man. He's a man who plays to win, no matter what. Are you like him, Mr. Lewis? Do you have your eye on the prize here?"

My heart pounds as I plot my next move. He's testing me now, looking to see why I'm really here and who I'm really loyal to. My conversation with Aaron and Jeremy plays through my skull. *You never know what a desperate person will do.*

I ignore my pounding heart and square up my shoulders as I try to channel every ounce of confidence I don't fully feel. "You better believe I do, Mr. Cummings. My family wins cases. That's what I'm here to do."

He slides back in his seat, a half-smile on his face. "Well, as you know, I can't wish you any luck here. But I wish you and your family nothing but the best, Benson."

Every word in that statement is loaded, from the word *best* to the fact that he's just used my first name. I know what I came here to find out, and it's making my stomach roll. But I can't think too hard about that right now. Right now, I need to see if I can pull any other information from this conversation. I plaster on my sharpest and most simpering smile; the one I used to use at boarding school when housemasters found my illicit CDs or chocolate collection. "I appreciate that, sir. Now, if you have a few minutes, would you mind if I asked you some quick questions about the ski resort? It has to do with the property borders for the land in question." He nods sharply, and I rattle off a series of questions about land boundary lines. Every question I ask can be easily answered inside the Devon Falls town hall, but I'm banking that Bill Cummings is a guy who likes to talk about what he owns. And my bet's right. He's more than happy to answer my questions. He even takes out a map of his property to show me exactly how much of this area of Vermont belongs to him.

"Now here," he says, as he spreads a large map over his desk, "you can see where I own property developments in the next county over. The ski resort was my first investment into this area of Vermont." He's in the middle of telling me about how he first decided to begin investing in ski areas when something on the map draws my attention. There's a road on this map that I haven't seen on any of the other town maps I've looked at. It starts at the north end of the ski area, an area that currently has no buildings, facilities, *or roads*, and travels over one of the hills on the west side of the land.

Looks like Jeremy and Aaron and I make pretty good detectives, because there's only one place that road can lead to: the Devon Falls Leaf Festival Center land.

Agatha Christie would be proud, I guess. But seeing near-proof that the land claim I'm representing is a scheme doesn't give me any sense of pride, that's for sure.

The sick, rolling feeling in my stomach spreads, and I know I need to get the hell out of this place. Bill's words are muffled in my ears as my eyes stay focused on that map. I force myself to breathe steadily and keep my poker face perfectly intact; the worst thing I could possibly do right now is give away that any of the energy in the room has shifted. And when Bill stops talking about his venture capitalism and his plans to own multiple ski resorts along the east coast, I look for the fastest way out of the conversation.

"I'm very grateful to you for meeting with me," I tell him simply as we wrap up the conversation and I stand to leave.

"I'm not sure I was any help," he says. "But I'm happy to answer any questions you have, Benson. Even if we are on opposite sides of this case. Your grandfather's always been good to me. I'll have to reach out to him, let him know we met." There's a warning in his words, and he watches me carefully as he says them.

"I'm sure he'd like that," I answer easily. "And in the meantime, no hard feelings when my firm wins this case."

"Of course not," says Bill.

And the smile on his face just then—well, it takes every ounce of self-restraint I have not to punch it off.

I drive almost recklessly back down the hill, trying to wrap my head around what I've just seen. I circle the ski area property, looking for further evidence, but that road I saw on the map definitely doesn't exist yet. Of course it doesn't. The people in this area know this land backwards and forwards. If a road suddenly appeared behind the ski area it'd be the headline in every paper for fifty miles.

No, that was definitely a map with future plans for the ski area. But who spreads their evil plans out on their desk?

Someone who thinks their old friend's grandson is either completely on their side or an idiot who'll never put two and two together. *Someone who's sure their plan is going to work no matter what,* my brain adds.

I should call Jeremy and Aaron. I should tell them what I've learned. I should make sure they know I'm safe, even if I'm not okay—not really. But I don't do any of those things. Instead, I let autopilot take over, and I wind the car down through roads that are already littered with pops of red and yellow and orange. Fall foliage season is already here.

Whether there will be a festival to celebrate these leaves lining the sides of the road is entirely another story.

Eventually, I end up at the parking area for the Devon Falls Leaf Festival Center. The parking area isn't massive, but it's big enough to support the crowds who arrive in Devon Falls every year to eat too much fair food and walk through leaves. I pull the car through the wide, open field and park it. I step out of the car and stare at the acres of land that stretch in every direction in front of me. Trees flank wide open spaces, each one in a different stage of turning. Some are still green with the colors of summer; others have already made the switch to bright yellow. One looks like a burst of red, a fire atop a grassy field.

I've never been here before. I've spent hours and hours looking at maps of this land. Talking about it. Studying its property lines. But this is the first time I've ever stood in the middle of it and stared around me, listening to the wind whistle and whisper in the tree's leaves.

I take my phone out of my pocket and I make the only phone call I can imagine making right now. He answers on the first ring. "Can you meet me somewhere?" I ask.

"Of course," he says.

"I was wondering when you'd come to see the Leaf Festival Center land."

Jack sits down next to me on the browning grass and hands me a paper cup. I take a sip of the liquid inside: skinny vanilla latte. Of course he already knows my coffee order.

"How did you know I would?" I ask him.

"Because you do your research all the way," he says simply.

It's late in the day now, and the sun's beginning to sink deeper into the sky. It sends out shards of light across the trees in front of us, cutting sharp lasers of brightness over the trails. "Have you come to every single festival?" I ask him.

"I missed a few when I was in med school and residency," he says. "Those were busy years. But every year that I could, I came back."

"Did you and Fiona always come together?" I'm saying all the wrong things right now, and I know it. There's so much more I should be telling him. So much more he needs to hear.

The man I'm representing is probably working for Bill Cummings.

He's going to take this land for Bill Cummings so he can expand his ski resort. There's going to be a new road here. Probably condos. Maybe a golf course. I don't know for sure.

I don't know if your festival will ever exist again. At least not the way it always has.

I should say every single one of those things. But I don't.

"Fiona loves the festival too," he explains. "Yes, we usually came together. If it happens this year, I'm sure she'll be here." He smiles at me wistfully. "But I don't want to make you talk about your case right now," he says softly. He leans back on one arm and moves to capture my mouth with his, and for a long moment I let myself forget everything about the festival and the ski area and Bill Cummings while I focus on the thrill of making out with Dr. Jack Lancer.

We finally pull away from each other, and he runs a hand over my cheek. "Are you okay?" he asks. "Are you getting a migraine?"

My head's been pounding since I left the ski area. I wouldn't be surprised if one were on the horizon. "I'm okay," I say softly.

Tell him. Tell him. TELL HIM.

My conscience chants the words, but then another vision takes place in my brain: my grandfather and father, standing here on these acres of land with me. They're congratulating me on winning this case and telling me they knew they made the right choice to hire me at the firm. My father is patting me on the shoulder the way he does with Linus and Daphne whenever they win a meet or a match.

He's telling me he's proud of me.

I can still win this case. I know I can. Nobody's made the connections I have between Bill Cummings and my grandfather. I doubt anyone else in town has seen Bill's map—or if they have, they haven't realized what it means. Everything I've discovered so far is circumstantial. And I'm not the town's lawyer. I don't work for them. I don't work for Jack.

I'm already crossing into so many gray areas here. I'm not actually a lawyer yet, so I'm not breaking an actual oath, and if I was an actual lawyer already, I'd be bound by the law not to commit fraud in court. But beyond that, I work for Lewis, Stillmer, and Gates, Attorneys at Law. I've wanted to work for them my whole damn life. I can't give up on that dream now.

Can I?

"What's up, Ben?" Jack asks again. His fingers are still on my cheek, and I can feel each individual callous on his fingertips as he strokes my skin softly.

There's that nickname again. I've always hated it before. But when Jack says it, the whole world seems to go a shade lighter. Everything shines in a way it never has before.

But Jack Lancer isn't my family. He'll never be my family. He's nothing more than my fake boyfriend, and I'm not sure why I keep letting myself forget that.

Whatever decisions I make next, I have to make sure I make them for myself. I've always made my decisions that way, and I can't stop now. People in this world let you down. The only person you can trust is yourself. That's a lesson I've learned over and over again.

"Nothing," I finally tell Jack. "Nothing's up. Nothing at all."

Chapter 16
21 Days to the Devon Falls Leaf Festival

Some places are meant for some people. —Jack Lancer

"Jackie!"

Milo's booming voice rings through the clinic as I'm packing up for the day. Malachai slips into my office, his eyes wide with something between panic and awe. "Uh, there are two guys here to see you," he says, his voice high. "And they're kind of giant? And I told them they had to wait, but they said—"

"I told him we'd find our own way." Milo appears in my doorway, beaming, and lands a hand on Malachai's shoulder. "Thanks for the intro, man. What's your name again?"

Malachai gets redder and redder as Sam appears behind Milo, looking dispassionately apathetic about everything around him, just the way he has for too long now. Malachai's gaze keeps moving back and forth between the two of them and landing hard on Sam, but Sam barely even glances at him. "Uh, Malachai?" he says. "Um, I mean, my name is Malachai?"

"Question or answer?" Milo asks, raising one eyebrow at him.

Malachai's eyes widen further. "Uh, answer! I mean answer? I mean, yeah, that's my name! Definitely answer!"

Milo smiles widely and holds out a hand. "Great to meet you, man. I'm Milo. And the surly blond guy behind me is Sam."

Sam gives him a small nod and then goes back to looking completely disinterested in the conversation. I inwardly sigh. Milo said that he thought Sam's new therapist was doing good things with him and that Sam might be making progress. I'm not so sure about that.

It's likely the two of them haven't landed on my doorstep just to say hello, so I guess I'll find out.

"What are you two doing here?" I make the rounds to give each of them a quick side hug and handshake, and Sam very nearly smiles when I get to him. "It's so good to see you both. Did I know you were coming?"

"Nope," Milo says cheerfully. "Your mom did, though. She said you wouldn't mind the surprise. We're here for the weekend. You're done for the day, right? Let's go get some grub. I'm starving, and that drive from I-89 is a bitch. We got stuck behind three tractors. You want to join us, kid? I mean, Malachai?"

Malachai's eyes are still traveling back and forth between the two behemoths who've taken over my tiny office, and I can't say I blame him. Milo and Sam know how to take over a room without meaning to. All three of us are large guys, edging toward six and a half feet. Milo's an athlete and an orthopedic surgeon, and he spends a lot of time at the gym. Muscles ripple through his arms and chest, highlighting his dark brown skin, and high cheekbones accentuate his light brown eyes. Sam is tall and used to be almost as muscular as Milo, but he stopped working out as much after he lost Chris. He must still be running, though, because his pale skin is slightly tanned and his blond hair is streaked with lighter shades. When the two of them show up together somewhere, they look like the cast of *General Hospital* just stepped into the room. I once saw a patient lose the ability to speak when Milo arrived in her room to do a consult.

"Oh! I'd love to." Malachai beams, but his face quickly falls. "But I can't. I have somewhere I have to be."

"Got class?" I ask. I'm not sure how Malachai keeps up with his busy schedule. Mom and Henri and I are constantly telling him we can adjust his hours if he needs more time to study, but he never takes us up on our offer.

"Um, kind of. Not exactly." Malachai glances at his watch and winces. "I have to run. See you tomorrow, Dr. Lancer!" He turns to leave the room and runs smack into Sam. "Oof!"

Sam looks surprised to find one hundred and fifty pounds of twenty-something hit his chest and then the floor. He helps Malachai up with a firm hand. "Careful, there," he says, in the same low, soft voice that I know has left more than one patient in his Emergency Department in New York begging for a follow-up.

Malachai says nothing. He just stares at Sam, still wide-eyed. Then he nods and flees the room.

I sigh. "He's still settling in. Anyway, what the hell are you two really doing here? I can't believe you didn't tell me you were coming!"

Milo drops into my mom's chair and throws his legs up on her desk. She won't care. She loves Milo; sometimes she loves him more than me. "Well, man, we heard you were dating again. Had to see this live and in-person."

"You and Mom have been texting." I sigh.

"She tells us the stuff you won't," Sam says calmly from where he's leaning against half my wall.

"There's a reason for that," I say wryly. "I suppose you all know that it's not real, right? It's just to keep Elijah's grandparents happy. Not that they're actually happy."

"Those asshole former in-laws of yours wouldn't know happy if it bit them on the ass," Milo says. "And your mom says you and your fake boyfriend are looking awfully tight these days. So, we had to come see for ourselves. Make sure you're not in over your head."

I frown as I think about how I rushed to the Leaf Festival Center to see Benson the second he called yesterday. It's absolutely true that I'm becoming more and more attached to having him in my life, and every day that attachment feels bigger and scarier. The upcoming trial for the land is looming over my head like a noose ready to capture my neck at any moment. I sigh. "Oh, I'm pretty sure I'm in over my head. It's probably a good thing you're here." Milo beams, and Sam nods almost imperceptibly.

The people of Devon Falls will forever know me as the child who ran through the streets here and colored the sidewalks with chalk, but Milo and Sam know me as an adult. We all came up through residency in New York City together and then stayed friends as our careers took off. The three of us have been through the hell of difficult rotations and eighty-hour shifts together. They were there for every single thing that went down with Fiona—they got me through it. I like to think Milo and I helped Sam get through losing Christian, but lately it seems more like we just kept him from drowning in his own grief.

I think he spends most days now treading water.

"Definitely a good thing we're here, then." Milo stands and slaps me hard on the back. "Call your fake BF. We've got limited time to meet him and tell you all the things you're doing wrong. Time to get this party started."

I roll my eyes as I pull my phone out of my pocket. "I'd tell you both not to scare him," I say as I start typing out a message to Benson. I've got no doubt he's busy, but hopefully he can take an hour or so to meet us at the café. "But I don't think you could if you tried."

Milo grins. "We'll see about that."

"You seriously call these guys scary?" Benson pulls himself up onto a stool next to me at Luis' bar and grins as he signals Ellis Ryker for another beer. "Please. I've been more afraid in mock trials. In undergrad. Of guys wearing pocket protectors and argyle."

"They're going easy on you," I tell him, but that's a lie. The truth is that Milo and Sam gave Benson the same assessing stare and twenty questions routine they've given almost everyone I've dated in the aftermath of Fiona. Everyone else either fell in love with one of them mid-conversation or nearly ran screaming for the hills. Benson just calmly gave them answers like he was sitting at a deposition table and then asked Milo if there was an actual reason he was flexing his triceps in the middle of a conversation. Sam laughed *out loud.* I was so surprised I almost spit my beer out.

Benson sends me a half-grin, just to let me know that he's fully aware I'm lying, and my heart speeds up in my chest slightly. It's embarrassing and concerning how much I want to lay him across the bar right here and now and do *very* not-for-public-spaces things to him.

Or take him back to the office and do them there. It's also embarrassing how hard I can get just thinking about that day I laid him across my exam table.

"Jack." Milo appears next to me with a plate of Luis' famous empanadas. "You gotta convince Luis to move to New York. He's wasted on this town.

"I like it here," Luis calls from down the bar. "But thanks for the compliment, man. Just for that you're getting an extra empanada in your next order."

"One for me too, please," Sam calls as he snags an empanada off of Milo's plate. I feel a rush of relief as I watch him start to eat.

There were so many days right after Christian passed when Milo and I would take turns begging Sam to take a bite of something. Anything. Days when I was half-convinced he was trying to starve himself to death out of sadness.

"So, Benson," says Milo casually. "Sam and I have begrudgingly decided we're going along with whatever you two have going on here. Mostly because Jack keeps staring at you like you're made out of some really good cheese." He gestures a hand at the two of us.

"A nice camembert," Sam adds around a mouthful of empanadas.

"But I do have one question that remains unanswered," says Milo. "Why the hell aren't we all singing you happy birthday?"

I whirl around to face Benson. "It's your birthday?" I blurt out. "Why the hell didn't you tell me?"

"Because I didn't want anyone to know." Benson glowers at Milo. "How did you know that, anyway? It's not like Luis checked my ID tonight."

"We have our ways," Sam puts in, surprising me. He holds his beer up for a toast. "Happy birthday."

"Whose birthday is it?" Luis appears around the corner of the bar carrying another plate of empanadas. "And why didn't anyone say anything? You know I've got cake ready to go in the back at all times!" He sets the plate down, and Sam and Milo immediately dive in like hyenas who've just found a recent kill. "So, who are we singing to?"

"No one," Benson says sternly. "There's no singing or cake about to happen here. I don't fucking do birthdays."

Luis knows Benson well enough at this point that he doesn't even blink at this statement, and to their credit, Milo and Sam don't either. "Why not?" I ask.

"Because I have to warn you," Luis adds. "We're very pro-birthday here in Devon Falls. Just ask the tree in the park that Amelia throws a celebration for every year."

"I came for the last one," Milo adds. "Very good ice cream sundaes, Luis." He salutes Luis with his beer.

"Thanks." Luis beams. "The key is making your own caramel. Oh, and I've been sourcing my ice cream from this local dairy that's developed a fantastic new production technique."

They start talking about churning processes, something Milo seems to know a surprising amount about, while I turn my attention to Benson. He's frowning down at his phone on the other side of me and slowly nursing his beer.

I know the face he's giving that phone. It's one I gave my own phone all too often after me and Fiona split. He's waiting for it to light up with a text or a call. With some kind of communication from someone.

And the screen is staying dark.

I gently ease the beer out of his hand and set it on the counter. "We'll be right back," I murmur to Sam, who seems to be only peripherally listening to the conversation about milkfat percentages that's currently taking place next to him. He gives me a slight nod.

"C'mon," I tell Benson. "We're going for a quick walk."

Benson sends me a skeptical look, but he doesn't argue or push back. He does give his phone one more look of something like longing before he slides it into his pants pocket. Then he pushes himself off the tall bar chair he's sitting on and follows me out the door.

On instinct, I lead him through the town and toward the bridge: the one above the falls where we first stood together and discussed our plan to fool the Maggios. I take Benson's hand loosely in mine, letting his fingers fall in between my own, as we set off down the sidewalk under a low fog that's clouding the chilly New England evening.

"Did you hear from your family today?" I ask gently. We're still thousands of feet away from the bridge, but Benson seems to know exactly where we're going, and he follows along where I'm leading him without missing a step.

"My stepmother. Sarah," he says. "She texted me. And sent a card, too. She always does. I'm not sure how she got the address for where I'm staying. She's pretty resourceful, though. Oh, and the twins texted me."

"The twins?" I ask. Benson's mentioned them before, but he never talks all that much about his family.

"My younger half-sister and brother. Linus and Daphne."

"Linus." The name settles itself in my brain. "That's your father's name, too. Isn't it?"

"Yes," Benson says steadily. "And my grandfather's name. And great-grandfather's, actually. Linus is the fourth in the line."

I don't ask the obvious question about why Benson, the oldest, isn't the one carrying that title. It's obvious enough that the answer would have to do with illegitimacy and bastard children, and I'm sure Benson's heard those phrases more than enough times in his life. But I have a better sense of who he was waiting to hear from in the bar just now. "Have you heard from your father? Or grandfather?"

We've reached the bridge now. There are no cars in sight, but I lead him down on the pedestrian platform anyway. The street-lights are projecting back on the water, giving them an ethereal quality in the falling darkness. Benson leans against the railing separating us from the water and stares blankly out into the loud rush of the falls. "Nope," he says, lightly popping the P on the end of the word. "Sarah signed the card from my dad. Some years he texts. Some years he doesn't. Grandpa thinks birthdays are a waste of time. Unless it's Linus and Daphne's birthday." He takes a long gulp of air that looks almost painful, and I wrap an arm gently around his waist. This being Benson, I expect him to tense up the way he sometimes does when I first touch him. It's like he has to keep giving himself permission to let me be close to him, over and over again. But this time he lets himself fall against my shoulder, his body molding itself to mine, as we look out at the falls together.

"One time," he says, "When the twins turned eleven, Grandpa rented an entire castle for a pool party he wanted to throw them. A whole fucking castle. It had turrets and everything."

I'm afraid to ask him what his eleventh birthday looked like. I don't have to, as it turns out. He keeps talking, surprising me and maybe also himself.

"I was at boarding school for my eleventh birthday. Sarah was in the hospital because she was pregnant and there were complications with the twins. Without her there to remind everyone, no one even bothered to email me. I fucking hate birthdays, Jack. Birthdays are bullshit."

I turn him gently in my arms until he's facing me. There's wetness at the corner of one of his eyes, and I wipe it away with one thumb. "That sounds like absolute bullshit," I agree. "And now that I know when your birthday is, I hope more than ever that I'll get to spend another one with you. I can really do it right next time. Luis' cake. Balloons. I can't promise a castle, but you'd be amazed what this town can do to the gazebo in the park with the right decorating budget. We'll make that tree's birthday look like a blip on a celebration radar."

Benson lets himself crack a smile, but it quickly slides from his face. "I'm not going to be here for another birthday, Jack," he says hoarsely.

"Yeah? Are you sure about that?" I tilt his face up and say the words that have been swimming in my head for days now. Maybe even weeks. "I know you've got plans, Benson Lewis. But plans change all the time. I've got a lot of recent experience proving that. And right now, right here, I wouldn't take back a single one of those changes."

I capture his mouth against mine, letting our tongues drift in and out of something that feels more and more like a dance every time we do it. Our hands begin to move slowly and carefully around each other's bodies, and I let mine wander down to his belt. We're both hard. I glance quickly around us, but the pedestrian platform is just as unoccupied as I'd expect it to be this late at night in Devon Falls. This entire place, this moment in time, belongs solely to the two of us. And I intend to make the most of it.

I take care of his belt first, and then slide my hand low into his boxers. He gasps into my mouth as I carefully grip the head of his cock and begin tugging, back and forth in the rhythm that I've learned he loves the best. I know exactly when to move my hand and flick at his tip, exactly when to take my mouth south and nibble at the skin on his neck. I know how to slide my other hand up his back exactly the way he likes. I know when he's getting closer and closer, and I tease him through the sparks of pleasure, nudging him back and forth toward and away from the edge while the falls crash in an even, steady beat behind us.

"Jack," he whimpers against my neck. "Jack. Jack, I can't—I'm going to—"

"I want you to," I whisper back. "Now." I move my hand back up to his tip again, pushing against it with the finger in the move that I know he loves. He lunges in my arms, letting go as I keep him locked safely between the space in my arms and legs, and I hold him close while every shake and shudder in his body sets a sort of mini-fire off in my own nervous system.

There's so much power in knowing I can make him feel like this. So much clarity.

Eventually his body comes to a rest, and he lays his head across my shoulder. "You didn't—" he starts to say.

"That was for you," I interrupt him. "Just for you. Happy birthday, Benson Lewis. I hope this is just the start of many better birthday memories."

He looks up at me. "What if my plans can't change, Jack? Even if I want them to? None of this is real. We're not real. Sometimes I even wonder if this whole fucking place is even real. So how can I change anything?"

It's a loaded question, and one I'm not sure I'm ready to answer. But I do my best.

I take a deep breath. What I'm about to say could scare him away; I know that. I think Benson will always spook easily. But it feels like the right time to take this risk.

"I think that some places are meant for some people. Some places find some people," I tell him. "And the moment you want this place and these people *and me* to be more than we are to you right now, all you have to do is say the word."

He takes another gulp of air, and then he nods. Slowly. Carefully.

But he doesn't say a single word on our walk back through the town.

Chapter 17
18 Days to the Devon Falls Leaf Festival

Villainy, as it turns out, isn't all it's cracked up to be. —Benson Lewis

All you have to do is say the word.

I've never been on the receiving side of a massive romantic gesture before. Hell, I've never been on the giving side of one either. So when Jack stood on a bridge with me and gave me the best birthday handjob I could ever imagine getting in my life just before he told me we can partner like swans in love if I want, I didn't exactly know what to say. Three days later, I still don't know what to say.

So I've done what I do best in these situations: I haven't said anything.

Jack doesn't seem upset about that. As usual, he seems to have infinite patience with me. Nothing's really changed between us. We had breakfast with his doctor friends the next day, and I managed to get through it with only one snarky comment about how Milo kept flirting with the entire waitstaff. We watched Elijah play at the school concert last night, and I got more hellos than glares from the rest of the audience.

Weeks ago I wouldn't have given two shits about those glares. But now that I've found what I did at the ski area, I feel differently about them.

I feel differently about every damn look Jack gives me.

You can't do this to him. To them. A little voice in my head, one that sounds suspiciously like Aaron Morin, keeps chanting the words on repeat. I've been placating Carter with daily research updates, but he's made it clear he plans to show up in Devon Falls at any moment now that we're only about a week away from presenting our claims in court. I've come up with plenty of arguments to support our case, but Ellie still has that death certificate on her side.

Tell her, Aaron's voice whispers in my head again. *Tell Ellie what you found. You owe her that. You owe the town. You won't be betraying anything. You can just casually mention this map you think you saw... and then Bill Cummings won't end up taking a whole lot of land that doesn't belong to him from a town that has done nothing but welcome him with open arms.*

"You got ants in your pants, honey? I keep telling you to just stop wearing 'em. It'll settle your energy," Ellie tells me cheerfully from where she's working across the archive room.

"I don't have ants in my pants," I mutter at my computer screen. "I'm just busy, that's all."

Ellie laughs. "Ah, yes. The busy Big Law life. What grunt work are they giving you now? How many hours are you planning to work after you head back and Big Law chains you to your desk again? I do not miss those days, I can tell you that much."

"You worked in Big Law?" I ask, and I don't even try to keep the skepticism out of my voice. I can't for the life of me imagine Ellie taking depositions for someone like my grandfather or sitting in boardrooms wearing full pant suits and heels. Most days it's a struggle just to get her to remember to keep her dress on.

"Honey, I *was* Big Law," Ellie says cheerfully. "For five years after I graduated I was climbing my way through that system. What is it the kids say? Kicking ass and taking names? I was doing all of that, and I was doing it well." She names off a massive law firm in New York that half of my classmates from Burlington U would have died to work for, while I sit there staring at her, completely in shock.

"You worked for them? What the hell happened?" I ask. I can't for the life of me connect the dots from how someone could go from one of the biggest law firms in New York City to owning a law office the size of a postage stamp in Devon Falls, Vermont. Absolutely none of this is computing for me.

"Nothing happened, exactly," Ellie says serenely as she tugs gently at the shoulder of the sweater she appears to be wearing under extreme duress. "Except that those assholes pulled one fast one too many, and I got tired of being the one to pull those fast ones with them. We staged a hostile attack on a mom-and-pop business started from scratch by a couple who'd been making ice cream their whole lives. They loved what they did more than anything. My clients got ahold of them and made sure they had nothing left of their business by the time we were done." She sighs. "I stared across a conference room table at those ice cream makers and I knew if I stayed in that world one second longer it was going to suck out my soul. You see, Benson, there are really only two irreplaceable commodities in life."

I'm glued to my seat, still trying to imagine Ellie arranging hostile takeovers and destroying ice cream makers with a flick of her pen. I don't interrupt her.

"Money and time," she goes on. "Those are the only two things you can't just up and create more of. Everything comes down to money and time. Almost every choice you ever make is a choice between one of those priorities. I looked at that ice cream maker and I saw that I had all my priorities out of order. I didn't want to spend my days crushing companies and making bank. I didn't want my lonely apartment on the fifty-seventh floor of my beautiful building in Manhattan. Those things fill up the souls of plenty of people. I'm just not one of them." She shrugs. "I took a weekend off and drove up to Vermont. Landed here by accident and met Amelia. I think you can figure out the rest." She winks at me as she stands up to stretch.

"I... you... what?" I'm stunned I'm just learning this now. I've been sitting in this tiny room with Ellie for basically weeks on end, and I never once thought to ask her about her work background or how she ended up in Devon Falls. It never mattered to me.

She was just the opposing counsel. Just the enemy in my story. And I was the villain of Devon Falls, here to win a case and bring money and prestige back to my family's firm.

No matter what.

Villainy, as it turns out, isn't all it's cracked up to be.

I stand up so fast I almost knock my chair over backward. "I have to go," I blurt out as I start gathering up papers and packing up my computer.

"Okay, honey," Ellie says cheerfully. "Do me a favor and pick me up some of that spaghetti Luis has on special today if you go by the café."

"I'm not going in that direction," I tell her as I pick up my backpack. I stop by the table where she's working and impulsively lean over to give her the closest thing I can manage to a hug.

"What the hell happened to you?" she asks as I stand up. "Have you been taken over by pod people or something?"

"It's starting to feel like that," I call over my shoulder as I head through the door, determined to get to my car as quickly as I can. Like Ellie says, time is a commodity.

And with traffic, it's going to take at least five hours to get to my dad's office in Boston.

I'm sitting in the waiting area near Mark, my dad's long-time secretary, when I hear them.

The steps.

Each one sounds like a swift smack against the flooring. No matter what footwear my grandfather wears, his walk sounds exactly the same. It doesn't matter what flooring is under him. Whether he's wearing wingtips on hardwood floors or socks on carpet, the sound of his walk always has the same rhythm. It's a sort of booming sound that seems to echo continuously in my ears whenever I hear it.

When I was a child, I used to dread hearing that sound. It usually meant my grandfather was coming in my direction, and his attention was rarely, if ever, a good thing. If he was headed toward my room in the giant mansion I lived in with him, I had most likely screwed up. Maybe I'd angered the nanny or done poorly on a test. Quite possibly I'd embarrassed the family by daring to exist in public without a mother who was married to my father.

My entire body stiffens, and I notice Mark wince when he hears the noise. He's worked for my family for a long time. I have no doubt he's been on the receiving end of Grandpa's wrath a time or two himself.

I brace myself for what's coming, but I can't stop my stomach from turning over when Grandpa appears in the doorway of Dad's office suite. Linus Lewis Jr. stands like a force to be reckoned with. He's well over six feet tall and broad shouldered, with dark silver hair and green eyes that seem to be able to stab right through you when he wants them to. And right now, they're laser-focused on me.

"Benson," he barks. "What the hell on earth are you doing here? You've got a job to do up in Vermont! Get the hell back there and do it!"

Mark looks like he's trying desperately not to shake in his seat. I know the feeling. I stand slowly, determined to keep my wits about me. I practiced for this. The entire drive down to Boston, I imagined what I'd say to my father when I saw him. I imagined what I'd say if the worst-case scenario happened and I ended up talking to my grandfather instead.

Worst-case scenario, here we are.

"Hello, Grandpa," I tell him as evenly as I can. I don't hear any shaking in my voice. Good start. "I needed to talk to Dad about the case I'm working on. I'm just waiting for him to get back from court. I won't be here long. I'll be back in Vermont tonight."

Grandpa glowers at me. "You're a week out from losing a case that I told you was important to this firm, and you're taking drives from Vermont to Boston without even checking in with Carter?" His face is practically red, he's so angry. Mark looks like he's trying to bury himself in his office chair. "Clearly your priorities are more than a little off."

Actually, Grandpa, I think. *I might finally have my priorities right for the first time in my life.* And then I make a decision.

I came here to tell my dad everything and ask him for help. He's never really been there for me in any way before, but what the hell, I figured. Maybe it was about time I started telling him when I needed something. I was going to march into his office, explain everything I knew, and beg him to help me figure out what to do. He's worked for this firm since he was in law school, and he doesn't seem to have lost his soul. At least not completely. People like Sarah don't marry guys with no souls.

So, I figured he was the best person to ask for help. But here I am, and once again, he's not here when I need him. And my grandfather, the man at the center of all my problems right now, is.

"Grandpa," I say, and I use the same voice I used the day I had to stand up in Devon Falls and tell the town I was trying to destroy their entire world. "Like I told you, I'm here about the case. But if Dad's not here, I'm happy to talk with you instead. I've just got some simple questions that I'm sure won't take long to answer."

His eyes narrow, but I can tell I've captured his curiosity. He's trying to figure out why I'm here and what questions I could possibly have. Linus Lewis isn't used to being the person in a room who's missing information. "Fine," he finally growls. "But you've got ten minutes. Time is money. You know that."

I do know. It's something I've been hearing my entire life. And something Ellie just reminded me of—but not in the same way Grandpa has.

Grandpa moves swiftly into Dad's office without even asking Mark's permission because Grandpa never asks anyone for permission to do anything—especially in his own law firm. I draw in another deep breath and follow him, forcing myself to let it out slowly as I close the door behind us.

Dad's office is an enormous space filled with high windows that look out over the tall, looming city of Boston. When I was a kid, I was enraptured with this office. My nanny would sometimes bring me here for lunch dates or short visits, and I'd stand at the windows, staring out at the city below me, certain that my father ran the entire world. That, I told myself, was why he never had time to spend with me. He was just too busy taking care of everyone else.

I'm looking out at skyscrapers, my mind trapped in the memories of those days, when Grandpa's voice snaps me back to reality. "Well? What the hell do you need, Benson? You know my time is precious. I've got better places to be right now."

You always do. I pull in another breath, steel myself to ask the question I haven't been able to ask for weeks, and I turn to face him. "What does Bill Cummings have to do with this land claim?"

I watch as Grandpa's face turns three separate shades of red before landing on a color that's really a purplish-red. Maybe mauve? Nobody ever gave me the set of fifty-two Crayolas, so I can't be sure. "What's this about?" he barks.

He's answering questions with questions; that means I've got him cornered. I cross my arms over my body, hoping that makes me look and feel more powerful than I actually feel right now. "This is about Bill Cummings' ownership of a ski area that could potentially benefit from annexing that land. And the fact that Arnie Blake may be attempting to take the land that belongs to Devon Falls on Cummings' behalf."

Grandpa's eyes narrow further and further as I speak. He's studying me carefully now, like he's not sure exactly who he's looking at. It's a feeling I know all too well.

It's a feeling that seems to spark through me every damn time I look at the mirror lately.

"Who I know, or where Bill Cummings owns land," Grandpa finally says. "Is irrelevant to this case, Benson. All that's relevant is winning our client back his family's land."

I do my best to keep every cell in my body from shaking as I answer him. "And what if the land doesn't rightfully belong to Arnie?" I ask.

Grandpa stares at me. "If our client says the land is his," he says carefully, "our only job is to prove his claim. Do you understand that, Benson?" His voice is stiff and darker than I've ever heard it, and I understand all too well.

This case has always been about Bill Cummings, right from the start. The Good Old Boys network started up the minute Bill decided he wanted that land. I still doubt very much that my grandfather knows the intricacies of what he and Arnie have been up to with paperwork—Grandpa would never dirty his hands that way—but I have no doubt he knows exactly who's paying for the many, many billable hours Arnie's racked up in the past few weeks. There's little doubt in my mind that when Bill Cummings left this firm there were handshakes around how and why. I wouldn't be surprised if whoever is representing him now is somehow connected to my family's firm.

I also understand that this is the moment where I have to make a choice. I can nod and smile and drive back to Devon Falls like the perfect Lewis family soldier Grandpa's always demanded I be, not that I've ever met that bar before. Or I can rebel. I can tell him that taking a festival from a town that's made it such a key part of its identity for over a hundred years is wrong. There's nothing moral or ethical about it.

And I understand that if I say that, there's a good chance my relationship with my grandfather, and my entire family, will be over forever. Whatever tatters our relationship was already in will go threadbare and fall to pieces in seconds if I tell him just how corrupt and wrong this situation really is.

I open my mouth. And no words come out.

"Sit, Benson," Grandpa barks, motioning toward two large leather chairs in the corner of the room. I feel like I'm stuck in some sort of field of quicksand I can't seem to edge my way out of, so I let myself stumble over to the chair and flop into it. Grandpa settles into the chair across from me with a lot more grace.

"I know you didn't go to a real law school, one that emphasizes rigor," he says, and there's no edge in his voice. In his mind, he's not insulting me or my school. He's just stating a fact. "So you don't understand how the real world works. That's my fault, clearly. I should never have let your father talk me into hiring you."

My heart lurches slightly. Dad is the reason I got this job. I'm still grasping at that piece of information, trying to make sense of it, when I realize Grandpa's still talking.

"But we are where we are," he barks. "So, I'm going to give you a lesson you should've gotten a long time ago." He leans forward in his chair and points a finger directly at me. "Keep your hands clean and don't ask questions that don't help you win a case. Those are two basic rules you've got to learn to follow if you're going to be successful in this business."

"Is that what you did?" I ask, my voice hoarse. "You didn't ask questions when Arnie Blake came here needing representation for a land claim and Bill Cummings nudged you to take him on?"

"Damn straight that's what I did," Grandpa says coldly. "I made sure the terms I arranged with both Blake and Cummings were advantageous to the firm, and I told them both we'd win. Because that's what we do in this firm, Benson. We win cases." He sits back, tenting his fingers, and eyes me. "It takes a certain something to be a winner. You've struggled with that in the past. I knew when I let your father talk me into giving you this case that I was taking a hell of a chance. But even I had to admit you've come a long way from the kid who couldn't even bring home a decent report card. I thought maybe some of the Lewis family genes were finally overriding whatever trash your father stupidly picked up in some bar one night. So, tell me, Benson: do you have what it takes to do your job here? Or do I need to send someone else up to Devon Falls?"

The implications of the phrase "someone else" are clear. If I can't do what Grandpa wants me to do here, I won't be invited to stay on at the family firm. This will be the end of my quest to prove to my family that I'm just as good as the rest of them. I'll be banished back to being nothing more than the family embarrassment.

My gut curls in my body at the thought. But if I do what I need to do to please Grandpa here, I'll never be able to look Jack and the rest of Devon Falls in the eye ever again. It's one thing to prove that the land the festival is on legally belongs to someone else. It's another to let some con artist take it in what's most likely a money grab that will only benefit him and his ski area.

I find I can't answer Grandpa. I just sit there, thinking of Jack. Elijah. Ellie. Amelia. All the people of Devon Falls. All the acceptance they've shown me, despite who I am and what I've done in their town.

Marion Stevenson even started giving me free cookies on Thursdays. And it has to be said: they're some of the best cookies I've ever eaten.

"Well?" Grandpa barks the word. "Can you do it, Benson?"

Something catches my eye: a picture on Dad's desk. It must have been taken when the twins were about four and I was fifteen or so. In the picture, Dad's hugging me around my waist and smiling. He and I are both wearing bathing suits. Sarah is next to him, leaning into the picture frame and squeezing my shoulder, and the twins are in front of the three of us, both of them making silly faces at the camera.

I remember that day so well. I was home from boarding school on a break, and Sarah decided we should all go stay at our family's cottage on Martha's Vineyard for a day or two. It was the first family trip I'd actually been invited on in years, and I was thrilled, even though I never told anyone that. The picture was taken on a day when Dad and I went bodysurfing and then dried out on lounge chairs while the twins built sandcastles around us and Sarah made us all laugh with ridiculous jokes and silly music she played over a wireless speaker. When she asked someone to take a picture of the five of us, I was the happiest I'd ever been. Finally, I thought, my picture was going to be on a wall in my Dad's house. Finally, other people would see me as part of the family.

But I never saw the picture again. I always wondered what happened to it.

"Benson?" Grandpa says again, his voice urgent and annoyed. "I need an answer here!"

Just then there's a quick knock at the door and Mark peeks his head in. "I'm so sorry to interrupt," he says. "So very sorry. But sir, your assistant needs you back in your office right away. She says it's an emergency."

Grandpa nods and stands. His eyes are trained on me in a glare. "Remember what I said, Benson," he says testily. Then he moves quickly out of the room, his shoes landing with that same noise that's echoed in my ears for so many years.

Mark and I both breathe a quiet sigh of relief the moment he's out of sight. Mark sends me a sympathetic half-smile. "Can I get you anything, Benson? Water? Coffee?"

I shake my head as I stand up. "No thanks," I say shortly. The only thing I need isn't here in Massachusetts. It's in Devon Falls, Vermont, and that means I need to get back there as quickly as possible.

I need to see Jack again. I need to see his face.

And then I'm sure I'll know what to do.

Chapter 18
18 Days to the Devon Falls Leaf Festival

It's the please, Jack *that undoes me. —Jack Lancer*

"Uncle Jack? You're being weird again."

Elijah says the words cheerfully and without malice, and I can't help but smile at him. "How am I being weird this time?" I ask him. He's been saying this a lot lately.

"You're humming again." He sends me a grin. We're walking down Main Street together, toward the café, where we're planning to meet Benson for dinner. "You never used to hum before. Did you know that?"

"Never? Really?" I ask. Elijah's an observant kid, and he seems to pay much more attention to my habits and idiosyncrasies than I do. If he says my humming is a recent phenomenon, I'll believe him.

"Nope," he tells me. He lifts an eyebrow. "Do you think you and Benson will get married someday?" he asks. "You've only been humming since you met him. If someone makes you hum, you've gotta marry them. Don't you?"

His question startles me more than I'd like to admit. Mostly because I did recently give Benson something somewhat equivalent to a marriage proposal, and he's never responded to it. I'm determined not to bring it up again until the land case is over and behind us in a few days. Then maybe Benson and I can finally have some space to figure out who and what we are to each other, separate from this town and Benson's conflicts with it.

The results of the case won't affect that, at least not for me. If this land legally belongs to Arnie Blake, I can accept that. And I like to think the town will come along with me on that point. In fact, I'm sure they will. Despite Benson's involvement in this land claim case, it's clear he's grown on the town in all the ways that matter. Marion Stevenson even gave him a free cookie the other day. And from what I could tell, the sugar and salt proportions in it were completely correct.

"Do you want me and Benson to get married?" I ask, determined to keep a conversational tone of voice.

"Sure, why not?" Elijah says. "Benson's great. And Aunt Fiona's probably going to get married again, so why not you?"

I somehow manage not to freeze where I am in the middle of the sidewalk. "What?" I ask him, and my voice comes out like a squeak. "Did you say your aunt's getting married again?"

"I think she's going to marry that guy she's been dating," Elijah says easily, obviously unaware that I'm about to go into shock next to him. "You know, the one she met in Rome? He sounds so cool. Aunt Fiona says he plays the drums! We're going to jam when they come back here to visit next month. How cool would it be if he and Benson and I all jammed together? You and Aunt Fiona could be our audience!"

And now I'm about to take back everything I've ever said about Elijah being observant, because I'm about ten seconds from having a heart attack and he hasn't even noticed. Fiona mentioned in a short text exchange recently that she was seeing someone, but I didn't realize it was serious.

Will they get married? Will their marriage stick? Will they have the children Fiona and I never had? Will they be the perfect couple we were supposed to be?

Those questions are whirling through my head, tornadoing past each other in a blur of confusion, and Elijah's still a flutter of conversation next to me, when my phone buzzes in my pocket. I pull it out, half-dazed and wince when I see who's texting me.

Conrad Maggio: Elijah's got a D in history? What are you doing about this, Jack? He's not answering my texts.

I stop in the middle of the street and make sure I take three even breaths. Elijah stops just ahead of me. "Uncle Jack? What's up?"

"What's your grade in history?" I ask, as calmly as possible.

Elijah winces. "Um, it's not great. But don't stress!" he quickly adds. "I've got it covered. I have enough points to get a C. I just need to—"

"A C? You're aiming for a C?" I demand as my phone buzzes again.

Conrad Maggio: We've been in touch with Eric. This needs to be addressed, Jack. He's spending too much time with his guitar.

"A C is all I need to stay in band!" Elijah throws up his hands, gesturing broadly. "And I'm doing way better in math now thanks to Benson. Seriously, Uncle Jack, you don't need to worry. I've got all this covered." He crosses his arms over his chest and grins like a Labrador retriever returning a stick.

I need to talk to Eric. Right away. I know Eric's always been looser than Conrad and Barbara would like where Elijah's school-work is concerned, but would he really condone Elijah shooting for a C? And what the hell would Fiona think of what I'm letting happen here? She's a former fourth-grade teacher, for crying out loud.

She doesn't even know, a voice in my head whispers. *Because she's in Italy, teaching English, with someone who would never let her nephew fail out of high school.*

That voice is snickering with laughter that echoes in my skull when Ellie appears in front of me and Elijah. "Yoo hoo!" she calls out as she walks toward us. "Are you looking for our dear boy Benson?"

"We're meeting him at the café," Elijah tells her.

"'Fraid not, hon," Ellie says. "I just saw Benson at the town hall. Jack, he said if I saw you to tell you he'd meet you at your office."

"Why didn't he just text me?" I ask.

"Something about his phone being dead? I'm not sure." Ellie wrinkles her nose. "Fool boy disappears all day and comes back looking like he's been hit by a truck. If that terrible family of his is torturing him again, I swear I'll—"

"Can you eat with Elijah?" I interrupt her quickly before she gets on a roll. This sounds like potential migraine territory, and there's no way I'm going to let Benson sit in horrible pain at my office waiting for me while Ellie goes on one of her rants, even if this rant is more than deserved. I'll just have to figure out this issue with Elijah's history grade later.

"Of course!" Ellie wraps an arm around Elijah's shoulder.

"Is Benson okay?" Elijah asks uncertainly.

"No worries, my little troubadour," Ellie soothes. "Your Uncle Jack will take good care of him. It's what he does."

Damn straight, I think to myself as I send Elijah the most reassuring smile I have and rush off down the street toward Lancer Family Medicine.

The office has only been closed for an hour or so. When I arrive at the steps of the wide porch that wraps around it, I at least get the sense that Benson hasn't been waiting for me long. He's still got his messenger bag over his shoulder, and he's sitting on the top step with his head in his hands, massaging desperately at his temples. His clothes are uncharacteristically wrinkled. I can tell right away that this day hasn't been kind to him.

"What's wrong?" I drop to my knees on the step in front of him, lifting his head to examine him closely. His skin is hot to the touch and his forehead is glossy with sweat. "Your head's hurting, isn't it?"

Benson doesn't answer me right away. Instead, he reaches out a hand to stroke my cheek gently. "I'm okay," he says in a choked voice. "Just needed to see you. Right away."

"I've been here all day," I answer gently. "Why didn't you come by?"

Benson's still staring at me like he's cataloging every single one of my features. Knowing the way his brain works, I suppose it's entirely possible that he is. "I wasn't here," he finally answers me softly. "I was in Boston."

I just saw him this morning. My eyes go wide. "You drove to Boston and back today?" I ask.

Benson nods slowly and steadily. Then he winces.

The wince does it for me. I'm getting him off this step. I lift him up into my arms, bridal-style, before he can protest, and head toward the door of the office. He mumbles something about being able to walk, but he quickly gives up and lets his head slump against my shoulder.

That's the moment when I know that whatever happened today was bad. Very, very bad.

Miraculously, I manage to maneuver the two of us through doorways and down hallways and into the exam room where Benson and I first made love. I wonder if he considered that to be making love. I know I did. I set him down on the couch in the room and stop to run a hand briefly through his hair. He leans into my touch. "Not a migraine, I don't think," he tells me slowly. "Just a bad stress headache. And I really, really needed to see you."

I want to ask so many things. I want to ask what happened today. I want to ask him what his family's done to set off the stress headache he's fighting now.

But I know better than to push Benson before he's ready. So, all I do is lean over to help take his heavy bag off his shoulder. I let it fall to the floor next to us as Benson takes hold of my arm.

"Need you," he whispers. "Inside me. Just like last time we were here."

"Babe, you're in pain," I remind him.

"You'll make it better," he tells me. His eyes are trained on me, and he's staring at me with that same intensity he was earlier. "Want you," he adds. "Right now. There." He gestures at the exam table. "Please, Jack," he whispers.

It's the *please, Jack* that undoes me. I lift him carefully again and carry him over to the exam table, where I set him down on the paper liner that someone—probably Malachai—has already laid across it. I should probably have second thoughts about defiling this room in my family's practice with Benson yet again, but right now my brain is trained entirely on him. I ease his polo shirt off over his head, stopping to tease his nipples and nip at his shoulders. He hisses faintly into my ear. "Yes," he adds in a whisper. "Keep going, Jack. Make me forget."

I hope someday I learn what I'm helping him let go of. I ease him off the exam table far enough to help him off with his boxers and pants, and soon he's completely naked except for his socks, splayed out in front of me and hard as a rock.

I lean over and take him in my mouth in one hard swallow.

Benson grabs my hair in his hands, tugging and pulling as he moans above me. I take him as deep as I can before I pull up quickly, making him gasp a little harder with every up and down motion I make. I swirl around the tip of his dick with my tongue, and he yelps into the silent space of the office.

"Need you, Jack!" he whimpers. "Inside me. Now."

That won't be a hardship. I'm hard as a rock myself and my cock is begging to be back inside of his tight body. I move away from him just long enough to hunt down some medical lube, and then I find my belt with shaking hands. I manage to get it undone and shove my pants and underwear down far enough to step out of them. I'm standing in front of him, the tails of my button up hanging by my dick, as I begin to ease two fingers inside of him.

"That's so hot," he says in a strangled voice. Then he throws his legs up over my shoulders, and I feel him surrender to the moment, to me, as I work to break and re-build and break and re-build him over and over again, one finger at a time.

"Jack! Please!"

He's begging now, more than ready, and I'm not going to last much longer. "Fuck," I hiss. "I don't have any condoms in here. I'll go find one and be right—"

"No." Benson shakes his head hard. "I'm negative. I was just tested recently. I'm not sleeping with anyone else. I know you're negative too." He takes in a deep and steady breath. "I want you all the way inside me, Jack. Just you. Nothing else."

I almost come just listening to those words. I've never been bare inside of anyone except Fiona. Just the thought of Benson's tight heat against my dick has me ready to explode. "Are you sure?" I ask. "I have been tested recently, but we've got condoms in the other room. I'm a doctor, for crying out loud. I can recite safe sex speeches in my sleep. I don't want you to feel like we have to do this."

"We don't," he agrees quickly. "But I want to. And I sure as hell know that you do too. Fuck me, Jack. Fuck me bare."

I take his words for the order they are and push into him. The feeling of each and every nerve inside his body against me—it's almost too much. Almost too intense. It's like I'm being swept into some sort of other-worldly scene as I move in and out of him, my thoughts on nothing but Benson and the intense perfection of this moment and the way my body feels inside of him. He reaches out to take one of my hands in his, and that's when I know he feels it too. This magic. This connection. This sense of this space and time belonging solely to us and this moment. I thrust into him, fast and hard the way I've learned he likes. I'm bent over him on the exam table, his legs still up over my shoulders, and I'm so deep inside of him right now that it's almost as if our bodies are merged. One. It's as if we could never possibly disconnect ourselves, no matter how hard we tried.

"Jack!" He nearly shouts the word. "Not going to last much longer."

"Me neither, baby," I tell him. I grip his hand harder in mine. "Come with me," I whisper, and then I wrap my other hand around his dick as I thrust into him with one final push. Every cell in my body seems to cry out in unison as I feel Benson come in my hand with the same white-hot intensity that's currently ripping through me. This is, without a doubt, the most intense sexual experience I've ever had. I don't ever want it to end.

Benson cries out over and over beneath me as we lose ourselves—or find ourselves? I can't be sure anymore—together. Finally, we're both spent, and I ease out of him carefully, gently, helping him lay back across the table as I stroke his soft skin from his cheek down to his stomach. For a long time the two of us are silent, meditating in the space of the sensations and energy we've created together. I lean over and kiss him again, long and hard, and when we finally break away he's staring at me with something like wonder.

I'm sure my facial expression is very similar right now. What the two of us just created here was like nothing I've experienced. It almost feels too big to even discuss, and I know if I tried I'd likely spook the beautiful man in front of me.

So I don't try. "I'll find something to clean us off with," I tell Benson. I lean over to kiss him.

"Not too well," he says, his voice husky. "Want to feel you inside me all night long."

And damnit, now I'm getting hard again. But my chub quickly dissipates as I watch Benson rub at his forehead.

I give him another soft kiss and move toward the door of the bathroom that's adjacent to the exam room. As I've learned, I've got to be careful how I broach this subject. "Benson," I say, "what's it going to take for me to convince you to see someone about these headaches?"

Benson flinches. Okay, maybe that was a bit too much at once. He sits up on the table slowly. "Grandpa used to say my headaches made me soft," he says, more to the wall than to me.

I turn around sharply, nearly dropping the box of tissues I just picked up. "Excuse me?" I ask, and I can't stop the harsh tone I know is in my voice.

Benson shrugs, still staring at the wall. "That's why my nannies stopped taking care of me when I got them. Grandpa said that real Lewises don't let things like headaches take them down and I was going to have to learn how to handle them myself. So I did."

"And that's what you're going to keep doing?" I throw my hands up in the air, and the box nearly goes flying. "Benson, you have to realize that's not normal! Your grandfather sounds like a sadist! If you'd just let me help you, we could get you better pain management. I promise you, we could fix this!"

Benson blinks hard. "You really think that?" he finally asks.

"I do." I cross the room and take his hands in mine. "We're a good team. Don't you think? Don't you see it too? I can help you with these headaches. You already do so much for me and Elijah. He just told me his grades are up in math." I sigh. "Of course, they're down in history, so I might have to take away some of his guitar time until we get that taken care of. He's such a bright kid. I don't see why he doesn't understand the importance of grades and school. But I know we can make him see that if we just stay on him, and—Benson? Are you okay?"

His eyes have gone slightly glassy, and he looks away as he slowly tugs his hands away from me. "You're going to solve all of Elijah's problems, huh, Jack?"

"Not exactly. Just help him to see what's important here; that's all." Wires cross in my head as I realize what Benson's probably thinking about. "It's not the same thing as what your grandfather did to you," I tell him. "I'm just making sure Elijah keeps all his options open. That's all."

Benson's still keeping his eyes on a far corner of the starkly white room. "Benson?" I ask. "Benson, you see what I mean, right? Please answer me."

Benson's gaze slides back toward me as he shifts himself upward to sit on the edge of the exam table before he pushes himself off it and starts getting dressed. "I see what you mean," he says quietly as he begins to make his way across the room. "I see exactly what you mean, Jack."

He doesn't look back as he closes the door behind him. And I'm left standing there, alone in the silence of the empty room.

Chapter 19

17 Days to the Devon Falls Leaf Festival

Winning used to be a lot more fun. —Benson Lewis

"You're really not going to tell Ellie what you found?"

Jeremy's voice over my speakerphone is high with dramatic concern. He may as well be talking about the latest episode of some soap opera. Which I guess isn't far off from what my life has become these days. "I was hired to win a case," I tell him and Aaron. "I think I forgot about that." I rub at my head, which hasn't stopped pounding since I left Jack's office yesterday. "In the end, does it really matter who the fuck is backing Arnie? He's my client. I need to do my best to help him win here. Anything else is irrelevant."

There's silence on the other end of the line. Aaron breaks it first. "You don't actually believe that, do you?"

"Look," I remind them. "None of us have found anything definitely proving Arnie Blake isn't exactly who he's claiming to be here."

"Except the sketchiest set of circumstances since the O.J. trial," Jeremy replies dryly. "C'mon, Benson. Aaron and I were just starting to think Devon Falls had magically made you human or something. Please don't tell us this was some kind of time-lapse spell and the clock just hit midnight and the pumpkin broke or whatever."

"Why would a pumpkin break?" I ask. "That doesn't even make sense."

"Seriously?" Aaron and Jeremy ask in unison. "You never saw *Cinderella*?" Jeremy demands.

"Is that the cartoon with the mice?" I ask. I vaguely remember Sarah putting it on for Linus and Daphne when they were little. I never saw many Disney movies. Grandpa used to call them "sentimental nonsense."

"Okay, we'll put a pin in that and plan a movie night. But Benson," Aaron says. "All cartoon retellings of fairy tales aside, have you fully considered the choice you're making here? If you follow this case through to the finish, there's a good chance you'll win. You'll be destroying a town tradition for a ski area's profits. What if you decide to stay there? Could you ever look anyone in the eye there again?"

A vision of Jack in his office yesterday, telling me about Elijah and his history grade, rings through my brain like a gong smashing into a bell. "I won't be staying here." I put the words together carefully, determined to make sure Jeremy and Aaron hear that I mean them. "As soon as this case is over, I'm leaving Devon Falls."

There's another long silence on the other end of the phone, but I don't need the time to reconsider my decision. I've been up all night making it, and I've got the mental pro and con lists to prove it. Dr. Jack Lancer and I were never a real couple and we're never going to be one. I know that for certain now.

Because at the end of the day, Jack Lancer's just like my grandfather. He's just like everyone else in my life who's found me lacking. Jack has his own vision of the world and what it's supposed to look like. Eventually, I won't match that vision. I won't want the migraine treatment he thinks I should get, or I'll fail at something he thinks I should try harder at. I'll disappoint him, and he'll make it his mission to fix me.

Because that's what people like Jack and my grandfather do. At least I have a chance to finally please my family. I'm so close now, right on the cusp of the praise I've been waiting for going on twenty-six years. But if I let myself fall all the way in love with Jack, I'll just be chasing that high the rest of my life. And odds are I'll never fully reach it.

Fuck everything about Devon Falls. I wish I'd never come here, and I can't wait to get the hell out, whether my firm wins this case or not.

"Listen," I tell Aaron and Jeremy, "I need to know right now that all the conversations we've ever had about this case stay between the three of us."

There's still more silence on the other end of the line, but I can practically hear the discussion I'm sure Aaron and Jeremy are having with their eyes right now. Aaron finally answers me. "We would never break your confidence like that, Benson. We're your friends."

Jeremy sighs. "Yeah. Not sure why, exactly, but there it is. Ow! Don't hit me, Aaron! Seriously, though," he adds. "I think what you're doing here is fucked up. But it's your mistake to make, not ours. We won't say anything to anyone."

Their words stab slightly at my heart. At least if there was some damning evidence out there proving beyond a shadow of a doubt what Bill's up to, maybe then I could go to my dad with that. I could point out that it's dangerous to move forward with the case on those grounds and possibly convince him and Grandpa to drop the whole thing in order to make sure they preserve the firm's reputation. But I also know Grandpa would have never attached himself to this case in the first place if he thought it presented any real danger to the firm. And as things stand, no one but Aaron, Jeremy, and I have drawn the lines between what's really behind

Arnie Blake's land claim. It's unlikely anyone else in this town will before the trial begins. Why would they? Ellie and the rest of this town think Bill's a hero in their story, not a villain.

Which means I'm stuck with the choice I had yesterday: my family or this case. This town, or my family. Losing or winning.

Winning used to be a lot more fun.

I clear my throat. "Thank you both," I say. "For all your help. I know you're both busy with your own shit, and I really appreciate you both doing research for me. Let me know how many hours you worked and I'll get payment to you as soon as I can. I–"

"Benson," Aaron interrupts. "We didn't do this for money. We did this because you're our friend. You don't need to pay us."

That's the second time he's used the word "friend," but the first time I've fully paid attention to it. "Friend?" I ask. The word feels somewhat strange on my tongue.

"Maybe frenemy first," Jeremy adds. "But I think we've graduated from that point by now. Somewhere around the time we started consulting on your sex life. Speaking of which, what happened between you and that doctor that has you so quick to give up all that great nookie you've been having with him? Did you finally have a bad orgasm or something?"

I wince as I think about all the mind-blowing orgasms I've had since I met Jack Lancer. But not even the memories of those soul-bursting moments are going to make me change my mind. I saw a vision of a future with Jack yesterday, and it was far too close to my past for me to keep moving forward. Not even with someone I thought I might be falling in love with. My only option now, I know, is to go back to the original plan. Win this case. Prove to my family that I'm better than they think I am. Go build a life in Boston, and maybe hope for a weekend on Martha's Vineyard with Sarah and Dad and the kids sometime.

And if thinking about leaving Jack behind here in Devon Falls makes my head pound with a kind of pain I've never really felt before—well, I guess that's just something I have to live with.

"That was never real," I tell Jeremy and Aaron gruffly. The words ring in my ears as the lie that they are. Because what Jack and I have may have started out as a "fauxmance," as Jeremy insists on calling it, but even I know it's become so much more than that.

You don't tell someone your deepest secrets in a fauxmance.

You don't trust someone to take care of you for the first time in your life in a fauxmance.

You don't go bare with someone in a fauxmance.

But it's a hell of a lot easier to tell myself this was all fake than it is to tell myself anything else right now. The truth is that I've always known exactly who Jack was, even when I didn't want to see it or admit it: Dr. Jack Lancer is just another fixer. Someone who fixed his last relationship right into oblivion without even realizing it. Someone who's about to drive himself right out of his nephew's life trying to fix him. Someone who would no doubt spend the rest of his life trying to fix me.

Someone just like my grandfather.

"I have to stay on this case. We were never going to work anyway. It is what it is." The words feel heavy on my tongue.

"Benson," Aaron says, "you didn't hang up when we called you our friends, so I'm guessing it's safe to assume you've accepted the title. Would you say that's fair?"

"I'm not getting drunk and telling the two of you all my deepest, darkest secrets," I warn them. "And Jeremy, no hugging in public."

"Lame," he complains.

"But yeah," I continue. "I guess... I am really grateful for the way you two have helped me. I know I don't deserve it after the way I've treated you both in the past. Yeah. Friends sounds okay," I add in a rush, because the words are a little hard to get out.

"Then I'm telling you this as a friend," Aaron replies. "A friend who honestly cares about you and your happiness. I know why this case has meant so much to you. But I hope you'll think hard about the choice you're making here. You know what the town potentially gives up if you win this. But have you thought about what *you're* potentially giving up here? About what you stand to lose?"

Last night I kept waking up thinking Jack was holding onto me, spooning me in his arms. I'd realize he wasn't there and feel immediately hollow. That same feeling of hollowness washes through me again as I imagine a world where I never feel Jack Lancer's arms around me. Where I never feel his fingers trace their way over my skin again.

I remember the crying in the courtroom the day we secured the injunction to stop the festival, and I wonder if I'll cry like that when I walk away from this town permanently. I'm not sure I've ever cried before. I'm not even sure if I know how.

"Believe me," I tell Aaron. "I've thought about it. I've thought about it a hell of a lot more than I should."

I hang up the phone, but that hollowness stays lodged within me all morning long.

"Damn," I swear to myself under my breath as I make the walk from my apartment to the historical society later that afternoon.

I was determined not to show my face at the historical society today. With the hearing tomorrow, I'm worried I won't even be able to look Ellie in the eye without accidentally spilling everything I think I might know about Arnie and Bill Cummings. I was absolutely determined to stay in my apartment all morning and finish putting together everything Carter needs there.

So naturally, I've discovered that I need copies of at least three documents I left over at the historical society. And of course, both Ellie and Henri are sitting there together, at the long table in the center of the room, the moment I walk in.

"You poor thing!" Ellie stands and rushes to throw her arms around me. "Are you okay?"

I'm so caught off guard that I almost drop my bag. "What the hell are you talking about?"

Henri clucks her tongue. "That fake beau of yours is walking around like the hamster he had when he was five died all over again. Hit in the street, the poor thing, and I swear I didn't even know a moped could go that fast. And I never did ask why anyone would be out walking a hamster."

I have absolutely no idea what she's talking about.

"We know the two of you say you were only pretending to be together for Elijah," Ellie adds. "But you were starting to look like Amelia and I did right before she popped the question at my favorite nudist retreat over in Plattsburgh. And as a sidebar, you never saw such a celebration."

My head is spinning now.

"What on earth happened?" Henri asks. "All Jack would tell us is that you're not answering his calls or texts. What's going on, Benson?"

The low throb in my head pounds as I try to figure out how to answer her. "I... well." I'm standing there, unsteady on my feet, trying to figure out how to explain the unexplainable to two women who would absolutely hate my guts if they knew the secret I've been keeping from them, when Elijah comes bursting into the room.

"Are you and Uncle Jack going to break up?" he demands. There's a guitar case over his shoulder and pure teenage rage in his eyes. "Why aren't you answering his messages?"

I do not have the energy for this level of angst today. "Elijah, I can't talk about this with you right now," I tell him.

"If you do, are you gonna stop tutoring me?" he demands.

Shit. I haven't even thought about that. "Elijah, I—"

"Please keep tutoring me!" he blurts out. "It's the only thing keeping my grandparents off my case, and they're definitely going to try and make me go to Florida with them if you stop. Plus, Uncle Jack hums when you're around! He never hummed before!"

"He hums?" Ellie asks.

"He does," Henri adds conversationally. "All around the office. Malachai thinks he's most on-tune in the mornings, but I say afternoons are when he's really at his best."

Jack hums now? The throbbing in my head is increasing steadily with every word the three of them say, and a quick flash of light off to the left of my vision alerts me that I'm probably not long for this conversation. The documents are just going to have to wait. There's no way I'm letting Ellie, Henri, and Elijah watch me collapse over a damn headache. "Elijah," I say, and I hope my voice doesn't sound as washed-out as it does in my ears. "I can keep tutoring you. But I'm leaving town after the trial anyway. You knew that was going to happen," I add slowly.

Elijah's eyes widen. "But you and Uncle Jack are dating," he says hoarsely. "I didn't think you'd just leave him—us—like that. I thought you liked us!" He turns and bolts out the door, grasping at his guitar as he goes.

"Elijah!" I call out, but the noise is too much for my fragile head. The migraine I saw coming bursts into fractured light in front of my eyes, and the steady throb in my head becomes a jackhammer of pain that slams into me with a force so hard I stagger backward where I stand.

"Benson? Benson!" I hear someone calling my name, but the sound is just an echo in between flashes of light and a pain so unreasonably terrible that I can feel myself collapsing under its weight. The last thing I hear as I feel my legs going out from under me are words that barely register inside my shattering brain.

"Call an ambulance!"

Chapter 20
17 Days to the Devon Falls Leaf Festival

Can you end something that never existed in the first place? —Jack Lancer

Time moves more slowly, I've already learned, when the future you were looking forward to begins to shift in front of you.

Benson and I had a big moment together last night. I was sure we did. Then, the next thing I knew, he was closing the door of my exam room behind him and barely speaking to me. He left me at the office with some mumbled words about needing to finish up some work and hasn't answered any of my texts or phone calls ever since. I even tried emailing him.

I hate using email.

I can parse enough of what went wrong to know it all started when I brought up Elijah's history grade. I'm not a complete idiot. I know Benson's sensitive to how I handle Elijah's school/guitar balance, and I don't blame him. But if he'd just let me explain, I'd tell him that I have no plans to rip Elijah away from his guitar the way Benson's family ripped him away from his. In fact, I have no plans to do anything involving Elijah's guitar time until I can talk to Eric. So far I've only been able to leave him messages.

But I can't tell Benson any of that if he won't speak to me.

Now I'm finishing up prescribing Tommy Schilling a new cream for his eczema and feeling every single second of the ticking clock on the wall of Lancer Family Medicine. Every step I take feels like I'm moving through molasses. Like I'm trying to force myself to move forward in air that's forever pushing back against me.

"You okay, Dr. Lancer?" Malachai finally asks after he has to repeat the same patient information to me three times.

"Yes. I'm sorry, Malachai," I tell him. Nobody deserves to have to work with me today. "I'm just tired."

Malachai nods sympathetically. "I definitely get that, sir," he says. "You don't have to apologize to me about that." Malachai's got dark circles under his eyes. I wonder if Mom and I need to talk to him again about cutting back his hours. But before I can mention this to him, the other Dr. Lancer herself comes bursting into my exam room.

"Jackalove," she says, and her eyes are dark with worry. "I just got a call from Henri. Benson collapsed at the historical society. They had to call an ambulance."

I'm out the door and running for my car before I even realize or remember that I'm running to the bedside of the man who may or may not be trying to end things with me.

Can you end something that never existed in the first place?

Devon Falls isn't big enough to have its own hospital. Fairlington Medical Center is the closest facility, and it's a thirty-minute drive. I have plenty of time on the ride there to let every single thing that's happened between Benson and me roll through my head on repeat. Everything Henri told my mother suggests that Benson was experiencing a severe migraine when he collapsed, and I'm already beating myself up for not pushing him to get treatment in place a long time ago. What kind of doctor am I?

By the time I get to FMC, I'm one giant ball of nerves. Luckily the nurses in the Emergency Department know me, and when I tell them there's a patient from Devon Falls I need to see, they let me through right away.

But when I push open the curtains of the small area where Benson's currently being treated, I almost wish they hadn't let me through so easily. I've been a doctor for a long time now, and I thought I'd gotten used to seeing people in pain, even people I care about. But the sight of Benson, lying there on that hospital bed, with an IV in his arm and his face pinched with agony, is almost too much for me.

He must hear my footsteps, because he tilts his head slightly toward me as I walk through the curtain and close it behind me. His eyes widen with something that's either surprise or more pain; I can't tell right away. "Jack," he whispers, and the desperation, the loneliness in his voice, is all I need to hear.

Right now, in this moment, it doesn't matter what happened in my office or why he's pushing me away. He needs me. That's all that matters.

I rush to his side, holding his hand as I give him a cursory examination. "I need to talk to the doctor and find out what they've given you," I tell him. "We need to talk treatment plans, and I want to make sure that they—"

"Jack," Benson interrupts me. I stop on the note of emotion in his voice. "You shouldn't have come," he says. He sounds dazed and almost shell-shocked.

"Of course I came, Ben." I sink down into the chair next to his bed as I run my fingers over his palm the way I know he likes. He sighs with contentment. "I would never leave you alone in the hospital," I add softly.

Benson's eyes go wet with tears. "You shouldn't be here," he tells me. "You can't be here... why are you here?"

Because I've fucking fallen in love with you. Those are the words I want to say. But are you allowed to say that to someone who was only ever with you as part of an elaborate ruse? Someone who's wrapped their soul up in every piece of body armor they can find? "Because I couldn't be anywhere else," I finally tell him, and the hoarseness of my voice seems to echo across the small space.

Benson stares at me for what feels like a long time, and he doesn't speak. Finally, I can't stay silent any longer.

"You can't keep doing this to yourself," I tell him. "Ben, I know how much your family means to you, but this needs to stop. You're killing yourself over them. Get some treatment. Let my mom help you. I know your grandfather gave you some toxic idea in your head that getting medical treatments for headaches makes you weak or some bullshit like that, but we both know it isn't true. Get your family out of your head. Stop working for them. Drop out of the case. Please, let us help you. My mom's on her way, and—"

Benson lets go of my hand. "That's what this is about?" he whispers. "That's why you're here? You came here to talk to me about dropping the case?"

"What? Benson, no!" I try to grab his hand back again, but he quickly pulls away from me. I lunge to make sure he doesn't pull out the IV that's attached to his arm. "This is about you and your health. This is about making sure you're not killing yourself for people who don't even care about you!"

Benson's eyes widen, and I wince. "I didn't mean it like that," I add quickly. "I just meant that you have people here who *want* to take care of you. You can't keep going on like this, Benson. You can't keep killing yourself for your family!"

Benson closes his eyes and turns his head slightly away from me on the pillow. "And you're going to make it all better," he murmurs into the cloth. "Just like you make everything else better, huh? Like you did with Fiona? Like you will with Elijah?"

I wince. "I thought you were angry with me last night. After I said what I did about Elijah's history grade."

Benson shakes his head. "Not angry," he mumbles. "More like sad. Yeah. Sad, I think." His eyes fill with tears again and he quickly blinks them away. "I was so stupid," he whispers, and I can't tell if he's talking to me or himself now. "For a minute I thought I could have something here. I thought I could have you. Maybe Elijah, and fuck, even Ellie and Henri, and the coffee and the Thai comedy nights and Luis' meatloaf. I thought I could have all of it."

"You can!" I tell him urgently. "You can have that, Benson! All of it! Just let me help you!"

He pulls in a large breath and shakes his head. His hands are shaking, I realize, but he jerks them away from me when I try to reach for them. "Jack," he finally asks me. "If we were together, is this how it would be? You always trying to fix me? Make me better? Trying to make me into what you think I'm supposed to be or do what you think I'm supposed to do?"

His words catch me so off-guard that I nearly jolt backwards in my chair. "What? What the hell are you talking about? Benson, I'm not like that. I'm not your fucking grandfather!"

Benson shakes his head. "Do you know," he asks softly, "how much torture homework is for Elijah? How much harder it is for him than it ever was for you? But you can't even let him take a C on an assignment and just go play the guitar. Nope. He's going to have to get As and Bs to please you. Always. No matter how many hours of work it takes. No matter how torturous those hours are."

His words swirl through my eardrums, dim and muffled. What the hell is he talking about? "Benson, he needs good grades. He's got to have future options. He can't rely on a guitar his whole life!"

Benson winces as he shakes his head slightly. "Or maybe he could, Jack. Have you ever even listened to him talk about his plans? He's got them, you know. He knows where he wants to study music and all the potential career paths he could take. He'll get the grades he needs to get to reach the future he wants. You're just not listening to him. Just like you didn't listen to Fiona."

The shock of Benson's words run cold through my veins. "What about Fiona?" I ask, and I can hear the darkness edging into my voice. Now he's fucking blaming my divorce on me, too? What the hell?

Benson at least has the decency to hesitate before he says his next words. "You did it then too, didn't you, Jack? Decided you knew what was best and just started bulldozing through with your plans. Before you'd even talked to her, I bet. Before you'd given either of you a second to grieve."

The words thrust through my chest the same way they did the first time Fiona said them. The first time our therapist said them. The first time Milo or Sam suggested that maybe I should slow down and stop making appointments. "I'm so tired," I tell Benson, "of people blaming me for trying to make things *fucking better*. What's wrong with fixing things, anyway?" I demand. "What's so wrong with me wanting to help you feel better, Benson? Or suggesting you let go of your fucked-up family?" Ellie's words from the church's doorsteps appear in my mind, a distant memory urging me to rethink what I'm saying right now, but I brush them away like I'm swatting a fly. Screw this. I've fallen hard for Benson Lewis. Fuck if I'm going to apologize for wanting better for him. I rub at my own forehead. "I can't believe," I tell him, "that you're saying all this. That you're telling me everything's my fault too."

Benson closes his eyes. "Not your... fault. Not exactly. But you really don't get it, do you, Jack? This thing you do? Running in, telling everyone how to make their lives better without even getting their input. It's the exact same thing my grandfather's always done."

He may as well have just twisted the knife that already feels like it's sitting in my chest. "I can't stay here," I murmur. "I can't do this again."

Benson blinks and slowly opens his eyes. They're wet and cloudy, and I see so many unfallen tears there. I struggle not to wrap him up in my arms—but how can I? How can I hold him and keep him safe when he thinks I'm anything like the man who's tortured him his whole life?

"Hand to your heart, Jack," Benson says slowly. "Are you going to let Elijah be the guitarist he could become? Even if it means him giving up on getting the grades you and his grandparents think he should get?"

I open my mouth to say yes, of course, that I'll support Elijah in whatever he wants to do, but I find I can't get the words out.

He has to do well at school. He can't depend on a rock star's salary.

I have to make sure he's successful in everything. It's what I owe Fiona and Eric.

But that doesn't make me anything like Benson's grandfather. Does it? I just want Elijah to be the best person he can be. I just want to help him. Just like I wanted to make sure Fiona and I could have the family we wanted. That's all.

This conversation is too much. It's all too familiar. I have to get out of this room before the walls close in on me.

I can't look at Benson as I rush away from his bedside and head for the nurse's station. Jackie, one of the charge nurses, looks up from her computer screen.

"Dr. Lancer?" she asks. "Is everything okay?"

"No," I tell her brusquely. "Everything's not okay. My patient is experiencing a serious migraine and needs to be seen immediately. Is Dr. Haslow on call today?" I trust Dr. Haslow implicitly. I know she'll take good care of him, at least.

"Yes, she's on call," says Jackie uncertainly. "But will you be taking over patient care here?"

I look over at the curtain surrounding Benson's bed, and I fight every urge in my body to swoop in, to make him better. To make all of this better. To make *us* better.

It's not what he wants.

"No," I tell Jackie. "He'll be in good hands with Dr. Haslow."

I leave Fairlington Medical Center, and I don't turn around as I walk away.

Chapter 21

15 Days to the Devon Falls Leaf Festival

Assholes aren't supposed to miss people. —Benson Lewis

"Hey, Benson! You're looking way better! Glad you're out of the hospital. Did you see all those gorgeous colors outside? Man, they have a leaf festival in this place for a reason."

Jeremy Everett pushes past me into my own apartment like he owns the place. "What are you doing here?" I ask, and I don't even try to rearrange the scowl that I know is etched across my face. I don't care if Jeremy and I are "friends" now. I didn't invite him here, and I sure as fuck don't feel like talking to anyone right now.

"Checking in on your well-being, sugarplum." Jeremy beams as he sets a grocery bag down next to the kitchen counter. "You just got out of the hospital, after all. And I see we aren't the only ones who were worried." His eyes pass over the table in the center of the room, which is covered in baskets and soup containers I need to put away. I found all of them in the hallway this morning. He picks up a note from the top of one of the containers and reads it aloud. "Here's some soup. Hope you feel better! We don't want you to win, but we know you're just doing your job. Love, the Rykers."

I snatch the note away from him. "I'm fine," I grumble. "I didn't need you to come visit."

"You sure about that?" Aaron Morin's voice is behind me now, and I turn to find him coming in through the open door with another grocery bag. "Because you look like death." His face is obscured by the heavy-looking bag, and Jeremy immediately rushes over to take it from him. Aaron smiles at him gratefully and gives him a kiss on the cheek. "My dad made you some of his famous brisket. It's better than chicken soup when you don't feel good, I swear."

"I feel just fine." I flop onto the couch while Aaron and Jeremy both study me appraisingly. I know what they're seeing: the dark circles under my eyes, the wrinkled sweatpants hanging low on my hips, the growing shadow of stubble under my chin. I saw it all in the mirror this morning. "No migraine symptoms since I left the hospital last night."

Jeremy starts unpacking things and putting them into the fridge—and either it's my imagination, or they bought the Devon Falls grocer out of orange juice—while Aaron makes his way over to the couch to sit next to me. It's the middle of the week, and he's wearing jeans and a t-shirt. I wonder if he took the day off to come see me. And shouldn't Jeremy be in class? "That's great to hear," he says. "Did the doctors come up with any kind of long-term treatment plan?"

"They prescribed me something," I mumble.

"And I'll bet hot money right now that you haven't filled the prescription yet," Jeremy calls from inside the fridge.

"I don't need medicine." I drop back against the couch. I don't feel like dealing with these two right now. I don't feel like dealing with anyone. I keep waiting for the phone to ring, watching it like it's a snake ready to lash out and strike. "I don't need anything," I mumble. And I don't. I'm an asshole, through and through. That's who I've always been. Assholes aren't supposed to need anyone. Assholes aren't supposed to miss people.

"I don't think that's true," Aaron says softly. And I close my eyes against the words, because they're right.

All I've wanted since the moment I found myself in an ambulance headed to a strange hospital was one person. When he showed up in my room there, I wanted so badly to latch onto him and hold onto him forever. Jack's arms were all I craved.

But I meant every word I said to him. I can't be with him. He can't be with me. He's the guy who swoops in to save everything and everybody, and I'm the hot mess who's about to be the ruination of this town. We were never going to work.

I had to let him go.

"Benson," Aaron says softly, "are you really going to be able to live with yourself if you keep moving forward with this case? Especially knowing what you do now?"

"I have a job," I remind him. "A duty. A duty to my client."

"You also have a duty to yourself," he says. "You are allowed to be happy, Benson. And since you've been here, in Devon Falls, you've been the happiest I've ever seen you."

"I don't actually dread your phone calls anymore," Jeremy says as he shoves another container in the fridge.

"Not helpful, babe," Aaron tells him.

"But it's true." Jeremy crosses the room and stands in front of me, his hands on his hips. "Look. I really do get fucked-up families better than anyone. I'm not sure what yours is all about, but I do know one thing: if you're in any way hanging onto this case and letting go of everything else you've got here because you're working for your family... well, maybe you should reconsider that. Talk to them. Tell them what's going on with you. What this case is doing to you."

"I tried that." My grandfather's pinched face and his low, angry voice crowd my vision. "Winning comes first in my family. It always has."

Jeremy nods slowly. "Well," he says, "what is it you want to win here, Benson?"

I slump into the couch. That's not a question I want to answer right now.

"Benson! Hey, you're up and about! That's great news!"

Right now I'm positive my face is etched into a shape directly the opposite of a smile. I was already in a piss-poor mood when I walked into Falling All Beans. But there's no way I can be rude to the kid whose family left chicken soup on my doorstep yesterday. "Thank you," I tell Belinda Ryker. "And hey, tell your mom I said thanks for the soup."

"Yeah, of course!" she says as she starts moving around the espresso machine without even asking me what I want. She knows my order. "Mom always makes sure someone has her soup when they get out of the hospital. She cares about people like that. And she only gave someone food poisoning that one time."

I make a mental note to eat from that container very carefully.

Belinda is just handing me my coffee when my phone pings with a notification. My heart shoots up into my throat as I see the line of text across my phone.

Vermont State Bar Results

Holy. Fucking. Shit.

I do my best not to shake as I take the coffee and make my way to the back of the shop. This is it. This is the moment. If I've failed, my family will probably never forgive me. If I've passed, then I know I've made it: I'm officially no longer the kid who barely got Cs in school and had to be sent away for "alternative education" because he was such a lost cause in the private school the rest of his family went to.

This is the moment I've been working toward, on some level, for most of my life. The moment I gave up my guitar for. And friends. And any kind of life outside of studying and work.

I'm terrified to open the email.

My eyes drift to the window and the doctor's office in plain view of the coffee shop. Jack should be working this morning. Any minute now, he'll walk up that porch and unlock the door, opening Lancer Family Medicine for the day. I could go sit on the porch and wait for him. Opening the results with him, I know, wouldn't be nearly as scary.

I gulp down a sip of my too-hot latte and let it burn down my throat. And then I open the email.

It takes a few minutes for the results to register from my eyes to my brain. I passed. I passed the Vermont bar exam.

"Holy fucking shit," I say out loud. I can't stop the burst of laughter that escapes from my throat. *I passed the bar!* All those nights and days of studying and stressing and panicking—they weren't for nothing. I really passed.

I stand up, then realize I have nowhere to go and sit back down. The one person I want to tell probably doesn't want anything to do with me right now. And I have no one to blame for that but myself.

But at least I can tell my family. I let myself smile, just a little, as I punch out a quick email and send it off to Dad and Grandpa.

And then I sip, and I wait. We may not be big on celebrations in the Lewis family, but surely passing the bar will garner some kind of excitement.

The first email comes quickly. It's from my dad. *I'm out of the office and away from my desk this week....*

What the fuck? He's not even in the office? I was wondering if he or Sarah had heard through Carter that I was in the hospital. I guess not; at least that explains why Sarah hasn't been blowing up my phone checking in on me. I was starting to wonder. I'm just about to try texting them both instead when my inbox pings with an email from Grandpa.

I tug in a deep breath, give myself permission to smile a little wider, and I open it.

I hope you didn't expect a medal for passing an exam with a damn fifty percent pass rate. What the hell is this I hear about the case being delayed because of some kind of medical emergency? Make sure you get Carter up to speed the second he gets there. The client's going to be very unhappy.

I drop the half-finished latte in the trash on my way out the door, and I make the hardest left I can. Because right now I don't think I can even stand to look at Lancer Family Medicine.

Chapter 22
13 Days to the Devon Falls Leaf Festival

You know it's a good party when three goats and an accordion player show up. —Jack Lancer

"I still think you should consider my offer."

I say the same thing to Sam every damn time we video chat, which is usually at least once a week. And every week he does the same thing: he frowns, sighs, and shakes his head. Every damn week. And then he says the same exact thing.

"I'm not ready to leave this apartment, Jack. You know that."

"I know how much that apartment means to you," I tell him patiently. And I do. It's where he made his home with Christian, and I know how many memories that place holds. But Milo and I worry he's become trapped in those memories. "You don't need to sell it. Milo and I will help you find renters. Mom and I could use the help here, Sam. The practice is growing." That's a little bit of an exaggeration. Devon Falls isn't getting that much bigger, and Mom and I can handle the patient load here just fine right now. But she's going to want to lighten her workload soon, and she's all for bringing Sam up here to work with us. She'd have Milo here in a heartbeat too if we could get him, but there's no way he's ever going to leave New York.

Sam sighs. "I just can't see leaving this place, Jack. Chris loved it here. New York was his life. Going to Vermont... I'm not sure I'm ready for that."

I start to say *I understand,* but the truth is that I don't. Breaking up with Fiona was incredibly hard, but she's still living and breathing and dating some guy in Rome. What Sam went through, losing the love of his life forever right in front of his eyes, has to come with the kind of pain I can't even fathom.

"I don't want to talk about me anymore," Sam says abruptly. "You and Benson really broke up, then? It's over?"

"It was never real to begin with," I remind him. "You know that. It was all just a show to hold off Elijah's grandparents." I wince as I imagine the phone call I have coming from them soon. The Devon Falls rumor mill travels fast. I'm going to have to scramble to explain who's taking over Elijah's tutoring and how I plan to successfully "single parent" without him. It's probably time I left a message for Eric catching him up, too. I just don't have the energy.

Right now all my energy seems to be going to basic everyday tasks, like getting up. Walking to work. Opening my fucking office. Making this phone call.

"Jack," says Sam, and I recognize the voice he's using; it's the one he uses when he's about to tell a patient something they won't want to hear. "Milo and I were talking. The way you were with Benson... we never saw you like that with Fiona."

"What's that supposed to mean?" I ask, but there's no heat to the question. I know exactly what he means, because I know exactly what he and Milo saw. It's the same thing I saw every single day I was with Benson.

Sparks. Heat. A sort of magnetism that felt like it could never be broken.

Except it has. And the dull, persistent ache that sits in my chest, the nagging questions in my head about where Benson is and what he's doing and how he's feeling—it certainly feels like some piece of me has been severed and taken. And for all the pain I felt when Fiona left, it never felt quite like this. It never felt so permanent.

So unescapable.

"You know exactly what I mean, Jack," he says calmly. "I know you do."

I stare across my desk at a photo sitting there. It's of me and my parents, and it was taken at one of the picnics on their lawn. I remember Benson sitting on that same lawn, playing guitar, his happiness lighting up the entire space. The light in his eyes that day made my whole body sing with a happiness I'd never felt before. "He made it clear," I tell Sam hoarsely, "that he thinks the same thing I know you and Milo secretly think. That I'm too much. Too overbearing or something. That I don't listen."

"Jack, Milo and I don't think that."

"Oh really?" I ask. "You don't think I railroaded Fiona with fertility treatments and adoption options? Or that I'm pushing Elijah too hard to get the best grades he can? You probably think what Benson thinks, too: that I should just let him live in migraine misery while his family walks all over him. And my concerns about his family have nothing to do with their legal case against Devon Falls, by the way." If Benson wanted me as much as I wanted him, I know we could find a way to navigate the issues with the land claim together. We could even find a way to navigate his goals for his career alongside my career in Devon Falls. But Benson obviously doesn't want to fight for a future with me.

"He accused me," I tell Sam, "of being exactly like his horrible fucking grandfather. Is that what you and Milo think too?"

"Oh, Jack." Sam sighs. "Milo and I think that you're one of the best people we know in the world. We think marriages take two people, and so do divorces."

There's a *but* coming here. I stew in silence and wait for it.
Only it doesn't come.

Instead, Sam says, "Did that therapist you saw with Fiona ever talk about vulnerability?"

I search the records of my mind, clawing through those painful and largely useless sessions. "Maybe. I don't know. I think she said something about that and me being too controlling."

Okay, maybe those weren't her exact words. But if I remember correctly, the language was more accusatory than I liked.

"Well, that grief counselor you and Milo finally convinced me to see—she's helped me a lot; you know that. And one of the things she always says is that most people don't like being vulnerable. We don't like feeling at risk. In danger. That makes sense, right?"

"Sure, I guess." I'm still not sure where Sam's going with all this.

"People tend to respond to danger in different ways: flight or fight, or freezing or appeasing, she says. And you, Jack, you're a fighter. I think you know that about yourself. When you see danger and the possibility of being vulnerable to it, you fight with everything you have. It's what makes you a great doctor. One of the best I'll ever work with." Sam's silent for a few moments before he speaks again. When he does, his words are quiet and clear. "In our first year of residency," he says, "there was a patient who refused surgery for a gallbladder issue. They said they'd rather live with the problem than go through the procedure."

My mind travels back through years of patients and illnesses and injuries, and eventually I land on a vaguely blurred face from early in my career. "I think I remember," I say slowly.

"The doctor we were working under told you to let it go. The patient had figured out how to live with the issue, and they were happy with the treatment you laid out. But you wouldn't let it go, Jack. You just kept pushing, determined that surgery could give this patient a better quality of life."

The patient clicks into place in my mind. "They asked to be switched off my care," I mumble. It was the first time that had ever happened to me, and at first I was crushed. I got over it quickly, though. I told myself that not every patient would always know what was best for them. And then I moved on.

"They did. Do you remember what Dr. Shartan told us when that happened?"

I gulp hard as the words re-register in my brain. "She said that sometimes caring for a patient is just sitting with them in their pain," I say quietly. I brushed off and buried those words long ago. I simply didn't believe them.

"When Christian died," Sam says, "I was so grateful to have you and Milo. You pushed me to get up. To move. To start over. To go on with life. And Milo—he let me wallow. He sat with me when I needed to be sad. Angry. What the fuck ever. He—"

"He sat with you in your pain," I whisper. I never did that. I couldn't stand to see Sam on the couch in his apartment, sinking into the sorrow of missing Christian. It was just too hard to watch. I'd haul him up off that couch and make him run, swim, take walks. I was the one who convinced him to go back to work. "Sam, did I push you too hard?" I ask, suddenly terrified. Am I the reason my friend still isn't back to being the person he once was?

"Hell no," Sam says, the force behind his words is like a rush of relief that races through my veins. "You and Milo were the balance I needed back then. But Jack—you were one very specific part of that balance. And now I wonder: did you ever just sit and mourn, when they told you that you and Fiona would never have children the way you planned? Did you ever give yourself a day—or hell, even an hour—to sit with her on the couch and be sad about what you'd both lost?"

I close my eyes against answering the question. Because Sam already knows the answer.

"Benson's right," I finally tell him, the words rough and calloused as they move through my mouth. "I do want to fix everyone. But I just... Sam, I just don't want anyone I love to fucking be in danger or hurt. I wanted Fiona—and hell, me—to be happy. To have the family we were supposed to have. I want Elijah to have the future he deserves. That's all I want for Benson, too."

I want Benson to have everything. I want to give him the whole damn world.

"I love him, Sam. I think I love him more than I've ever loved anyone. Or ever will."

"I know," Sam says softly. "You're such a good person, Jack Lancer. But sometimes, Jack, love is sitting with someone in their pain."

I sigh. "Fuck, Sam. I'm the one who's supposed to be all sage-y on these calls, remember?"

Sam barks out a laugh. "I can't be a hot mess every single second of my life. I'd never get any coffee made. Listen, though: I really hope you won't give up on whatever you and Benson have. Because the only thing I know for certain is that you don't ever want to be staring back at the best days of your life wishing you could live them over again. Not if you don't have to."

He says the words so calmly, so dully. Like they're embedded into him. Like they're words he lives every single day. "Oh, Sam. I'm so sorry."

"There's nothing to be sorry for. You and Milo have always done everything you can for me," he replies. "And you still do. Hey, I have to run. I'm being paged. Keep me posted on what you do next, okay?"

"Bye, man." He clicks off, and I set the phone down carefully on the desk in front of me.

Sometimes love is sitting with someone in their pain.

What the hell does that even look like?

I'm trying to figure that out when Elijah comes bursting into my office. "Uncle Jack! Malachai said you didn't have any patients. Are you busy?"

I rub some of the tiredness from the corners of my eyes. "Not too busy for you. What's up?"

"Benson passed the bar!" He flops into the chair in front of the desk and immediately starts raiding the candy dish there, looking for strawberry Starbursts.

"What? How do you know that?" I pull one of the pink candies from the stash in my top drawer and hand it to him.

"I saw Ellie on the way home! She said to tell you. I'm not sure how she found out. Something about a little bird in Burlington telling her or whatever."

I smirk as I imagine the network of birds Ellie probably has in place to get her information when she needs it.

"She said I should tell you," Elijah goes on as he unwraps more Starbursts. "And then I asked her if it was a big deal and she said it's a really, really big deal. And I know you and Benson are like in a fight or whatever, but obviously you don't want to be, so I was thinking: what if we, like, threw him a party or something to celebrate? Maybe then he'd remember how much he's into you and you two could get back together or something! How great would that be?"

I sigh. "I don't think it works quite that way, Elijah." But Sam's words echo in my head yet again. Maybe this is my chance to tell Benson that I heard what he said in the hospital. That I'm trying to learn, and I haven't given up on us.

Hmmm.

"Well, maybe we should do it anyway. Even if you two still keep fighting." Elijah shrugs and starts hunting through the candy jar again. "Benson always makes a huge deal out of it whenever I pass a test, or even when I don't pass but I try my best. I think we should do the same thing for him."

"You really like him, don't you?" I ask.

"Yeah." Elijah shrugs. "He's kind of like the only person around here who gets me, except maybe for Pat. No offense, Uncle Jack, but you don't know what things are like for me in school. Dad doesn't really either. Grandpa and Grandma definitely don't." He frowns, and then his face lights up as he digs out another pink candy from the bowl. "Benson does. And I'm pretty lucky, because you and Dad and Aunt Fiona all like me the way I am most of the time, even if you don't get me. But I'm not sure Benson had people like that. That must have sucked. A lot."

"I can't even imagine how much," I mutter as I think of Benson's face in that hospital room. He's been through so much loneliness. So much pain. And I can't fix any of it.

But I sure as hell can show him that he's not alone anymore. And that he's surrounded by people who like him exactly the way he is.

People who don't need or expect him to change one damn thing about himself.

"Let's throw a party." I stand up and toss a bag of Only Pink Starbursts across the table to Elijah, whose face instantly lights up. "Go get Henri. She'll know what to do."

"Sweet! Let's get your dad to barbecue. And I bet Luis will make some pies. Oh, and do you think your mom could hook up her sweet sound system? I've gotta DM Pat!"

I'm not even sure where I fit into this plan, and I'm not sure that matters. All that matters now is that I show Benson Lewis that I'm in love with the gruff, snarky, stubborn, porcupine-spirited, guitar-playing person that he is—exactly as he is. That I can be vulnerable enough to stop and sit and listen and not try to change or fix one damned thing about him or his life if that's not what he wants me to do.

And if any group of people can help me do that, it's the town of Devon Falls.

You know it's a good party when three goats and an accordion player show up.

By the time most of Devon Falls has assembled on my parents' lawn, that's only the tip of the iceberg of who's attending the occasion. The goats are Esme Desdine's. They're part of the goat yoga classes she regularly leads, and she felt they would add to the energy of the party. Right now, they're entertaining a group of elementary schoolers at the edge of the lawn while Elijah and Pat's band tunes up on the patio. Arlo Decker is here decked out in his clown outfit, and I heard that Elmore Tran is going to perform his stand-up act for us later. Mom's decorated the whole lawn with solar fairy lights, and dad has a pile of hot dogs ready to go on the barbecue. Henri and Luis are standing at the buffet table arguing over which pie to serve first while two of the youngest Ryker kids wrestle under the table.

The accordion player is some friend of Ellie's from her nudist group. He's walking around the edge of the lawn serenading people with what sounds distinctly like the chords of the happy birthday song. I have a feeling he missed the memo about what we're celebrating today.

But that doesn't matter. All that matters is that Benson's going to walk into this party at any moment. All that matters is the look on his face when he sees that we've all come out to celebrate him.

Mom crosses the patio to stand next to me. "I did wonder," she says thoughtfully, "if I'd ever see you fall in love again after Fiona."

"Me too." I sigh.

She squeezes my hand. "He's a prickly one," she says. "But then, so was I when your father met me."

I squeeze her hand back and let her smile fill me with something that quells the nervous energy creeping through me right now.

"Shhh!" Henri calls out. "They're coming! Everyone quiet down!"

The crowd around me goes silent as we listen to the footsteps making their way through my parents' house. "I still don't understand why we're here," Benson says. "What did you find at the Lancer's house that has anything to do with the land claim?"

"Stop being impatient," Ellie reprimands him cheerfully. "Now, c'mon. Just step through the backdoor."

Benson pushes open the door slowly, and his eyes widen almost comically as everyone on the lawn shouts "SUPRISE!" loudly. Even more impressively, we're actually in unison. His eyes drift to the large hanging banner that Elijah and Pat made. CONGRATS ON PASSING THE BAR! (BUT YOU'D STILL BE AWESOME IF YOU FAILED IT) the banner proclaims in neon pink and green letters.

They nearly ran out of room on the right side trying to fit all that in. But Elijah and I agreed the parenthetical phrase was important.

The look on Benson's face just then is like nothing I've ever seen before. It's like someone has put the only present he's ever wanted right in front of him, and he can't quite believe that the thing he wanted so badly even exists in the world.

His eyes move through the crowd over to me, and then they lock onto mine, and I feel it: that magnet between us, drawing him toward me.

It takes what feels like a century, but is probably only twenty minutes, before he makes his way through the crowd of well-wishers and over to me. "You did this?" he asks. There's a half-smile on his face I know all too well.

"*We* did this," I tell him. That seems important: him knowing for certain that I'm not the only one here who sees what's beautiful inside of him. "Benson, I know I've made plenty of mistakes rushing to fix things and people when fixing wasn't what they needed or wanted. I understand that now. But I don't think I've ever seen anyone—or anything—as clearly as I see you in this moment. If you give me another chance, I promise I won't be another person who's out to make you into something you're not. I'll spend every damn day listening to you the way I should have been listening right from the start. I'll spend the rest of my life trying to show you that no one could be more perfect for me than you. Exactly the way you are."

Benson's eyes widen and he blinks suddenly, fast. "Jack," he whispers. "Oh, Jack."

"Benson!" An oblivious Luis rushes in between us with a back slap and congratulations, and it isn't long before Benson's surrounded by people telling him they're impressed, and they wish he was a shittier lawyer but congrats anyway, and soon we're separated by an entire town that came out to celebrate someone they were never supposed to like in the first place.

Benson and I don't get that moment back. But there's another moment shortly after that, when our eyes lock again, perfectly in time, and just then it's like we're the only two people in the backyard.

Thank you, he mouths through the crowd.

It's a moment of my life that I'll be happy to live over and over.

Chapter 23

12 Days to the Devon Falls Leaf Festival

So do you want me to talk or not? You need better clarity in your directions. —Benson Lewis

No one's ever thrown me a party before. Not a real one. Not for anything.

A full twelve hours after the town of Devon Falls, a town I arrived in solely to destroy, threw me an epic party to celebrate that I passed the bar, I still can't believe that this place, or these people, exist.

I still can't believe Dr. Jack Lancer exists. Or that after everything I've said and done to him, he'd rally the town to throw a low-key rager for me.

There were goats. Clowns. Elijah's band played. Some asshole even brought an accordion. Luis made his meatloaf, and Jack's dad hugged me and said he hoped I was incredibly proud of myself. Jack's mother even gave me a congratulatory handshake, and I spent most of the evening with a ball of something in my throat—feelings, maybe? I'm still not sure.

My father still hasn't even acknowledged my email about my bar results. But somehow the town of Devon Falls found out I passed the bar, and everyone came out to celebrate, less than forty-eight hours before my firm is scheduled to stand up in court and try to take away one of their most beloved institutions.

And Jack was there, standing at the center of the best thing that's ever happened to me.

All I fucking wanted to do was run across that party and launch myself into his arms like a star in a bad rom-com. But I couldn't. Not yet. Soon, I hope. But not yet.

First, I have to fix my fuck-ups. I have to fix what I've done to this town. I understood what Jack was telling me last night, and that message meant more to me than he may ever know.

But the truth is that I haven't earned any kind of unconditional love Jack Lancer wants to offer me. Not when I'm embroiled in a long con to destroy the town that's given him, and me, so much.

I finally know the answer to Jeremy's question: I know what I want to win now. I want Jack. I want Devon Falls. I want those things above all else.

And that means I've got to get his town's leaf festival back.

"Okay," I whisper to myself. I stare at the email I've drafted, re-reading just to make sure I've made myself one hundred per-cent clear.

Dear Mr. Lewis:

I am writing to inform you that I am resigning from Lewis, Stillmer, and Gates, Attorneys at Law, effective immediately. In my professional legal opinion, the firm's handling of the Blake case has been unprofessional and calls into question the ethics of the firm itself. I no longer wish to associate myself with your organization.

Best,

Benson Lewis

P.S. Grandpa, you read that right: I quit. You should re-think what your firm is doing in Devon Falls. Immediately. Also: you're a pretty shitty grandfather.

I read through the email one more time. And then, without another thought, I hit *send.*

Immediately I feel every muscle in my body relax. Twenty-five years of stress and tension seeps out of me like the stains bleeding out of a bleached bedsheet, and I feel as fresh and new as that clean sheet.

And now, the hard part: I have to talk to Ellie. I have to tell her what I know. I've spent most of the morning pep talking myself up to this, because I know what I'm risking here. Ellie and the rest of Devon Falls may never speak to me again after they find out how far I've let this case go. Even if Ellie's able to use what I've discovered to her advantage—and there's no guarantee she can—it's highly unlikely there's going to be a leaf festival this year. Autumn has descended heavily on Devon Falls, and at this point it's likely too late for the town to hold the festival even if Ellie pulls off a miracle in court.

For the first time in over a hundred years, the Devon Falls Leaf Festival won't be held this year. All because I chose to keep supporting this case even after I knew it was probably a scheme.

That's something I'll always have to live with. But at least I'm finally ready to do everything I can to make things right.

Will Jack still want to be with me after he finds out the whole truth about my part in this land claim? That's a question I don't have the answer to. But it's a risk I'm going to have to take.

I spend the rest of the morning getting ready for the day and preparing for the hard conversations I'm about to have, and it's almost two hours before I finally lock the door to my apartment and step out into the hallway. What I have to explain to Ellie isn't something you do over the phone, so I'm hoping I can find her at either her office or the historical society. I'm making my way down the stairs, silently reciting the speech I've planned to share with her about Bill Cummings and what I know and what I still don't. I hit the last step before the stairwell as I wonder again what the odds are that Jack and I will ever have a chance at a relationship after I tell him what I've known all these weeks.

Then I feel an arm wrap around me and press a piece of cloth against my nose and mouth.

Everything goes dark.

"I never tied a guy up before," a voice says.

"Me neither," says another one. "Bill, you should give us jobs like this more often."

Someone sighs. "Gentlemen, we're not animals. We're in the business of persuading people to come along with our vision, not threatening them."

"Then why do we have this guy tied up here?" That's the first voice, I think.

The world comes back into focus slowly as I open my eyes. My head is pounding, but not in the way it usually pounds. This is much more localized. It's a throbbing, centralized pain right in the middle of my skull. I see the wooden slats of an older building, and there's cement underneath my feet. I'm tied to something—a pipe maybe? As more details come into focus, I realize I'm probably in an out-of-use barn.

"Well, Darius," says a voice I now recognize as Bill Cummings', "I've had someone monitoring this fellow's communication. Our last conversation left me concerned that he wasn't working on Arnie's land claim case with as much fervor as one would hope. I'm sorry to say he sent a very disturbing email this morning to his colleagues suggesting he will no longer be an asset to our case. As it also seems clear he's about to share information we'd rather not have shared, it seemed necessary to remove him from the equation entirely."

They're standing at the other end of the barn, about thirty feet away from me, completely oblivious to my small movements. This seems, I decide, like a good time to take further stock of my situation. My arms are tied to the pipe behind me, and my legs bound in front of me. I've been gagged with something that looks and tastes like an old handkerchief.

And here I thought people only ended up bound and gagged against pipes in movies. My life started out like a Netflix series, and it sure as fuck looks like it's going to end that way. Because these guys haven't blindfolded me, and I've listened to enough true crime podcasts to know what that usually means: they don't plan on me being alive long enough to identify them.

As I focus my thoughts around the ache in my head, the situation before me becomes clear: Bill Cummings found out I was about to betray him. And now I'm fucking tied up in a barn.

"Hey, look who's awake!" Voice Number One rings loudly inside my skull, and I wince. A pale-skinned guy with a long beard and a thinning hairline comes rushing over to me. "Bill, he's up."

"Thank you, Norton."

Norton? Definitely didn't have this guy pegged as a Norton. Movie writers always name their bad guys much better than that.

Bill crosses the dusty barn floor to where I'm sitting, cautiously placing each step with his wing-tipped shoes. He crouches down in front of me. "You know," he says thoughtfully, "your grandfather clearly has underestimated you. He's always said that you're a bit of a disappointment as far as intellect goes. But you're the only one who noticed the connections between the ski area and the land claim. Not that anyone else at your firm would have been looking for those connections, of course. They know what they're paid to do: win a case. You, my friend, are apparently not so wise in that area."

I don't even bother trying to respond through the gag. I'm not rewarding this sub-par confession with any kind of sub-par mumbling.

Bill stands again and crosses his arms. "It's a damn shame it has to come to this. I've always liked your grandfather. Unfortunately, even he's not aware of what's at stake here. He doesn't know what I've invested in this ski area. He doesn't know how much time and energy and money I've put into this silly, backwards town, with their ridiculous festivals and absurd statues."

There's something to be said for bad confession speeches, I guess. At least I'll go out knowing what I died for. And it definitely looks like Aaron and Jeremy and I were right all along, and I'm about to die because some asshole acquaintance of my grandfather over-invested in a ski area and couldn't make his money back.

Bill sighs. "The sad truth is that I need that land far more than the town does, which is something I didn't realize until I was a bit in over my head with this project. But it doesn't matter, really. From what Carter tells Arnie, the chips are still stacked in our favor. I have a very good forger on my books. I'm sure you're quite familiar with their work by now." He studies me carefully. "Sadly, you've become all too familiar with this case, and this town, for your own good. If you're resigning from your position at your firm, I have to assume it's only a matter of time before you mention your findings to someone else. And I simply can't let that happen. So I'm going to need you to disappear."

"Aww, man," says Darius. He's got a baby face, a spotty beard, and he's wearing a Red Sox baseball cap with a Yankees t-shirt. Given those teams' rivalries, it's amazing he's lived long enough to try and kill me. "Does this mean another hit-and-run, Bill? They're so fucking boring."

"They're quick to cover, Darius," Bill says matter-of-factly. "However little this man's grandfather thinks of him, he'll no doubt be quite disturbed by his death. I'm also given to understand the town has developed something of a liking for him, oddly enough. We know I'll need them on my side once Arnie acquires his land. So we have to be sure there's no possible way to link us back to Benson's death. You two are quite skilled at covering your tracks with hit-and-runs." He sends me a wry smirk. "So silly of you, Benson, to try walking alone on a strange road in the mountains. I can't imagine what you were thinking. It's so very dark here at night; so very easy for an accident to take place."

"Are you saying people might ask questions, Boss?" Darius asks nervously. "They never usually ask questions."

"Well," says Bill, "usually the people we take care of aren't much liked, Darius. This one, despite his personality, is quite well-liked, it seems. But it doesn't matter." He shrugs nonchalantly. "My associate who's been watching his communication will send out a carefully worded email suggesting that Benson will be taking some time away from Devon Falls and the legal profession to take stock of his wants and needs. Benson will explain that he may return when he's had some time to think about his future. It's so unfortunate that shortly after he sends those emails he'll go for a walk on a dangerous road." He frowns. "There might be some suspicions about his demise, but it won't matter. We won't leave behind anything to confirm suspicions." He tilts his head at me. "I want you to know, Benson, that I'm truly sad things had to end this way. You've made quite an impression on me. It's too bad you let yourself forget what's at stake here."

Part of me wishes I could tell this asshole that it's thanks to him I've finally figured out exactly what's at stake in all this. But I'll never give him the satisfaction of hearing me mumble through this gag.

"I'll leave you in the very capable hands of my colleagues here. You'll have a few hours to wait before it's dark enough for them to take care of you. At least you'll have some time to consider how all of this could have been avoided if you'd simply done the job you'd been hired to do." He leans down to face me directly. "But take heart. You did what no one in your office with their fancy Harvard and Yale degrees could do. Perhaps Burlington University deserves more credit than it gets."

I keep my face as even as possible as he stares me down. I'm determined not to give him the satisfaction of seeing any kind of anger or fear from me, even though my heart is pounding in my chest and every cell inside of me feels like it's shaking. I'm no expert in how one stages a hit-and-run, but I can't imagine the next few hours of my life are going to be very enjoyable. Will Darius and Norton at least knock me out before they kill me? What does being hit with a car even feel like?

Bill moves closer to me as he carefully releases the gag from part of my mouth. "Nothing to say, Benson Lewis?" he whispers.

I decide now, more than ever, it's time to lean on my inner asshole. "Do you want me to talk or not? You need better clarity in your directions. Because the gag's sending the wrong message if you want me to be chatty."

He tilts his head back and laughs. "You've got fire! Shame you've also got such a developed moral compass."

"Yeah?" I lean forward, doing my best to ignore the spiking panic rolling through my body. *You're going to die no matter what you say now,* I remind myself. "Well, here are my final words, then: the town of Devon Falls is worth twenty of you. They'll beat you eventually. They will."

He shakes his head and laughs again. "Such youthful naivety," he tells Darius and Norton. He snaps my gag back into place. As he turns and steps away, a pressing, horrific thought enters my mind: I'm going to die without ever telling Jack I love him.

"Hey, boss?" Norton passes something to Bill that I recognize as my cell phone. "This thing's blowing up with texts from somebody named Aaron. He's freaking out that no one's answering. I think Benson told him he quit his job." He frowns.

For just a moment, Bill lets a scowl show through in his expression. "We'll have to cut that off at the pass. So to speak, of course." He turns to me again, cocking his head. "You know," he says, "we could make this easy for you, or we could make it very painful. Perhaps, if you'd be willing to help us craft a message to your friends putting their concerns quickly at bay, we might be willing to take the easy route."

And just like that, there's a glitter of hope in front of me. It's so tiny: barely the thinnest of cracks in a wall of darkness. But light's coming through. I see it.

If I can play this right, maybe there's a chance I'll get to see Jack again. Maybe there's a chance I'll get to tell him that I'll do anything to spend the rest of my life with him.

It's a one in a million shot. But I'm going to do the best I can with it.

I swallow a gulp of air. "Okay," I tell Bill. "Okay."

And then I grab onto hope with both hands.

Chapter 24
12 Days to the Devon Falls Leaf Festival

Get to Benson now. —Jack Lancer

"It doesn't make any sense."

Mom and Henri are crowded around my computer with me. I didn't intend to be surrounded by people while an email broke my heart into a thousand pieces. But according to Mom I made a noise like a dying cow when I opened it, and now the two of them are gathered around me while I slump in my chair, trying to parse the words in front of me.

To the folks of Devon Falls–

I know we've gotten close since I've been here, but I need some space. I resigned from the firm today. I'm going to step away from Devon Falls to try and get some clarity. I hope I'll be back to see you all again someday, but I can't say that for sure. Whatever happens, I hope you all know how much I've enjoyed my time here.

Best,

Benson Lewis

I was up all night waiting for a text or call from Benson. Something, anything, telling me that we're not as over as he said we were in that hospital room.

Spoiler alert: the only buzzes from my phone came with political texts asking for donations. The causes were worthwhile, but I still ended up nearly chucking my phone across the room on the fourth reminder that whales really need my money right now.

I'm trying so hard to be patient. To not be Fixer Jack. But it's been so fucking hard when all I wanted to do through that entire party was grab Benson in my arms and kiss him. And now, less than twenty-four hours later, this is the first piece of communication I get? A mass email to pretty much everyone in Devon Falls on Benson's address list saying that he needs some time away to think? Even worse, it's a mass communication that barely sounds like him. "I know we've gotten close." What the hell? Since when does Benson Lewis talk like that?

I really thought we had a moment at that party. I really thought he heard what I was trying to tell him. I thought so many things.

"I guess I was wrong," I whisper to myself. Except it's not really to myself, because four hands immediately pat me on the shoulder.

"It's going to be okay, honey," Henri says.

"We need to track that boy down and demand an explanation," says Mom. "What on earth is he thinking?"

I drop my elbows onto the desk and let my head fall into my hands. "I love you both, but let's be honest here. No one's tracking Benson down for an explanation, and this isn't okay. This is just how things are supposed to be, I guess? But I don't get it!" I throw my hands up and stare at my laptop, willing the words in front of me to say anything else. "Resigning I could see. But stepping away now, and asking us all for space? After last night? And why the hell is he writing to us like some kind of used car salesman?"

"I'll have you know my favorite brother is a used car salesman," Henri says evenly. "But he does kind of talk like that. All stiltedly cheerful."

"Since when does Benson sound cheerful? Or stilted?" I ask. Henry sighs, and Mom shakes her head.

"Call him, Jack," she says. "Call him. You deserve to know what's going on here."

I want to. I want to so badly. But I can't stop thinking about all the mistakes I've made when I pushed Benson and others too far. "Mom," I say miserably, "someone I worked under in residency used to say that the best doctors know when to correct something and when to leave imperfections and problems alone."

Mom nods. "I'd say I agree."

I stare at the cursor on the screen, which is currently blinking on a blank reply email to Benson. "I'm worried I might not know how to make that choice anymore," I tell the computer screen in front of me.

Mom grips my shoulder tightly with one hand. "Jack Alan Lancer," she says. "You are the best son and colleague I could ever ask for. Do you make mistakes? Of course. We all do. But please believe me when I say that I am one hundred percent certain, beyond a shadow of a doubt, that you know what the right choice is here."

I nod as I draw in another breath. And then I let myself imagine.

I imagine dinners at Luis' with Benson across the table from me, ordering terrible meatloaf and making sarcastic comments about our town statues.

I imagine holding his hand at open mic nights on the square. I imagine listening to him play guitar there. I imagine cheering for him after every number. I imagine making requests for his set late at night when I'm in bed with him.

I imagine more furtive afternoons in my exam room. I imagine memorizing every inch of his body, one day at a time.

I imagine telling him I love him every single day. Every single hour. Every single minute, if that's what it takes for him to know for certain that I'll never want him to be anyone other than exactly who he is.

And then I imagine a world where Benson disappears from each of those scenes—and I immediately know what choice I need to make. "Henri, can you hand me my phone?" I ask.

She claps her hands and squeals excitedly. "Oh, there's going to be a reunion! I'm just certain of it." She slides my phone across my desk just as Malachai peeks his head into the office.

"I'm so sorry to interrupt, Dr. Lancer," he says. "But two people are here to see you. All the way from Burlington! They say they know Benson. And they need your help."

A sandy blond head appears behind Malachai's. "Sorry to shove our way into your office," says the stranger now standing right in my doorway. "Hi, I'm Jeremy Everett, and this is my boyfriend Aaron Morin. We're frenemies of Benson Lewis. And we think he's in some kind of deep shit trouble."

"Explain this to me again." Maggie Sefferson, the county sheriff, squints at Aaron's phone. "You think he's in trouble because he said, 'I know we've never been friends' in this text?" She shakes her head slowly. "That sounds an awful lot like Benson Lewis to me."

I look over her shoulder at the message we've all been staring at since Maggie arrived at my office porch twenty minutes ago.

Benson: Hey, man. No worries, I'm fine. Going to go off the grid for a bit and get some space. I know we've never been friends, but thanks for everything you've done for me anyway.

"I know, right?" Jeremy says effusively. "That's exactly what most people would think! But the thing is, Aaron and I had this *moment* with Benson a while ago. Like some deep dramedy shit, and he was all 'I'll call you my friends now.' It was kind of a big deal for him."

"Right," Aaron adds. "Benson doesn't forget or just skip over things like that. If he said it, he meant it. There's no way he'd send me a message like this after saying that to us. It just doesn't fit. And that, along with what we just told you about Bill Cummings—"

"Listen here," boys," says Maggie. "You have to know that Bill Cummings is a stand-up member of this community. He sponsors our local scout troop, for crying out loud. You really want me to believe that he's... hell, I'm not even sure what you want me to believe here. Are you honestly trying to tell me that Bill Cummings might be trying to make Benson *disappear*?" Maggie's my mom's age. She's got straw-blonde hair and a face covered in freckles, and right now every freckle is wrinkled with confusion as she stares back and forth between the two "Burlington strangers," as she called them when she first walked up to us.

"We don't know that exactly," Aaron says patiently. "All we know for sure is that there's a connection between Bill and Arnie Blake and that Benson found a map suggesting Bill wants to annex the festival land for his ski area. But no one at his firm shared his concerns about the case. That's the reason he quit. Well, one of the reasons." Aaron glances across the porch at me. "If he was going to leave, he certainly would have told someone about what he'd discovered before he left. He wouldn't have just told everyone he was disappearing and then shut off his phone."

"I knew that email didn't sound like him." I'm pacing the porch now, fear growing inside of me at every step. So many threads are tying together in my head. Benson's questions about Bill. That strange and impersonal email. "Maggie, that email wasn't from him. Something's off here. I think they're right."

Maggie shakes her head. "Well, I'm not sure what you all want me to do. We can go talk to Bill Cummings, see if—"

"No, that'll tip Bill off if he does have something to do with this." I shake my head. "Shit. Let's think about this. Based on these emails, we have to assume that if something is wrong here, then Bill's goal is to make Benson disappear before he can, um, say anything." I gulp down the bile that rises in my throat at the thought of what kind of danger Benson might be in right now. I can't think too hard about that. Not at this moment. I need to keep my head clear and my thinking logical. That's the best thing I can do for Benson at the moment. "But no one's even seen Benson today, and his car is gone, and—"

"Update," Mom interrupts. "Henri's post on the town message board asking if anyone's seen Benson went viral. Viral for Devon Falls," she adds when Jeremy's eyebrows go up. "No one has, but Shelly Shoalski did mention that she spotted Norton Fletcher coming out of Benson's apartment building earlier today. She thought we might ask Norton. But it occurs to me now that—"

"Norton does maintenance at the ski area," Maggie finishes, pursing her lips. "Yes, indeed he does. Okay, all, I think we need to follow this spool of fishing line. If Norton is involved in this, it seems all the more likely the ski area could be as well. But searching that place without tipping Bill Cummings off is no easy task. Hmmm."

"Uh, excuse me?" Malachai, who's standing on the edge of the porch looking slightly green around the edges—and I feel that look deep in my soul right now—raises his hand like he's in class. "I have an idea. But it might get me in trouble if I say it out loud. And I'm not sure it means anything anyway. So, I'm not sure I should."

I'm still processing that statement when Maggie shakes her head. "Son, if you have any idea that might help us figure out what the hell is going on here, I suggest you say it out loud. Immediately."

Malachai glances around the circle of faces staring at him and shrinks back slightly. "Please, Malachai," I say, and the tone of my voice has more than a little begging in it. "If you might know something, please tell us. Please."

Malachai pales but straightens his shoulders. "Um, I kind of didn't have a place to live for a while? It's a long story," he adds when multiple eyes go wide at once. "Anyway, I used to do some odd jobs for Norton and Darius Fletcher at Darius's scrap yard. And when I got a little desperate for a place to stay, I sort of crashed at this barn on Darius's family's land. He didn't know I was staying there." He wraps his arms around his body like he's holding himself together. "But then one day I figured out that they were dealing meth out of it. They found out I found out, and I had to leave. I stopped working for them and I never told anyone because—well, they're not always the nicest guys."

"That's an understatement," Maggie mutters.

"Anyway, that barn," Malachai goes on. "It's really hard to get to. Very secluded. Plus, it's huge. No one ever noticed what Darius and Norton were doing. It even took me a while to figure it out, and I was staying there. And. Um."

"Yes?" Maggie prompts.

Malachai shudders. "When Norton found out what I knew," he says quietly, "he told me that if I ever told anyone, he'd make sure I disappeared into that barn and never came out. He said he'd made it happen before."

I'm on my feet and rushing toward Maggie's car before Malachai can even finish the sentence. I've got one thought in my head right now. Everything else is just white noise surrounding me.

Get to Benson. Get to Benson.

Get to Benson now.

Chapter 25
12 Days to the Devon Falls Leaf Festival

There aren't a lot of times in your life when poorly etched graffiti gives you an aha moment. —Benson Lewis

I think it's safe to say, at this point, that I'm going to die today. I think it's also safe to say that I'm not built or equipped to handle life-and-death situations like this. I'm really starting to regret taking swimming as my elective at my fancy boarding school. Maybe fencing would have at least given me some kind of skill to get out of this mess.

Not that there are many sabers to be found in a dark, dank Vermont barn somewhere in the middle of the mountains.

I've spent the last two hours tied to this pipe while Darius and Norton skirt the edges of the barn mumbling to each other and doing shit that looks only slightly less sketchy than kidnapping local lawyers. I've placed a guess that they're running meth.

They also made it clear when they saw me struggling against my ropes that they have no real qualms about doing bodily harm; Darius planted a pipe down hard on my wrist to make that point. My arm is throbbing now, along with my head, but I stopped worrying some time ago whether it's broken. At least I have plenty of other things to focus on to keep my mind off the pain.

Like the fact that I am almost certainly going to die in this barn without ever getting to say "I love you" to the first and only man I've ever loved in my life.

I'm fairly certain I've gone through all five stages of grief as I've mourned that loss. I spent some time in denial; that was when I fought my ropes and got a pipe to the arm for my trouble. I went through a serious bout of anger that involved shouting until Norton threw yet another pipe in my direction. I did some bargaining when I made all kinds of promises to any higher power that might be listening regarding all the ways I'll be better if I get out of this alive. Given my rather assholish approach to life, the list was long.

And then I spent some time in depression, thinking about all the things I really am sad I'll never get to do better or differently. I'll never get to apologize to Aaron and Jeremy for being such a dick to them when we worked together. I'll never get to tell Ellie that I'm grateful for all I've learned from her in the short time we've known each other. I'll never get to tell Luis how much I fucking love his meatloaf.

And I'll never, ever get to tell Dr. Jack Lancer how much he changed my life. I'll never get to tell him that he made me see what's possible in the world.

I'm not going to lie: I cried a little at that point. As quietly as I could, because I didn't want to give Stupid and Stupider the satisfaction of hearing me. And when I was done, I'd reached something like acceptance.

Now the sun in the right of my peripheral vision is beginning to dip lower in the sky. It's turning a dusky purple, shaded with orange and yellow. When my dad first sent me to boarding school in Vermont, I remember being terrified. I was at a school for problem students. I was in a new state and knew absolutely no one. And I didn't have my guitar; Grandpa had refused to let me put it into the car as I'd packed for the trip.

I never saw my guitar again.

I remember sitting on my new bed, alone in my cardboard box of a room, almost shaking with fear. And then, out the window, the sky painted color over color in front of me. I watched those colors crisscross around and top of each other until I stopped shaking. And when the sunset was over, I resolved that whatever came next, I wouldn't let it beat me. I'd win. I'd show my Grandpa once and for all that I was a winner.

Now, I think of that moment as I watch a purple fade to a light pink slowly before my eyes. When it disappears into darkness, I'm ready. Ready to say good-bye.

I was never a loser, I silently tell Grandpa. *I know that now. I'm sorry it took me this long to realize it. I'm sorry you never will.*

At least before I died I did what I could to make sure Elijah had more people who believed in him than I did. I won't leave much else of a legacy, but at least I'll leave that.

I turn away from the window just as the final glints of sunset cast through it, lighting microscopic pieces of dust and something else: an old side of the wall, carved with something I can't quite make out at first. Then the light from the sunset hits the wall just right, and squarely carved letters appear there, like magic.

B + J

My heart pounds in my chest as the letters take complete shape in my vision. There aren't a lot of times in your life when poorly etched graffiti gives you an aha moment. But right now, I swear I'm having what I can only describe as a moment of perfect clarity. Suddenly, I see my situation in a very different light.

I've always been a fighter. From birth I've fought to be wanted, worthy. Now that I've finally found a person, and place, that sees me as both, I can't stop fighting. I can't give up on myself now. I've got to try harder.

And if I die anyway? Well, at least I went out trying.

Darius and Norton are having a conversation at the other end of the barn. It looks somewhat heated; maybe they're trying to figure out which side of the whole Yankees/Sox debate they land on. Whatever they're talking about, they're not paying much attention to me. I'm guessing that the silent slump of self-pity I've been sitting in for the last hour has them convinced they don't have to keep that close of an eye on me.

Hopefully I can use that to my advantage.

I push my hands up against the ropes binding them together and white-hot pain immediately shoots through my left arm. I bite my cheeks to keep from calling out and force myself to take slow, even breaths until the pain recedes to something I can think past. Maybe living with an untreated migraine disorder for twenty-five years is finally working to my advantage.

Okay. So wrestling with the rope isn't an option right now. Time to get resourceful and look for Plan B.

I slowly, carefully turn my head, studying the metal and wood surrounding me. It occurs to me that it says a lot about how much these guys don't see me as a threat that they still haven't blindfolded me. I hope I can make them regret that choice.

I notice a glint of something out of the corner of one eye, and my heart speeds up slightly with excitement. It's not much at first glance: just a spot where two bars have been welded together into a T formation. But one end of the bottom bar wasn't welded perfectly, and the slide of it is sticking out slightly. And it's sharp.

And it just happens to be right next to my bound ankles.

Score. I have to approach this carefully, though. Darius and Norton have made it quite clear what's in store for me if I piss them off again.

"I dunno, Dar," Norton is saying. "We already fucked up with that kid who was working for us. I still think that might come back to haunt us. You really want to get more people involved with this operation?"

"The kid's not going to say anything," Darius insists. "We scared the hell out of him. And you've got to stop stressing. This expansion is gonna be smooth as good butter, and then we'll have control over this whole county." They move out of my range of hearing as they start plotting what I can only assume is the expansion of their meth empire, and I decide this is a good time to move myself two or so inches to the right. They're clearly not paying any attention to me.

I brace myself for the jarring sensation this level of movement is going to create in my arm, and when I'm sure I'm ready, I go for it.

I start the mildly agonizing process of slowly shifting myself against the pipe I'm tied to. I take things as slowly as I can, determined not to attract attention or cry out whenever my arm sends sparks of fire through my body.

B+J, I recite to myself. *B+J*. You can do this, Benson. *B+J*.

It feels like hours, but it's probably just a few minutes before I'm directly in front of the pipe. I keep one eye on Darius and Norton as I set my ankles in front of the sharp end there and start moving my legs back and forth. And then, the most amazing thing that's ever happened to me begins to happen right in front of my eyes: the rope starts to split.

Holy shit.

I bite my cheek again to keep from crying out in amazement and keep up the slow, steady process of moving back and forth carefully while the rope slowly divides itself in front of me. A sliver of hope is glinting through a doorway I was certain was closed, and I can feel my heart speeding up with each small movement.

I'm coming, Jack. I'm coming.

I'm so focused on what I'm doing that I lose track of almost everything else around me. So I nearly jump out of my skin when I hear a low voice whispering in my ear.

"You think you're smarter than us, don't you?"

It's Darius. And he's holding a gun to my head.

"Norton," he says. "You see what this fucker's up to? We can't wait with him anymore. We gotta get rid of him now."

Norton frowns and shakes his head nervously. He's got his arms crossed in front of him, almost like he's holding himself together. "We have to do what Bill says, Dar. He says hit and run. We gotta go hit and run."

"Naw." Darius scoffs. "Fucker was disrespecting us, Norton. We gotta do it now, man."

Norton studies me, narrowing his eyes. This is it for real, now, I think. I know Norton well enough already to know he doesn't have it in him to disagree with his brother. My minutes were numbered the moment Darius held this gun to my head.

I tried, Jack. I hope you know I tried. I hope you know how sorry I am that things worked out this way.

And I'm so sorry you'll probably never know how very much I wanted a future with you.

Norton gives a quick jerk of his head—a nod. Darius cocks the gun, and I close my eyes against the way the sound rings in my ears.

"Goodbye, Jack," I murmur into my gag.

And that's when I hear something slam.

I whip my eyes open to see a tall blonde woman, wearing a uniform and holding a gun in her hand, standing next to the door at one end of the building. "Drop the gun! Hands up, Darius Fletcher!"

Darius jerks in surprise. For a moment I'm sure he's going to shoot me, but then a body comes at him from behind. There's a long moment of chaos and a massive rush of people around me, and I lose track of what's happening.

"Darius, you're under arrest!" I hear someone call out. "You too, Norton! I always knew you two were no good. No one's a fan of the Sox *and* the Yankees!"

And then Jack Lancer himself is kneeling in front of me, running his hand down my cheek as he gently removes the gag. "Did they hurt you? Benson, where are you hurt?"

This has to be what people walking through the desert, desperate for water, feel like when they see a hint of civilization. For a moment I'm sure I'm looking at a mirage. "Jack?" I whisper. "Are you really here? Fuck, Jack. I'm so sorry about everything. I wanted to tell you that at the party, but I had to fix things first. I had to make some shit right. I've got so much to tell you Jack. And I'm so, so sorry. I—"

And then Jack leans over and claims my mouth with his. The world explodes in a rush of fireworks as everything I was so sure I'd never have again is suddenly mine for the taking. And take it all, I do, kissing him back hungrily.

We finally come up for air. There's bustling around us and the crackling of a police radio, but all I see is Jack. He's all that matters right now.

Maybe forever. I hope.

"I could never let you leave without hearing you play guitar again," he whispers.

Hope has never felt brighter or clearer.

Chapter 26
7 Days to the Devon Falls Leaf Festival

People aren't supposed to look attractive in hospital gowns. —Jack Lancer

"Do you need any more pillows?"

I hover next to Benson, ready with a stack of three fluffy throws. I've been trying to stress the importance of elevation during his recovery. I'm determined to make sure he's in as little pain as possible while his wrist heals up. Benson casts a fond smile at me as I perch on the edge of the couch cushions.

"Jack, my arm may as well be on the top of the empire state building by now." He points to his wrist, which is casted and wrapped in dark blue bandages and currently laying across a stack of four high-quality down pillows. "I'm fine," he adds softly. "Really."

Unfortunately, that's not true. Not yet. There are black shadows under his eyes. He's woken up at least three times each of the last two nights, yelling with nightmares. It's hell not being able to do anything to make him feel better except hold him tightly in my arms. And I can't even hold him as tightly as I'd like, because those bastards who kidnapped him broke his scaphoid bone with a pipe.

But I've been doing it. I've been holding him as tightly as I can, sitting with him in his pain. Learning to be *vulnerable,* even it fucking sucks. Listening when Benson needs me. *Just* listening.

Well. Mostly just listening. I'm not an entirely reformed fixer; I may be crafting a revenge plan or two in my head. "If I ever get my hands on them," I mutter under my breath. Benson rolls his eyes, but he's still smiling.

"They're in jail, Jack," he reminds me. "And they're not getting out anytime soon."

That's true, at least. Maggie found enough evidence in that barn to rain down charges on Darius and Norton. "That bastard Cummings better not either," I tell him as I begin gently sliding extra pillows behind his neck.

Benson frowns. "I sure as fuck hope not," he mutters. Bill Cummings was arrested as well, and he's currently being held without bail, but he's telling everyone who'll listen that he's been wrongly accused of having anything to do with Benson's kidnapping. Benson will probably have to testify at trial if there's going to be any chance of Cummings doing actual time.

At least Benson's family's firm isn't representing him. Benson has been ignoring all the phone calls and texts he's been getting from them, and I don't blame him one bit. If I ever do meet any of them, it will be a damn miracle if I get through the encounter without punching someone's lights out.

"Okay." Dad steps into the living room, rubbing his hands on a tea towel. "I've put all the casseroles the town dropped by into the chest freezer, and I've got a hearty chicken soup simmering on the stove for you to eat tonight. I made a roast and put that in the fridge, and there's some homemade bread in the box. Why are you both laughing?"

"Nothing, Dad." I stand up so I can give him a hug. "I was just thinking about how it's nice to be ready for an apocalypse."

Dad hugs me back, hard. "I'm just so happy to see you two together like this," he says, and when he pulls away, he rubs at the corners of his eyes. "I've never seen you so happy, Jack. After everything that just happened, I'd cook up the food from every farmstand within three miles to see you looking like this." He moves past me to lean over Benson and plant a kiss in the center of his forehead. Benson's face turns the color of a tomato. "Now," Dad tells him. "Listen to your doctor and keep resting up. I'll see you both tomorrow." He waves at us over his shoulder as he exits the living room. "No hanky-panky yet, you two!"

Benson groans. "I've been out of the hospital for days," he whines. "When will there be hanky-panky again?"

"Soon." I nearly growl the word. It's been an almost impossible task keeping my hands off of Benson since the moment I knew he was safe. All I want to do is show him again how very much I want him to be mine.

People aren't supposed to look attractive in hospital gowns. But I swear, I spent all twenty-four hours of Benson's hospital stay trying not to jump him.

Benson sighs. "Fine," he mutters. I sit back down next to him on the wide couch, and he winds his good hand into mine, stopping to trace his fingers over and across my palm. "Ellie's coming by later," he tells me. "Just to keep up the whole Grand Central Station thing we have going on here."

I swear, the entire town of Devon Falls has stopped by since Benson got out of the hospital. He was terrified everyone would be angry at him for not doing more to stop Bill Cummings earlier. But Devon Falls is Devon Falls, and everyone welcomed him back with open arms. I'm sure by the time they're done gossiping about this whole thing, the stories people tell will have Benson wielding a saber at Bill Cummings on the top of a mountain or something. And nothing would make me happier than the town continuing to celebrate him. Benson deserves a little hero worship.

"She's going to offer you a job," I tell him. Ellie basically telegraphed this move to the town when she opened up a position for another associate in her office but only advertised it in one place: the local paper. Since Benson's the only other lawyer who regularly reads *The Devon Falls Chronicle*, this was more of a symbolic gesture than anything. Benson's face when he saw the ad made me love Ellie more than I already did.

Benson circles his fingers around my hand again. "I've been thinking," he says slowly. "I know you and I have basically been really, actually together for maybe seventy-two hours. And I don't want to rush things. But do you think, if I took the job, I could move in here with you? I don't want you to feel pressured, of course and–"

I answer by leaning over and kissing him as hard as I dare.

When I pull away, he sends me a disheveled grin. "Then I'm going to take the job," he says. "Mostly so we can do that every fucking day."

"Good answer," I whisper. I lean over for another kiss, but Benson interrupts me. "You really think the town's forgiven me?" he asks. "I mean, I did ruin the festival this year."

"You didn't ruin it. Bill Cummings did. And anyway, it's still going to happen, Ben."

He shakes his head. "It won't be the same," he mutters.

That's true, unfortunately. With all the bad publicity circling him, Arnie Blake has dropped his land claim completely. We've heard he's also being questioned by police. But it's already October, and there won't be time for Devon Falls to pull off the epic festival we're used to seeing every year. The planning time just isn't there. Right now, Henri, who's the long-time festival coordinator, is hoping the town can at least pull together the basic, most iconic events and sights of the festival. It's sad, sure, and the town will feel the loss this year, but I wish Benson would stop feeling guilty about it. "It's not your fault," I remind him again. "You have to stop blaming yourself for this, babe. I mean it. You're still getting over your concussion. The last thing you need to do right now is give yourself a migraine stressing about our leaves." I run my free hand gently over his forehead. "The festival is happening. That's what matters," I tell him softly.

He sweeps his face around to kiss my hand. "I've been meaning to tell you, actually. When your mom stopped by yesterday, I asked her if she could get me an appointment with that friend of hers. The one in Burlington who specializes in migraine treatment."

"Yeah?" It takes every ounce of self-control I have not to hop off the couch and do a dance. I know some part of me will always want to come shouting in, guns metaphorically blazing, whenever something's wrong in Benson's life. But I'm also so very glad he talked to my mom on his own, without me even mentioning it. "That makes me really happy, babe," I tell him softly. "You know how much I hate seeing you in pain."

"That's a lot of the reason I did it," he says. He twines our hands back together. "That, and I finally have a reason to go. A real reason. If we're going to be together, I want to enjoy every moment I have with you. I don't want to spend a single second in bed. Okay, no, that's not what I meant. I definitely want to spend *a lot* of my time with you in bed. I just don't want to be in there with a fucking migraine. You know what I meant, right? I mean–"

I lean over and kiss him again before he gives himself a migraine trying to explain.

"Holy crap. I still can't believe we were involved in your actual *rescue mission*, Benson. Will you include us in your tell-all? Is someone making a movie about you yet?" Jeremy Everett leans toward the video call screen, grinning, his boyfriend by his side on a couch in their living room. The two of them have been video calling with Benson almost every day since the incident. I snuggle next to Benson on the couch and wave to them. "Hi, sexy doctor!" Jeremy calls. "Great to see you again."

"Really good to see you again, *Jack*," Aaron says, as he playfully shoves Jeremy in the side before kissing his cheek. "And it's even better to see you sitting up, Benson. How are you feeling today?"

Benson blushes pink as I rearrange the pillows under his arm again. "Pretty good, thanks. It's still kind of weird for me that you three all know each other now."

"You know what they say," Jeremy chirps. "The family that stops a kidnapping together stays together. Plus, Jack has to be our new bestie now that your fauxmance isn't a fauxmance anymore."

"Fauxmance?" I ask.

"It's not a word," Benson says as he rolls his eyes.

"It is absolutely a word. Did I tell you it's actually in multiple well-respected dictionaries? I checked."

"Of course you did," Benson replies wryly, but he's smiling.

"I like it," I tell him. "But I like what our fauxmance brought us even more." I lean over to give him a soft kiss on the lips, and Jeremy wolf-whistles. "Thank you," I say as I pretend to bow my head to the screen. "You two are still coming to visit us for the festival, right?" I've had some time to get to know Aaron Morin and Jeremy Everett since they first ran headlong into my world, and every interaction makes me like them even more. Aaron's even temperament and Jeremy's effusiveness for, well, everything, makes for a great combination, and their loyalty to Benson is something I'll never stop appreciating. It's not lost on me that we might never have realized he was in danger if Aaron and Jeremy hadn't parsed his coded text message so perfectly. Elijah already loves them, and I can't wait for the rest of the town to meet them at the leaf festival.

"Wouldn't miss it, Doc. I've already primed my Instagram audience for pictures in front of the poop emoji statue. And I believe I heard something about a parade?"

"My whole family's coming," Aaron adds. "Briar and Jamie already have plans to write about it on their blog." I haven't met those two yet, but I keep hearing about them. Jamie's Aaron's brother, apparently, and I've gathered that he and his boyfriend Briar have a blog where they mostly write about romance novels. "I checked that out," Benson says. "Jack got me some of their book recommendations, actually. Briar said maybe I could video call into their book club."

"Oh yeah? Which books?" Aaron asks. "I just read *Lost Hope.*"

Benson always perks up when he talks to Jeremy and Aaron, and I sit back and enjoy how relaxed and happy he is right now. Benson's told me some of the stories of what happened when he first started working with them, and I know he has serious regrets about the choices he made back then. The three of them had a long conversation about that while Benson was in the hospital, and there were some pretty tearful apologies on Benson's part. Aaron and Jeremy were quick to tell him they were more than happy to move on.

"The past is in the past," Aaron told him. "Friends don't hold grudges."

"If Taylor and Katy can patch things up," Jeremy added, "we've got nothing to worry about.

Elijah had to explain to me what he was talking about.

Aaron's explaining the itinerary he created for their trip to Devon Falls when Elijah comes bursting into the room. "Hey, J and A!" He waves at the screen excitedly. "Um, sorry to interrupt, but my grandparents are here. They said they need to talk to us."

"Did we know they were coming?" I ask Benson.

"We did not," he mutters.

Jeremy grimaces. "Yikes. That sounds like the exact opposite of fun. Prepare thyselves, friends. We'll call you tomorrow, okay?" Benson nods and ends the call just as Conrad and Barbara Maggio step into the living room. We go through the usual greetings while I try to ignore the way my stomach's twisting at the sight of them. I haven't had to deal with them much in the last few days, and it's honestly been a welcome reprieve.

"It's good to see you up and about, Benson." Conrad Maggio very nearly smiles as he says the words. Nearly. Next to him on the loveseat, Barbara gives Benson a weak nod.

"Right?" Elijah bounces over to the sofa where Benson is sitting to hand him a glass of water. It's the fifth one he's given Benson in an hour, and the side table is starting to look like an ocean. Elijah's proving to be an enthusiastic caretaker. "Can you even believe he got kidnapped? I thought that stuff only happened in movies and shit. Pat thought I was lying when I told them!"

"It certainly has been a busy week in Devon Falls," Conrad says. He clears his throat. "That's part of the reason we wanted to come over, actually." Barbara nods in agreement. "Elijah, would you mind making me one of those ham sandwiches you made for Benson?"

Elijah rolls his eyes. "That's code for 'leave the room so you can talk about me,' right? Fine, whatever. But I'm putting more mustard on it than you like." He leaves the living room in a flounce.

"That was subtle," I tell Conrad as I take a sip of coffee. Looks like I'm getting another dressing down over Elijah's grades.

"Well, we have some good news." Barbara claps her hands together. "But we didn't want to say it in front of Elijah in case things don't work out. We wouldn't want to get his hopes up. But Eric may be home this week!"

"Really?" I ask. With everything that's going on, I've managed to miss some calls from him, and I haven't checked my email in days.

"Eric thought you might be missing his messages," Barbara adds. "So we let him know we'd tell you. It's not guaranteed. But he says things look very good."

"Elijah's going to be thrilled." A pang of something moves through me, and Benson reaches over from where he's lying next to me to rub my back. He sends me a slight smile.

It's going to be okay, Jack.

It will be strange not to have Elijah rattling around the house, testing my musical knowledge and playing loud riffs of Foo Fighters first thing in the morning. But it won't be lonely. Benson will be here with me.

And, I suddenly realize, this means we might have the house *all to ourselves.*

Hmmm.

I'm still processing this realization when Conrad starts talking again. "We wanted to speak to you both," he says. "We've appreciated that you've done more than Eric ever did to keep Elijah on track with school. Of course, there are still improvements to be made there. We're hoping you'll both help us convince Eric to rethink how he encourages Elijah in the future."

"Yes," agrees Barbara. "His grades are up since you've been working with him," she tells Benson. "Now, of course, they'd be even better if he'd spend less time with the guitar, but—"

"No." I interrupt Barbara before she gets a chance to go any further. Benson's eyes go up in surprise.

"Excuse me?" says Conrad.

"No." I take another sip of my coffee. "No, we're not going to ask Eric to rethink anything. I'm assuming Benson and Elijah will keep up the tutoring sessions, because they both enjoy that time together." Benson nods enthusiastically. "But Elijah's a great kid with enormous musical talent. His father sees that talent and lets it shine. Neither of us is going to interfere with that. I certainly won't anymore."

Conrad shakes his head. "Jack, I thought you saw all this more clearly now!" he says.

"I see things very clearly," I tell him. "I see that your daughter is in Italy and rarely speaks to you. I see that you're constantly fighting with your son. I see that you're pushing your grandson away for not being who you want him to be instead of getting to know him for who he is. I see that if you don't start rethinking your expectations for the people you love, you're going to lose them all."

Benson's staring at me now, blinking in something like wonder. But I'm not done.

"You two seem to think that it's my fault Fiona and I divorced. But you know what I realize now? I realize Fiona grew up in a house with expectations she could never fully meet. It's no wonder she and I fell apart when I started running around with even more unreachable expectations." I shake my head. "You know what's odd? Benson and I only started up what we have now to make the two of you happy. We weren't even really together in the beginning. But he's taught me so much since then. I see things so much more clearly since I met him." I lean over to kiss Benson again, gently, as I squeeze his hand tightly in mine.

"Thanks, Jack," he whispers.

"Thank you," I answer. "Thank you for everything, Benson Lewis."

"What do you mean the two of you were never together?" Conrad demands. "And you can't both seriously think that there's any long-term future for Elijah in guitar!"

That's when Benson speaks up for the first time.

"Mr. Maggio," he says. "Can I tell you a story? It's about a boy, and a boarding school, and a guitar he never saw again. And I think you may need to hear it."

I hold his hand, and I listen to his story. I listen, and I fall even more deeply in love with Benson Lewis than I already am.

Chapter 27
3 Days to the Devon Falls Leaf Festival

I still haven't decided if it's hell or heaven having your doctor-boyfriend nurse you back to health. —Benson Lewis

"I can't believe we're closing the office for a town meeting again," Jack grumbles as he jogs down the steps of Lancer Family Medicine to meet me.

"Last time that happened it worked out pretty well for you, didn't it?" I pinch his ass as he hits the bottom step, and he whirls around to pull me into his arms.

"Guess it did," he mumbles. "But the odds of any meeting being as good as the one where I met you are slim to none, I'd say." Then he kisses me so hard we end up pressed up against one of the porch rail posts. The happiness that floods through me every time Jack kisses me lifts me like a balloon.

"Ugh, don't stop," I say, swatting him gently when he pulls away.

He smiles and kisses my cheek. "Are you sure you're up to this?" he asks me. "It's barely been a week since you were released from the hospital, and your arm was bothering you last night."

"I'm fine," I tell him. Okay, that's not totally true. My arm aches every evening, and I've got an appointment with a psychologist in addition to my appointment with the migraine specialist because my nightmares of being held in that barn don't seem to be going anywhere. "Right, I'm not totally fine," I admit brusquely when Jack looks at me skeptically. "But I'm going to be okay, Jack. I promise. And I want to see what this meeting is all about. Amelia's post said it was urgent."

"I can't believe you read the town message boards now," Jack says as he takes my good hand and begins walking with me. People pass by us, waving and murmuring together. Speculation is running wild about why this meaning is being held. Every idea from aliens to new menus at Luis' has been floated on the discussion boards today.

"That town discussion board did save my life," I point out to Jack. "You all might never have found me if someone hadn't posted there that they'd seen Norton coming out of my apartment."

His face darkens slightly. "Thank goodness," he whispers. I think he's about to lean over and kiss me again—and then we'll see if we can actually kiss and walk at the same time—when Ellie comes rushing up behind us.

"C'mon, lovebirds!" she calls. "Can't be late! This one's going to be important." She rushes by us, power walking.

"You're not the boss of me yet," I remind her, grinning.

"But I will be come Monday. You better be there bright and early, youngin! No later than noon. Heaven knows what kind of funny business you two like to get up to in the morning." She speeds down the sidewalk.

"If only," I tell Jack wryly.

He sighs. "I promise, funny business is coming. But you've still been healing, and—"

"I know, I know. 'Rest is the key to recovery.'" I still haven't decided if it's hell or heaven having your doctor-boyfriend nurse you back to health. Especially when your doctor is someone as methodical and careful as Jack Lancer.

I swear, if he stands over me to take my pulse one more time I'm going to start humping him. I just can't be that close to his package without wanting a hell of a lot more than his hand on my wrist.

The town hall is packed, and Jack's mom and dad, or Maria and Alan, as they've been insisting I call them, wave us over to two seats they're saving for us. "Henri said not to worry about getting her a seat," Mom says when we arrive at her side. "I'm not sure why, exactly."

The answer to that question becomes clear when Henri appears at the front of the room. "Everyone quiet down!" she calls out. "I've got important announcements to make."

The entire town goes silent, because this is Henri. Harry, I notice, is sitting in the chair directly to the right of the small stage, listing slightly in his seat. He jerks upright when Henri starts talking, and he sends her an encouraging grin.

"Friends, I have exciting news. Some benefactors heard what happened to our little leaf festival this year. They stepped in and used their connections to ensure we can throw something more like our usual festival—and they've done far more than that. By my calculations, this is going to be the biggest festival Devon Falls has ever had!"

There are gasps and shouts from the audience. Hands shoot into the air as people begin to call out questions. Henri quiets them down with a quick gesture.

"Our very kind benefactors have strong connections in the party planning community in Boston. With their help, we've been able to secure all the tents, vendors, and rides we've had in past years, along with so much more. They've even hired an event planner to work with me! Can you imagine? Me working with an event planner?"

"Who's the benefactor, Henri?" someone calls out.

"My dancers still won't be ready in time. But I'm so excited we'll have the festival back!" Irene Cooley shouts.

"I can't believe this! What incredible news!" Burt Busby gets to his feet and begins clapping. That starts a wave of excited shouting, whooping, and laughter that doesn't end until Henri finally signals for everyone to quiet down.

"We have a great deal of work to do to make sure we hold the festival we know and love," she says. "And, of course, we owe a great deal of thanks to the people who are making this happen. If you'll all turn around, I'd like you to meet them."

"I can't believe this," I mutter to Jack. "Shelling out this kind of money to plan a last-minute event is no joke. Who's doing this?"And then I turn around and get my answer.

Standing at the back of the Devon Falls Town Hall are my twin half-siblings, my stepmother, and someone else.

My father.

"It's so good to see you!" Sarah swoops in for a hug the moment the meeting is over and I'm able to find her at the back of the hall. "We've been so worried! Your poor arm. Oh, am I hurting you?"

"I'm okay," I tell her. She smells like lilacs and soft sweetgrass, just like always. "My arm's going to be fine."

"Can we sign your cast?" Daphne gives me a side-hug and peeks at the bandage covering my wrist. "I have some great silver and gold markers I could use on that dark blue."

"Sure. Elijah signed it," I tell her. I point to the name ELIJAH drawn with white-out pen on one end of the cast.

"Who's that?" Linus asks. He slides his phone into his pocket—and I'm around him enough to know what a rarity that is—as he comes to study the name. "Why's there a guitar next to it?"

"Elijah's my nephew," says Jack. "He's about your age. Benson and I are dating." He wraps his arm around my waist. From the way he stiffens slightly, I know he's waiting to see exactly how my family will react to this.

I'm sure it's not easy showing a whole new side of yourself to the world when you're in your thirties. I appreciate how easily and openly he does it with me.

"Cool," says Linus. He pulls his phone back out of his pocket and steps off to the side of us as he starts scrolling. Daphne rushes off, telling us she needs to get her markers out of the car.

"It's wonderful to meet you, Jack." Sarah beams. "Just wonderful. I'm so excited to get to know you. I'm Sarah."

"My mother," I blurt out. Her eyes widen at the word, and she blinks fast, beaming at me.

"Yes, that's right," she says. "Yes. That's exactly right." She reaches out to squeeze my hand.

"And I'm Benson's father." Dad puts his hand out for a shake. Jack eyes it for a moment before he reluctantly reaches out his own hand.

"Benson," Dad says quietly. "I'd like to talk with you. Could we take a quick walk together?"

At first, I'm not sure what to say. I can count on a few fingers the number of times my father and I have ever had a serious conversation together, just the two of us. Jack leans over slightly to whisper in my ear.

"You don't have to go, you know. And if you do want to, I'll be right here waiting the whole time."

It turns out that's all the encouragement I need to follow my father out the door.

We end up sitting at one of the picnic tables behind the town hall.

"I owe you so many apologies, Benson," Dad says. "I need to start there. I know I need to start there. Sarah's been telling me that for years." He shakes his head. "When I heard you were in the hospital, I was terrified. So very scared, Benson. And then you wouldn't take my calls, and I wanted to get up here right away, but I was worried you wouldn't see me." He gulps in a deep breath. I've never seen my father look like this, I realize. Nervous. Unsure of himself. "And I wouldn't have blamed you one bit," he adds miserably. "Not one bit."

"I might not have agreed to see you," I tell him simply. Because it's true. And I'm done lying to my father about what I want.

"Sarah and I heard what was happening to the festival here. We decided it was the least we could do after what the firm nearly did to this town. And to you."

"The firm, Dad?" I ask quietly. "Is that who did this to me?"

He sits up straight and shakes his head. His brown eyes are watery and dark. "No, Benson," he says. "This is all on me. Well, me and your grandfather. But his part in all this is on me too. When I was a kid, you know, he wasn't quite the way he is now. Or maybe he was, but my mother softened him, I think. I grew up differently than you did." He bites at his lip. "When you were born, I was such a damn mess. I wasn't ready to raise a kid on my own. I thought I was doing the right thing, letting them take over. But my mom passed before you were even a toddler, and Dad got harder and harder over the years after she was gone. I should have done more back then, Benson. I should have done more to figure out how to be a father to you."

I don't answer because I don't know what to say. He should have done more. But I think I understand now that he couldn't.

Some people just do the best they can with what they have.

And sometimes, it isn't enough.

"After I met Sarah, I started to see all the ways I'd gone wrong with you," he goes on. "I vowed to do better with the twins. But you were already *you*, this grown and fully formed person I felt like I hardly knew. Sarah wanted us to be more involved in your

life, but your grandfather fought her every step of the way on that."
He sighs. "And what I'm about to say is terrible, son," he goes on
quietly. "I hate even voicing it out loud. But the honest truth is
that I've avoided being the person you needed me to be for a long
time because it's awfully damn hard to look at your kid and know
you probably screwed them up for life. Especially when they look
back at you. Right in the eye."

I gulp down the bile rising in my throat. "Grandpa?" I ask. "Is he
sorry? About everything that's happened?"

Dad frowns. "I don't know, actually. He and I had an argument.
I quit the firm."

"What? What the hell, Dad? You quit?"

"I did." Dad nods sharply. "I don't regret it. Your grandfather
and I disagreed about our parts in all this. He certainly won't work
with Cummings anymore, or have anything to do with him, but
he can't seem to acknowledge his own role in everything that
happened to you here. He insists that he was never aware of
Cummings' intentions and that he gave you the advice you needed
to hear when you asked for help. He still thinks it was in the best
interest of the firm to take Arnie's case. And when I heard all that,
I realized I couldn't work for him anymore." He shakes his head
again. "Turns out it only took you nearly dying for me to see what
Sarah's been trying to tell me for years. I'm so sorry, Benson. So
very, very sorry. I know I can never say that enough, but—"

"It's okay," I cut him off abruptly. He looks up at me, surprised.
"What?"

"It's okay." I draw in a breath and look across the yard, at the
door of the town hall. Jack's standing there, arms crossed as he
talks to Sarah and his mother. He's watching me from the corner
of his eye—I can tell. When our eyes meet briefly, he winks. *I'm
here*, he mouths.

"I don't know if I can forgive you," I tell my dad. "At least not
right away. But I've done some pretty shitty things to people too.

And I've been lucky enough to get second chances from so many of them. Even this entire town." I shrug. "So, I want to try. I want to try and start over, if we can. Maybe we can both be better people than we were."

Dad takes my hand in his. It's cold and clammy, but just feeling it against mine sends an instant rush of *good* through me.

And when he leans toward me, I let him hug me. I even hug him back.

My eyes meet Jack's, and I look forward.

Chapter 28

0 Days to the Devon Falls Leaf Festival

I told you, it's not a Devon Falls party unless at least three goats show up. —Jack Lancer

"It's kind of exactly what I imagined and nothing like what I imagined at all," Benson says.

"I get that," I tell him. I think I do, anyway. I've been looking at Devon Falls Leaf Festivals for so long—since I was in the womb, I guess—that it's hard for me to really imagine having expectations for this festival or seeing it for the first time. But looking at the wonder in Benson's eyes right now makes me feel a little like this is the first time I've ever laid eyes on the magic that happens when Devon Falls comes to celebrate the beautiful show autumn puts on in our little corner of the world.

We're standing at the entrance gate. It's a little fancier than usual this year; it's a giant white tent decorated with hanging lights shaped like red, yellow, and orange leaves. The lights are already lit in anticipation of the falling twilight. We step through the gate to find ourselves staring down a long path decorated with piles and piles of what look like freshly fallen leaves. Signs point out all the different "leaf walks" you can take if you follow the path to the trails that shoot off from the end of it and into the surrounding woods. The path itself is surrounded by everything I remember from my childhood, the days when this festival was an ubiquitous part of my existence.

There are the food vendors, ready and waiting to serve culinary delights baked and cooked into every leaf formation possible. A large stage has been set up where the main events, including Elijah's band's performance, will take place. Another large tent promises contests featuring everything from leaf painting to leaf crochet work, and rides are set up on the other end of the field. Tomorrow those rides will be filled with the excited screams of the kids on the Tilt-A-Whirl. I wonder how long it will take for Dusty Ryker to throw up.

"What's that?" Benson points to the southwest end of the festival area, where fencing has been set up. Goats ramble between the fences, stopping to prance and head-butt each other.

"It's the play-with-goats area," I tell him matter-of-factly. "I told you, it's not a Devon Falls party unless at least three goats show up."

"Naturally," says Benson dryly.

I just shrug while I do my best not to stare at his ass. He looks so good. He always looks good, but he looks especially good tonight. He's wearing a navy blue suit over a white linen shirt. The suit hugs every part of his body perfectly, and all I want to do is wrap him up in my arms and carry him right back home to bed. I glare at the cast peeking out of the end of his shirt. It's kept me from doing everything I want to do to him, I'm sorry to say. We've fooled around a bit, but I've so far managed not to cave to demands for more. I've been too worried about the possibility that he could re-injure himself.

But it's been some time now since he got out of the hospital. He hasn't needed his pain meds in days. He keeps assuring me he's ready.

And tonight we're both dressed to the nines—or at least the sevens—for the dinner celebrating the return of the Devon Falls Leaf Festival. More spotlights and fairy lights are popping on around us in the darkening night as we stand together on the path, and Benson seems to glow in the reflecting beams.

Tonight, I want nothing more than to show him exactly how happy I am to have him in my life. How grateful I am that I didn't lose him in that barn.

"Jack?" A voice I haven't heard over my shoulder in a very long time suddenly sounds in my ear. I take a breath and turn, and there she is: Fiona. Standing between Eric and a man I've never met before.

"Dad!" Elijah's voice from across the festival grounds is so loud and wildly excited that the area goes nearly silent.

"Hey, Jack," says Eric cheerfully. "It's really good to see you again. Gotta say hi to my kid! Talk to you in a minute. Elijah!" he shouts.

Then he takes off running across the brown, crunching grass in the direction of Elijah, who's running toward him. They meet right next to a giant pile of leaves, and Elijah jumps into Eric's arms as Eric lifts him into the air. Eric holds tightly to his son, and it's not hard to see, even from where we're standing, that they're both crying.

The entire crowd of people around us erupt into applause. Benson bangs one hand against his cast excitedly as he leans into me. "Man," he says. "I think I'm gonna cry. Look at what a sap you've turned me into, Jack."

The man standing next to Fiona clears his throat. "Hi. I'm Trevor, Fiona's boyfriend. You must be Jack."

"I am. And this is Benson Lewis," I tell him without preamble. "My boyfriend."

Fiona gives me a small smile from underneath her brunette bangs. "It's very nice to meet you, Benson," she says. "Elijah says the sweetest things about you. I can't wait to get to know the man who makes Jack smile like that."

It's probably not every day someone hopes for their ex and the love of their life to meet. But I'm surprised to find I can't wait for them to get to know each other.

"So I hear you told off Mom and Dad."

"I don't know if I'd put it like that," I tell Eric. We're sitting at one of the many white-clothed tables dotting the area around the stage now, waiting on the final course of the reopening dinner. A Vermont chill hangs in the air, and I'm grateful for the outdoor heaters set up by the fancy caterers Benson's family hired. And I'll certainly be grateful for the opportunity to cuddle Benson next to the fire when we get home tonight.

"That's what they told Fiona," Eric says easily as he sips his beer. "They were all butt-hurt at first; you know how Dad gets. But now they're telling E they're going to pay for him to go to some fancy music camp next summer. It's like you performed an exorcism or something. Or maybe a lobotomy."

I laugh so hard I actually snort.

"Anyway, Jack," says Eric, "thanks for taking such good care of my kid while I was gone." We both glance over to the side of the stage, where Elijah and Pat are geeking out over some amps and other equipment the event planners set up. "Hell, I would have been excited if you'd just kept Mom and Dad off his back. You went one giant step further."

I sigh. "Honestly, Eric, I can't take most of the credit. I made plenty of mistakes along the way. Luckily, I had a lot of help." My eyes drift to Benson, who's found Elijah and Pat on his way back from the drinks table. He's pointing at some piece of equipment while Elijah and Pat peer at it excitedly.

"I hear there's a story there," Eric says, grinning. "Something about you pretending to date him just to keep my parents off your back? I'm guessing Elijah doesn't know that, though."

"He doesn't. Most people don't, actually."

"Benson told me," Eric clarifies. "I like him, Jack. A lot. And I know Elijah does too. But I'd hate to think my kid and I got you trapped in something you don't want to be in here."

"Definitely the opposite," I tell him. "More like you and your kid accidentally helped me find the love of my life."

Eric looks a lot like Fiona. They have the same dark brown hair and deep brown eyes, and the same dimples when they smile. Those dimples are on full display now as Eric's grin widens and he raises his glass to me.

"To you, then, Jack," says Eric. "To you and Benson. You know, I was pretty crabby when you and my sister broke up. I liked you as part of the family. But I'm really glad you found someone who makes you this happy."

"Me too," says that voice again—the one I used to know all too well. Fiona's standing next to me. "Trevor and I have to take off soon. Want to dance, Jack?"

The music switches to something upbeat and cheerful but not too fast. I take Fiona's hand and follow her to the dance floor that's been laid out across the hard ground. We quickly find ourselves in the predictable embrace and movements of people who've been dancing together since they were fifteen. "I'm glad you came back home," I tell her. "It's been a long time."

"I really wanted to be here for Eric's homecoming. And then I got word that my ex-husband had started dating the man who was out to destroy Devon Falls."

I laugh. "Yup. That about sums it up."

We take a turn in time to the music, and Fiona smiles at the table where Benson's just sat down with Eric. "I like him a lot, Jack. It seems like you two are good for each other."

"I hope so. I really do." I take a breath. What I have to say next isn't going to be easy. "Fiona, I owe you an apology. When we went through what we did… I honestly thought I was handling it the best way I could. But I've learned a lot since then. And I want to say that I'm sorry, for not stopping and listening and being there for you or myself when we both needed that. I think—I think I felt guilty, you know? I knew we couldn't have children because of me, and I felt so fucking guilty about it I was determined to move heaven and hell to fix things. But in the process, all I did was push the two of us further apart. I didn't see it then, but I know now that I made a lot of mistakes rushing to do what I thought was right when things got hard for us. I'm sorry about that. Truly, I am."

"Thank you, Jack," Fiona says softly as we spin together again. The bridge of the song begins to play behind us. "But I hope you're not putting what happened to us all on yourself. There's a lot I could have done differently. I'm sorry, too, for my own part in what happened. And I think we both know that if we were meant to go the distance, we would have fixed our mistakes. Together."

We both look back over our shoulders at the table where Trevor's now sitting next to Benson. The two of them are chatting comfortably, and Benson says something that makes Trevor laugh. "Trevor seems nice too," I tell her as the song ends.

"He is," she says simply. We hug quickly, and when we separate, I don't feel anything like loss.

"That's our last song of the evening, folks!" Albert Byley, sheep farmer, owner of the record store where Elijah works, and some-times-DJ, ends the music to a raucous applause. "Now it's time for what we've all been waiting for: we're going to announce the Leaf Festival Royalty for the year!"

Fiona laughs. "Are they still doing that?"

"Yup. They changed the titles to make them less gender-specific, but every year they still pick two people. Both still lead the parade."

"Remember the year we did it? The cow behind us kept trying to get ahead and poop all over you."

"Mildred the Menace," I remember as we leave the dance floor and return to our table.

"Thank goodness you're back," Benson mumbles to me under his breath as soon as I arrive in the seat next to him. "No way I was going to make it through this speech without making sarcastic comments to someone. Which poor suckers are getting stuck with being leaf royalty? Imagine having to wear a leaf crown to lead a parade!"

"I don't have to imagine it," I remind him. "I did it."

"Oh, believe me, I know. I'm having coffee mugs made from the pictures. Your mom got me copies."

I make a mental note to put salt in her coffee on Monday. And then blame Jeremy Everett, who first shared that idea with me.

"Here we have it, friends. The winners of this year's Leaf Festival Royalty crowns!" Albert slides open the envelope and beams at all of us. "Look at this! A repeat winner! And our town's newest member!"

"Still laughing?" I ask Benson as I take his hand in mine. He looks completely stunned, face red and eyes wide, as I stand and pull him to his feet while our names ring out over the loudspeaker. "C'mon, babe. Time to get your crown."

The audience stands and applauds wildly for us as we make our way to the stage, and I make sure Eric takes plenty of pictures of Benson smiling when they place a leaf crown on his head.

We get home late, primed with energy from the evening. Benson's suit is mussed at the neck, his hair disheveled from his crown, and we're barely in the front doorway before I decide I can't wait another second to take him to bed.

"Need you," I whisper in his ear as I press him up against the hallway entry table. "Need you now."

"Need you right back," he tells me as he attacks my mouth with his and the buttons on my shirt with his fingers. It's like time is moving quickly and in slow motion all at once as we work our way down the hallway, kicking off shoes and tackling each other's shirt buttons. We've barely made it to the stairs when I run out of patience. I sweep him up in my arms and carry him up the staircase, desperately holding onto my focus as Benson nibbles and nips at my earlobe.

I rush us into the bedroom, tossing him to the bed so I can take his pants down and swallow him in as few movements as possible. "Fuck, that's my favorite doctor," he moans, and if I wasn't already hard as metal before, I sure am now. At the rate things are going between us, I'm going to have to build an exam room in my house. My dick likes the thought of that too, and it lets me know by straining painfully against the zipper of my pants.

Benson tugs at my hair with his good hand and cries out, wild and reckless beneath me. "Inside me!" he begs. There's no way I can deny him, or me, one second longer.

I get our shirts off while he leans over to push my pants down. He shucks his off and finds the lube in the bedside table. Then he stares me down, stroking himself, as he hands it to me.

"Get me ready, Doc," he tells me huskily.

I know I'll never tire of this feeling: the sensation of sliding any part of myself into Benson Lewis. I prep him as slowly as I can, determined not to let us both get so into the moment that this ends up not feeling as good as it should for him. Soon I have him writhing on one finger. Then two. Then three. And then—

"Doctor," he begs. "Now. I need you."

The feeling is mutual.

I lift his legs up, take my fill of him spread out before me, gorgeous and perfect, and then I thrust into him.

Time's a blur after that. The world reduces down to me and Benson, to the sensations of being buried inside of him and then sliding in and out of his perfect tightness. I hold onto him hard, feeling every gasp, every moan, every shudder, every shake. And when I'm sure he's not going to last much longer, I take him in my hand while I let myself go.

He calls my name as I call his. The words echo together in the dimly lit room, and then we fall into each other on the bed, a heap of sweat and hard-won perfection.

It's the middle of the night when I hear him wake up. But not with a nightmare, thank goodness. "Jack?" He whispers, drowsy with sleep. "The festival. Is it over?"

I wonder what he's been dreaming about.

I pull him carefully against my body. "No, baby," I whisper in his ear. "It's only just beginning."

THE END

Thank you for reading *Fauxmance in the Falls*. WANT MORE Jack and Benson? Find out how Jack makes good on his promise to put maple syrup on *everything*. Grab their bonus scene at this link: https://tinyurl.com/fauxmancefalls

Turn the page for more titles from J.E. Birk!

More Books by J.E. Birk

Find all of J.E.'s books at www.jebirk.com.

Curious about Sam and Malachai? They star in *Forbidden in the Falls*, the second book in the Devon Falls series.

Want more of Jeremy and Aaron? They star in the book *Counterpoint*.

Interested in Jamie and Briar, the romance bloggers? Grab a copy of their book, *Booklover*.

You can also get another glimpse of Jack in *ILYBSM*, an M/M/M holiday romance written with Rachel Ember and Leslie McAdam.

If you're looking for a darker, angstier read, you may enjoy *The Worst Bad Thing*. Please heed the content warnings in the author's note!

About the Author

J.E. Birk was raised in Vermont and is now adulting in Colorado with intermittent success. She is a long-time lover of stories, and she writes and reads in worlds where imperfect characters find their happily ever after. Snag free bonus content and stay up-to-date on J.E. Birk's news and releases by signing up for her newsletter at www.jebirk.com.